BOOKS BY CINDY PACKARD

THE MOTHER LOAD *1986*

HELL'S BELLS *1983*

The Mother Load

THE MOTHER LOAD

Cindy Packard

Atheneum 1986 NEW YORK

This is a work of fiction. Although the locales exist, the characters frequenting them do not.

Lines from "The Second Coming" are reprinted with permission of Macmillan Publishing Company from *Collected Poems* by W. B. Yeats. Copyright 1924 by Macmillan Publishing Company, renewed 1952 by Bertha Georgie Yeats.

Library of Congress Cataloging-in-Publication Data

Packard, Cindy.
The mother load.

I. Title.
PS3566.A29M67 1986 813'.54 85-47636
ISBN 0-689-11577-6

Published simultaneously in Canada by
Collier Macmillan Canada, Inc.
Composition by Heritage Printers, Inc., Charlotte, North Carolina
Manufactured by Fairfield Graphics, Fairfield, Pennsylvania
Designed by Kathleen Carey
First Edition

For Harvey, my better third.

Contents

Prologue . . . Hackles 3

Nights of Calipash 5

Barnyard Bernhardt 19

Dramatic Exits 28

In Search of a Christmas Story 40

Fowl Play 49

The Coming Rage 56

Of Sperm and Men 62

Leger de Main 77

Warts and All 88

The Newlywed Game: Hide and Go Seek 104

House of the Living Deadbeats 119

Forgive Us Our Debts . . . 127
Privileged Information 136
Back in Harness 145
The Road to Hell . . . 157
The Merry Moppet Mob Scene 163
Mother Teresa Takes the Stand 174
Awaiting Sentence 182
Mother Maude 188
Open Season on Marriage 198
The Smoking Gun 206
Life in the Fire Lane 213
People Who Read *People* 222
The Dogsbody Shuffle 228
Milady Malingerer 239
Lost in Translation 248
The Legacy 255
To Tell the Truth 264
Ménage à Trois 274

The Mother Load

Prologue . . . Hackles

"You look familiar," said the interviewer as he flexed a rubber band between his thumb and forefinger.

"Do you read *People* magazine?" I asked unhappily, knowing another job was about to vaporize before me.

"Well, sometimes."

"It's not true."

"What's not true?"

"I didn't push my so-called famous husband down the steps of the New York Public Library."

"I beg your pardon?"

"They said I did, but I didn't."

"I see," he said hesitantly.

"Well, I mean, really. If bodily harm had been my intention, would I have pushed him directly into the arms of his girl friend a mere four steps below?"

"I . . . uh . . ."

"Hell, no, I'd have gotten a good clear shot at the full length of those granite steps."

Nights of Calipash

I come from independent stock. My mother, Orin Delaney, was the ill-fated naturalist photographer. The pictures taken seconds before the rhino trampled her made an arresting spread in *National Geographic*. The fact that it was a prized white rhino did little to lessen the impact—dramatic or otherwise.

If Mother had lived to see the enlargements showing the rhino's beady eyes boring down on her with such demonic urgency, she would have been happy with the shot—regardless of the cost. Rhinos, her editor reminded us, somewhat apologetically, were one of her favorite photographic subjects.

Mother was not the only one who felt the visceral impact of the rhino's horn. At the age of thirteen, I was motherless.

I didn't see Mother all that much when she was alive, so I was surprised by the enormity of my loss. Life with Orin

Delaney was a series of limited engagements. It seemed she was always packing for another continent. Her love swept down on us in cascading, though intermittent, waves. When she was abroad, I knew we were in her thoughts. Cryptic cables from Tierra del Fuego or Mombasa or Nepal arrived at odd hours. And then there was the flow of packages containing items useful to our "education": strange lumps of rock, tribal beads, carved bones, prayer rugs, intricate craft work.

All the same I would have preferred a standard-issue mother like my friends'. Their mothers smelled of cinnamon and geraniums and excelled at baking chocolate-chip cookies, sewing on merit badges, and nagging about dirty rooms.

Mother was not of this mold. Most people were surprised to learn she had four children. Like the wildebeest she photographed, Mother appeared to give birth on the run, leaving the rest of us to mop up. Apparently believing that a mother's primary function was to ignite her child's sense of adventure, she was an exotic tour guide of the mind and digestive tract. Her stories were told with vivid and sometimes gruesome flair. But far from igniting my sense of wonder, they often engendered recurrent nightmares.

My friends, reared on Peter Rabbit, thought my mother most wondrous. But, after a day of watching her move like a gale through our lives, they could retreat to their own snug nests. When a problem arose in their lives, their mothers were willing to help. They did not say, "Use your head, Mallory—that's what it's there for," and depart for another continent.

Father declared us "Mother's province" and rarely intervened. I suspect he wasn't much interested. Often times he got our names wrong. Finally he resorted to "kidlet," apparently thinking the blanket term affectionate enough to hide his disinterest. Father was rarely home, but when he was, we were expected to revolve around him like adoring satellites. We were not to intrude on his peace of mind. Problems were to await Mother's return.

Father got and gave his affection elsewhere. Known to his adoring fans as *the* Sean Delaney, he was a famous English actor of middling talent. Father was never knighted or Oscared. His roles ran to the heroic. Our father had downed the Baron von Richtoven, won the battle of El Alamein, and led the Allied invasion of Normandy beach.

Later I learned he was less than honorable, though I suppose it wasn't his fault women were attracted to him. If anything, the camera blunted his good looks. Father was devilishly handsome with thick black curly hair, green eyes, and an elegant jaw. His laugh, the sound of jangling wind chimes, was his best feature. If Mother minded Father's females, she kept it to herself. Once, when a particularly juicy bit of gossip reached our ears, Mother sighed and said, "As creatures go, women are easily besotted."

My parents made an incongruous couple. Father was every inch the thoroughbred. Mother was more a sinewy quarterhorse. She wore her carrot-colored hair pulled back in a french braid, but hanks of it were forever springing loose. Makeup was declared "an unholy artifice." I suspect she reasoned that with all the star-struck beauties at my father's disposal, it would be folly to compete.

Father remembers meeting Mother on a train during the war, but he must have been thinking of someone else. Mother claims they met before the war, on a dance floor in London. From this disputed origin developed a life more apart than together.

As a child I would watch them come and go. One year I kept score on a calendar. If both were home on the same day, it counted as an error. Wasn't the point to steal home and not get caught by your spouse?

Occasionally they had rows of theatrical proportion. The anger would echo off the plaster walls for days, even after one or both of them had left. On these occasions I was shaken but not alarmed; I knew they spent too little time in each other's company ever to get seriously angry.

The obvious connection between my parents was the camera, though even there they worked on opposite sides of the lens. Father's work was on the west coast, while Mother covered the world. Rather than live somewhere expedient, they chose a spot two hours north of New York City on the east bank of the Hudson River. The advantage being that it was inconvenient for everyone.

Home was a Gothic revival "cottage" that sprawled seemingly in every direction—twenty-one rooms in all, not counting the verandas, second- and third-story porches, and sun rooms. (Designed as a summer house, it caught every little breeze that came down the Hudson. In winter the porches funneled arctic gusts into our bedrooms.)

The mother I knew was not a fanciful woman. I've often thought buying this house must have sucked all the whimsy out of her. Father called it "The Delaney Delirium." It had been built in the 1860's when Romantic fervor reigned along the Hudson. The architect, we were told, died in an asylum. The Delirium had four turrets, nine gables, fourteen fireplaces, seven porches, three crenellated towers, several pointed arches, and no basement. For exterior decoration there were diamond-paned windows, finials, crockets, cusp foils, wooden spires, crenellations, scroll work, stained glass, and hand-carved vergeboards. Inside were carved columns, mahogany-paneled walls, ornate fireplaces, and general frippery. And amid the Victoriana there mingled enlarged photographs of wild animals, Makonde sculpture, bronzed Buddhas, and panels of Japanese art.

Most old houses have their own personality, ours had a voice. At night it sang—or keened. On stormy nights, you could almost believe it was the trees slapping against the windows or the wind off the river clanging the swing set. But on calm nights, there was no mistaking it. We suspected it was the ghost of the architect dragging his asylum chains across the floorboards. My brother Gerald told skittish housekeepers it was his mad Aunt Rosalyn imprisoned in the north tower.

When Mother was away, our days flowed in an easy stream. But the minute she set foot in the house, it was as if a chemical reaction had been loosed. The air became charged with electricity and expectation as we each prepared to parade our latest triumph. Like most families, my siblings had diverse interests.

Ned, the youngest, was a sports junkie. If it wasn't round and didn't bounce, he simply wasn't interested. Mother appreciated Ned's aptitude for sports but tried to broaden his base with activities of the mind. They played chess, Pente, and an abstruse Arabic game Mother had found in her travels.

At six, Maude loved anything that flew, from bombers to bats. She spent her days devising "Maudeflight"—flapping her arms vigorously, nose into the wind. She used umbrellas, bedspreads, plumed capes, and oversized kites in her repeated efforts to fly off the roof of the veranda. Maude was plucky and I hated her for it. Nor was I wild about the fact that she shared Father's dark Irish looks. She and I were as alike as 'in' and 'out.' At eight, I was a tall, reedy kid with red hair and prominent knee caps.

Gerald, the eldest, had two years on me. Even as a ten-year-old, he looked like a terrorist, with clumps of ungovernable red hair striking out in all directions. His talent was for vivisection. Gerald was not above inducing brain death in small animals with a hammer. Mother seemed to regard his nasty attitudes as a natural rebellion against her interest in wild life. Rather than forbid his experimentation, she took a different tack. Although he was perfectly capable of reading, she read aloud to him—not humanist tracts or moral sermons but Thurber and Benchley.

I was the only child without apparent talent or direction. I may have looked like Mother but there the similarity ended.

My ambitions were tame. Some days I wanted to be a hairdresser, some days a Good Humor man. Purposefully, I dragged my heels against the current of maternal stimuli: her extravagant house; her lessons in everything from calligraphy to genetics to roof thatching; her field trips to museums, obscure and renowned. In my bid for attention, I became the hothouse bud that refused to flower. This distressed my mother considerably. What was I doing with my life? she asked with annoying persistence. I could not or would not answer.

With both parents largely in absentia, someone had to see the children were fed. We went through housekeepers like most families go through bathwater. If the Delirium with its aged plumbing and wiring was not enough to discourage them, Gerald certainly was. He put bats in their rooms and left decapitated animal carcasses on their pillows. Many of them fled at first light. Triumphantly, Gerald would wire both parents demanding their return. But Father was on location, and as Mother pointed out, she could not return from Ceylon in the blink of an eye.

The agencies soon despaired. By then we had a reputation and the locals wouldn't touch us either. Mother was forced to be inventive. She secured Hannah from the work-release program of a nearby prison. Decapitated squirrel carcasses did not faze Hannah. She ruled by corporal punishment and threatened to "cut us up" if we told Mother. Stupidly, she left welts on Gerald. And while Mother might have dismissed such bruises on the rest of us as the results of childish roughhousing, she knew none of us could get the better of Gerald. Hannah was sacked, a stray relative was brought in from Des Moines, and Mother was off again.

Once, when Gerald had routed yet another housekeeper, I offered my services. I was eight at the time and quietly enthralled with the prospect of mothering. From what I could see, the hours were good and the vacations frequent. Rather like playing with dolls, I imagined. (I was not allowed to play with dolls, they "fostered a dependent mentality.")

Mother was appalled by my offer, to her it smacked of stunted imagination.

"This is your ambition in life? To be a mother?"

"Yes," I answered stoutly.

"And?"

"And?"

"Isn't there something else?"

"No."

"Nobody is just a mother," she retorted.

"Harriet Nelson, June Cleaver, and Margaret Anderson are just mothers!"

"Who on earth are they?" she asked bewildered.

Mother had never heard of my idols. "They are mothers. On TV."

"Mallory, you know perfectly well that television is unrelated to life. Don't you want to be someone?"

"Like you?"

"Right."

"No. I think I just want to be a mommy. Can I go now?"

Soon biographies of Madame Curie, Amelia Earhart, and various suffragettes began to appear on my bedside table. I took to sulking and refused to play with my friends, who, at any rate, were deeply involved in their Barbie dolls.

"What do you want to do with your life?" Mother asked again and again. The question resounded in my head. When I answered her with a blank stare, Mother would impatiently prod, "Use your head, Mallory."

I could not profess an interest in biochemistry or architecture just to appease her. She would have insisted I begin training immediately. Maude and my brothers, refining their acts with each passing day, always had something to show—a new dribble technique, a neatly vivisected squirrel, or a fresh compound fracture. I had nothing.

Exasperated by my lack of initiative, Mother made the decision for me when I was ten.

One spring night, the family—minus Father—sat around the large oak table trying to avoid a dinner of calipee and calipash.

"Now, who can tell me which is which?" asked Mother.

"If we can tell, do we have to eat it?" asked Ned.

"Certainly."

"Oh," he answered glumly, continuing to push the two jellylike masses around his plate.

"Father lets us eat Chef Boyardee," complained Ned.

Mother ignored him. "Calipee and calipash both come from the same species. Would anyone like to hazard a guess?"

"The yellow one looks like solidified pig's gas," Gerald ventured.

"Wrong species," Mother corrected amiably.

"Definitely reptilian," I said with loathing.

"Very good, Mallory."

"We've plenty of good reptiles at the Delirium if that's what you hunger for," Gerald remarked dryly.

"You can eat those any time, and I am given to understand that you do. However, these are a rare treat. The yellow one, calipee with two *e*'s, comes from inside the lower shell of a turtle. Calipash, the greenish one, comes from under the upper shell."

Ned groaned and went to fetch the ketchup. "Get the barbecue sauce too," Gerald directed.

Mother yielded our palates and moved on to a round of "Name that Beast." "Name a dog that doesn't bark," she began.

"Hamlet," answered Maude. It was true our family dog did not bark. Nor did he fetch, roll over, or perform other doglike feats. Hamlet was little more than a diseased rug given to frequent farting.

"She meant a breed," said Gerald disinterestedly.

"Dingoes, native to Australia," I answered.

"Good, now what can kick like a mule, give a realistic imitation of a lion's roar, and hiss like a snake?"

"Gerald!" Maude exclaimed.

"True enough, dear, but not the answer I am looking for. Here's an additional clue: The first born often feeds on the other unhatched eggs."

"Gerald!" Ned asserted.

"No dear, if that were true, you all wouldn't be here, would you? Use your head."

"Ostriches," I guessed.

"Excellent, Mallory. You have a real talent for this." The statement hung in the air between us. I expected a cartoonist's balloon to be drawn around it.

"Mallory . . ." she said in an ominous tone, "you'll be a zoologist!"

"But . . ." I protested, struggling to marshal an argument, "I'm afraid of wild animals." None of Mother's children shared her passion and respect for wild animals. Given a free hand, Mother would have brought emus, oryxes, and Siberian tigers home from her journeys. But in deference to Immigration, she contented herself with a domestic menagerie. At one time or another, we had had horses, goats, fish, chickens, hampsters, snakes, rabbits, pigeons, frogs, ducks, dogs, swans, canaries, turtles, sheep, cats, gerbils, lizards, deer, pigs, and a cow. Most of these creatures found their way into the house at some point, and an unfortunate few found themselves under Gerald's flying scalpel.

But with Mother determined, the odds against me were overwhelming. "Oh, all right . . ." I relented. After all, how much could a ten-year-old zoologist be required to do?

* * *

Within the week, I regretted my vocation. Who could have guessed that veterinary science would involve so much shoveling? Mother dismissed the high-school student who cared for the animals and put me in charge. At first I was mesmerized by the sheer volume of manure. Then I studied the different varieties, from guano to pellets to plops.

I put the animals on a diet, reasoning that it was the excessive intake of grain, hay, and kitchen scraps that was producing so much excrement.

Mother returned from a photographic assignment in the Galapagos Islands and pitched a fit. "I can see the pigs' ribs!" she exclaimed indignantly. "Fury tried to eat my shirt!"

"Yes, it is a very becoming shade of wheat."

"Mallory!"

"Oh the animals are fine. A bit peckish but perfectly healthy."

"Peckish? This is not Treblinka-on-the-Hudson! Restore full rations immediately."

I was still halfheartedly taking care of Mother's menagerie three years later. One early summer afternoon a man came to the Delirium. He asked for my father.

"He isn't receiving visitors," I said warily. Father was, in fact, a week overdue. Inclement weather in the Australian Outback had delayed the shooting of *Glory March*. I had no idea when he'd be home.

"It's very important that I talk with him," the man said urgently. "May I come in?" I was alone in the house. The latest housekeeper, a Holy Roller, had left in a huff three weeks earlier. We had not bothered to wire our parents. At that age we rather enjoyed our freedom.

"Father left strict instructions that he was not to be disturbed," I said, through the mesh of the screen door.

The man awkwardly shifted balance and put his hands in his suit pockets. "Are you Mallory?"

"Yes," I said guardedly.

"Your mother has spoken of you."

"You know Mom?"

"I'm Ted Haskell, her liaison at the magazine."

"*National Geographic*?" He nodded. "Do you have any proof?" He opened his wallet and searched for a while.

"Here's my Blue Cross card."

It listed his employer's group number. "Okay," I said, opening the door.

He sat in the main living room, turning a straw hat in his hands. I wondered why he was so nervous. I went to get him some lemonade. He drank it quickly and put the glass down on the mahogany table. I remember worrying that it would leave a ring in the wood.

He stood up and paced. I grabbed the glass before it could do much damage and took it to the kitchen.

When I returned, he had sat down again. "When do you think your father will be available?"

"Well the truth is, Mr. Haskell, he's not here. He's in Australia. I'm not sure when he'll be back. It could be days or weeks. Mom should be home in two days though."

"Oh dear," he muttered and began pacing again. "Are there any adults about?"

I straightened to my full five-feet-ten-inches and said, "Perhaps I could help. I can certainly take a message."

"I don't know what to do," he said miserably.

"Can't I help?" I persisted.

He sat down and, staring at his shoes, said, "Honey, your mom is dead."

I stared at him for a long time, uncomprehending. He must be speaking of someone else, I thought. Mother, for all her comings and goings, would never leave us.

"She was charged by a white rhino. I don't know why she didn't run; she stood her ground and kept snapping, professional to the end. She even managed to save the camera," he said with awe.

"My mother is dead," I repeated stupidly. He nodded. "No!" I said adamantly. I could feel my head fill with a silent scream. Come back, Mother. You win. I'll be a nuclear physicist or a violinist or anything you want! Just come back.

Ned came home first that evening, cursing a broken string that had ruined his tennis match. Mr. Haskell had gone. Maude and Gerald followed close on Ned's heels, arguing as usual.

I couldn't tell them.

Mother had never been mine. I had always had to share her with my ambitious siblings. Perhaps she had loved them more for their accomplishments. Now I alone knew Mother was dead. There was a certain power in the knowledge but one I was unwilling to wield. I didn't want to be the one to take Mother from them. For who could take her place?

The next day a package arrived. My brothers and sister picked over it before I got to see the contents. Maude laughed and turned and hurled an object at me. "This must be for you, Barbie."

I saw an African cloth doll sailing through the air. I fought the instinct to catch it and let it drop at my feet. A message from the dead. Mother had never approved of dolls. I had outgrown the urge to play with them. Why was she sending one now? I looked around uneasily at my brothers and sister.

They were fighting over an assortment of malachite. Did she really expect me to raise her three children? If Mother's menagerie had taught me anything, it was that I had no natural talent for nurturing.

Surely she had seen that.

Father had barely gotten through the door three days later when I hit him with the news. I had been bursting with silent grief and could bear no more. Father bellowed one long agonizing wail and slumped to the floor. His response seemed exaggerated. Was he passionately wounded or merely a bad actor?

His keen brought my brothers and sister on the run. I looked at him. He shook his head and made a gasping sound. It fell to me to tell them what no one wanted to hear.

Barnyard Bernhardt

After Mother died, my father folded up like an old tent. When decisions had to be made, he was unavailable for comment. "Send all bills to the accountant," he said as he retreated to his bedroom, apparently assuming we would have the good grace not to disturb a man in his underwear.

When he had not emerged in over a week, I brazened in after him. His face spoke with horror of my breach of etiquette. "Kindly remove yourself."

"But there's green stuff oozing out of the cistern. And Ned has a spiking fever . . ."

"Enough!" he barked.

"I can't do this by myself," I wailed.

" 'Give me my robe, put on my crown; I have immortal longings in me.' "

"What?" I asked uneasily.

"Shakespeare, you silly tot. Now, plump my pillows. And close that window. I feel a chill coming on."

Gerald might have bullied us into shape, but two nights after learning of Mother's death, he simply took off. If it was possible to assign degrees of grief, Gerald seemed hardest hit. The manner of Mother's death was so gruesome he felt his obsession was in some way to blame. At the time there was no one rational enough to explain that it was Mother's obsession, not his, that had gotten her killed.

Mother's death punched holes in my life. I missed her fiercely. Not so much her warmth and laughter, which would have been expected, but her will. With her gone, I had no one to resist. Father didn't care what I did with my life as long as his needs were attended.

The supply of casseroles and one-pot suppers from concerned friends stopped soon enough. On automatic pilot I cooked and cleaned, trying only to keep the family alive until Father came to his senses. Mother was right; television was unrelated to real life. I doubt Donna Reed herself could have pulled my family together. Lord knows my efforts, gleaned from years of faithful viewing, failed.

Months passed. Father remained in royal hibernation. Each day I would take him his meals, shave his face, draw his bath, and change his sheets. It was as if he thought he was putting up in a world-class hotel. He complained about the food and the "valet service" and said the barber was "ill-mannered."

Seven months after his abrupt departure, I spotted Gerald coming up the drive. The Allies had landed.

But if I was expecting liberation, I was sadly disappointed. Something bad had happened to Gerald, who seemed astonishingly chastened. He slept for days at a time.

I came downstairs one morning to discover all the furniture had been moved during the night. Several rooms were stripped clean while others could barely be walked through for the congestion. Gerald, wrapped in the remains of a Hopi rug, was in the kitchen eating a raw onion sandwich. I said nothing. If he wasn't crazy himself, then this was a ploy to drive me round the bend. Either way there didn't seem to be much point in discussing it.

The following morning the furniture had been moved again. The piano was in the kitchen. I marveled at the logistics but still said nothing to Gerald, who was using the piano top as a carving board for his onion.

Clutching a box of stale doughnuts, I left for the barn. The barn had become my emotional dumping ground. I wailed as I poured the grain, screamed as I pitched the hay, and complained loudly to any pig who would listen.

" 'Turning and turning in the widening gyre,' " I muttered to the goats. " 'The falcon cannot hear the falconer; Things fall apart; the centre cannot hold.' "

Ned hadn't spoken a word since Mother's death. Even the school psychologist couldn't get him to speak. He lanced all of his balls with an ice pick and started wetting the bed. Father was playing Camille. Maude had become a Jesus freak. Gerald was afraid to leave the house. And I was quoting Yeats to barnyard animals.

My family was sliding toward the edge of the earth and I could not stop them.

It was many months before my father invited us into his chamber for any purpose other than room service. Propped up in bed, he was wearing a green silk dressing gown and a blue cravat. In a most solemn manner he informed us he could no longer bear to live with the memories in this house. He was "decamping for the coast." We could join him if we wished.

For a moment I didn't understand. All this time, while I had been waiting for him to get dressed and save us, he had thought we were doing nicely. Now he was leaving. It was true his physical absence would merely ease my load, but I was too young to be a single parent.

Gerald tossed an onion in the air and caught it with his teeth. I went to phone the realtor.

No one, it seemed, was in the market for a Gothic monstrosity. Father finally let it go for a fifth of its value as a home for wayward girls. They even agreed to take Mother's menagerie. The animals were to be used as an object lesson in nurturing. It hardly seemed fair but then what did these days.

Father preceded us to California and set up house in a tiny pink bungalow. What had been tolerable idiosyncrasies in a twenty-one-room mansion quickly became unbearable outrages in a four-room bungalow. Ned was so provoked by the close quarters that he began speaking—not, however, in a tongue anyone recognized. When he wasn't talking gibberish, Ned cried. Maude's incessant benedictions angered everyone. If Mother's death had turned me away from God, Maude's preaching finished the job. We were at one another's throats all day long.

Gerald helped matters somewhat by leaving again. I suspect that, in his heart, Father would have been happy if we all followed suit. Apparently, we too reminded him of Mother.

Eventually he realized we were not going to oblige him

and disappear, so he moved us into a larger though shabbier house on Wilmet Avenue. No Hollywood glamour for us. Father's income had dwindled considerably. With Mother's death, something had snapped in his body chemistry. His looks began to coarsen. Starring roles were no longer offered.

Father remarried the first year we were in California. I was fifteen and, Electra conflicts aside, not overjoyed with the bride. Father introduced her one evening as I was dishing up Spam and canned pineapple.

"This is your new mother, Velma."

"Pleased ta meet cha," she said. Velma looked nineteen, but even she, with her platinum ringlets and rosy cheeks, was no stranger to motherhood. Her maternity gown had a deep "V" neck with sparklers swirling round the bosom.

Ned, wiping the sweat from his palms, tried to look manly.

"Harlot!" spat Maude.

"Naw, honey, Harlow. Velma Harlow. I'm a actriss."

Velma was not with us long. Wilmet Avenue was not her idea of Easy Street. But while in residence, she grabbed what perks she could. Having assumed I was her handmaiden by right of marriage, she thought nothing of waking me in the middle of the night to fetch "French Peekan" ice cream. I complained to Father who was, as usual, unhelpful. I suspect even he was rather embarrassed by Velma.

Two days after I got my driver's license, Velma went into labor. Father was away on location, so it fell to me to undertake the wild ride to the hospital. Velma was not one to suffer in silence. Her pain made an indelible impression. Pregnancy was a condition to avoid at all costs.

Velma named the baby Tiffany. Had it been a boy, she probably would have named him Frederick of Hollywood.

Tiffany was a sickly little thing, given to bouts of colic. Devoid of maternal instinct, Velma bounced her as if she were a bottle of seltzer gone flat. I regarded the baby with empathy but knew better than to offer assistance.

Velma took off when Tiffany was three months old. I came home from school to find the baby red with anger on the sofa, a note pinned to her diaper. The pin had opened, sticking Tiffany in the ribs. I sighed, dropped my books, and picked up my newest charge.

When Father returned from the studio that night everyone was in bed. I handed him Velma's note. He read it and smiled for the first time in months. "And Claire?" he asked.

"Who's Claire?" I was genuinely bewildered.

"The baby," he snapped with exasperation.

"The baby's name is Tiffany."

"No, we will name her after Claire."

"Who's Claire?" I asked.

"I can't see that it matters to you," he snapped and left the room.

Father lost interest in Claire moments after he renamed her. He made no provision for her care. Perhaps he honestly thought babies changed their own diapers. I missed several weeks of school looking for a sitter. It was easy to see how Hannah had entered our lives.

As the search proceeded, my demands eroded daily until all I wanted was a woman who could walk and speak English. I had to settle for less.

Maria hailed from an undetermined country south of Texas. She worked from eight to three, during which time Claire slept like an angel. And why not? She was up most nights deviling my sanity. I tried to get Maude interested in child care but she would have none of it. Maude had left the church and was now seeking shelter in the back seat of boys' cars.

While my family spun in its eccentric circles and my school friends reeled from the effects of fun, sun, and alcohol, I was changing loaded diapers. No one else seemed to think this untoward. When I yelled at Maude to help, she rolled her eyes skyward and stomped off to her bedroom. On the rare occasion that she or her brother did help, the job had to be redone. It was easier to do it myself.

On graduation day I had intended to break free of my family—college back east or a tramp steamer heading west. This was no time to be picky.

But I couldn't do it to Mother. While the family was hardly flourishing under my care, it was always possible it could get worse. Indeed, it seemed to be heading that way. Father began talking of "night visitors," but as he had always longed to play in *Macbeth,* I ignored him. The night visitors told him Gerald was in the grips of a terrible power. Given Gerald's nature, this could not be considered a newsflash from the netherworld. But two days later, we received a postcard. Gerald claimed he was doing research for a pharmaceutical company. He advised us to stockpile lysergic acid before the prices rose.

Claire was three and still not paper-trained. All the dreadful Delaney habits had filtered down and intensified in her. No one would have anything to do with her. They called her Claire de Looney and left the room before she could bite them. Mother would have admired Claire's spirit. I loved her but happily would have lived without her.

I was only eighteen, but my days were those of a middle-aged suburban housewife. From six to seven a.m. I prepared breakfast and packed lunches. From seven to eight, I cleaned, did laundry, and barked at my brother and sisters. From eight to three, I looked after Claire as she tore around the house destroying whatever order I had just imposed.

From three till six, with Claire in tow, I chauffeured Ned to sporting events and fielded the complaints of Maude's teachers. Maude had become a problem child, and as Father was working (at least periodically), it fell to me to hear the school's grievances.

Maude disclaimed any need of my "retarded maternal interference." At the time she made this statement, she was sleeping with the football team. As an eighteen-year-old virgin, I was woefully ill-equipped to counsel her, but someone had to do the job. Maude was notably careless, and sleeping with a football team could produce little tight ends.

I was fighting Nature. At sixteen, Maude was a black-haired beauty and very ripe. The only intelligent thing I could do was get her to a gynecologist. The doctor would not give her birth control without parental consent. Wresting Father's signature was easier than I had anticipated. I told him it was a release form for Ned's soccer team. He did not bother to read it. Even if he had, I'm not sure he would have objected, which was probably what had sparked Maude's behavior in the first place.

When I suggested she try another method of gaining Father's attention, she asked, "You mean I should try the guys in the Thespian Club?"

"Maudie, you could sleep with Lassie and he wouldn't notice. You'd do a lot better going back to your 'Up in the Air Junior Birdman' routine. Father tends to notice falling bodies more readily than girls spreading their legs. Just a matter of what he's used to, I guess."

"I hate him," said Maude.

"Of course you do. We all hate him. That's why we've stuck to him like barnacles for so long."

"No, I *really* hate him."

"You can't afford to really hate him. Hate him in moderation like the rest of us. Now, go worship Ra at the beach like a good little heathen."

"That's no fun," she groused.

"I wouldn't know," I answered as I lugged another load of diapers down the basement stairs.

Dramatic Exits

Two years later the most beautiful words in the Latin language, in loco parentis, set me free. Maude's sexual mores were now in the hands of Bennington College. Gerald had resurfaced to collect his college fund and was pursuing his love of slime in the pre-med department at Northwestern. All I saw of Ned were the dirty clothes he sloughed off seasonally.

And Claire, the littlest albatross, was enrolled in all-day kindergarten.

I was twenty years old, in the prime of life, and I had no idea what to do with myself. The sudden absence of constraints was terrifying. Seven years of involuntary servitude had dulled my wits. For one week I just sat, waiting for the luxury of idleness to flow over me.

Inactivity is a tricky thing. Mother's voice floated through the years demanding, "What are you doing with your life?"

The question had lost none of its wallop. On one level I needed to be true to Mother's creed of professionalism. She would have wanted me to study. But I was the wrong age for college: too young socially (still a virgin) and too old mentally (mother of four). I simply couldn't see myself wearing a freshman beanie.

The answer came to me in a dream, rather like Father's night visitors. It seemed so wrong and yet inescapably right. I wanted to be an actress.

Most of my life, I had wanted to be somebody else—the daughter of a living mother and a loving father, the master of my fate, the belle of the ball. Acting would allow me to be anyone.

I knew Father would object. And surely somewhere Mother was beating her brow. But I also knew it was the only answer. I applied to the American Academy of Dramatic Arts in New York. They arranged an audition at their Los Angeles branch. I went straight from the audition to call Mother's old lawyer and arranged for the release of my college fund.

A month later, Father was presented with a fait accompli.

He looked at me with arched brows and laughed with condescension. "You? An actress? What an imbecilic notion!"

I said nothing, waiting for his anger to dissipate.

"Well, look at you!" He propelled me to a mirror. "There! I ask you. Is that the face of a star?"

Staring back at me in the mirror, beside the mocking glance of my Father, was the face of a tall, lean, reddish-blond-haired girl whose best feature was her father's green eyes. Her nose was straight, her cheekbones unnoteworthy, her skin faintly freckled, and her lips a bit full. The man had a point. Had I not received an acceptance letter from the academy that very afternoon I might have wavered.

"I don't intend to be a star."

"How very convenient."

"I meant I do not intend to act in pulp. I will be a serious character actress. One who lends reality to a production," I answered earnestly.

Father reddened. "It's pulp that's kept you in britches."

"Be that as it may, I aspire to higher things," I retorted.

"What makes you think you can act?"

"I've read a lot about technique," I answered lamely.

Father guffawed. "You haven't a lick of a chance."

Time for the trump card. "I was accepted by the American Academy of Dramatic Arts on the basis of my audition last month."

"Balls! You were accepted on the basis of being Sean Delaney's daughter."

That struck a raw nerve. The comedy portion of my audition had been less than awesome. "I sincerely doubt it," I lied. Even if it was true, didn't he owe me that much? I hadn't had a scrap of affection or even a thank you from him in twenty years.

My face must have hardened with righteousness.

"Oh, very well, I suppose you have to do *something.* I can't take care of you forever," he conceded.

"No, I've been pampered long enough," I replied dryly.

The irony escaped him. "You'll study at the Pasadena branch."

"I leave for New York at the end of the week."

"Bloody hell!" he swore. "I'll not have you there." No, he would have me here, where I could continue starching his shirts.

"I'm going."

"You won't get a brass farthing from me," he thundered. "And I'll not have you using my name."

"Fine. It doesn't exactly open doors anymore."

I arrived in New York in the late summer with two suitcases and a passel of hopes. As the bus had sped along the interstates, I remembered the trips Mother and I had made to the city years earlier. I couldn't wait to get back to the broad avenues, the horse-drawn carriages, the Russian Tea Room, the Museum of Modern Art, the Planetarium, Schraffts, and of course, Broadway.

I stepped off the bus and frowned suspiciously. The pungency of diesel fumes and heated garbage blasted my senses. I felt the dream doing a quick slide and fought my panic. Stowing my suitcases in a locker at the terminal, I headed for Broadway.

Kids who made James Dean look like an angel festered in bunches on the sidewalk. Here the air smelled of spoiled meat and, undeniably, sewage. The side streets were littered, too. Cars were double parked, motorists jammed their horns. A Dodge van ran into a Buick. The drivers erupted from their vehicles hurling insults and defamations at one another. I watched in alarm. No one else seemed to pay them any attention.

Down Forty-sixth Street, I looked for the theaters where I had seen *Peter Pan, The Music Man,* and *West Side Story.* They were gilded in my memory, but now in the fading daylight, they resembled sad old ladies brought down by Time. I felt a surge of loss, named it Excitement, and moved on.

While living in California, I had fantasized about my New York apartment. It was a garret perched, illogically, atop a Park Avenue penthouse. If such a place existed, I never found it. My apartment search was conducted far from the broad avenues of my childhood visits. Even the unfashionable areas were prohibitive. Uta Hagen, my idol, may have lived on $6.50 a month when she started out but not in the $300 cubbyholes I had been inspecting. Nowadays, Uta's monthly stipend wouldn't even cover a week of Twinkie dinners.

As students were considered reprobates by any landlord worth his credit rating, I took to lying. Eventually I sublet a "studio" apartment in the Ukrainian section, Twenty-sixth and First. The room had no windows as it had been subdivided from another apartment. The water ran rusty, the tub had rings that resembled a geological survey, and the "kitchen" was a hot plate. But it would be my own private domain—all for $190 a month. I toasted my independence and the aroma of boiled cabbage with a bottle of Brill's Best Champagne.

The academy was located between Thirtieth and Thirty-first on Madison Avenue, a moderate hike from little Ukrainia. The building itself, designed by Stanford White, was imposing. Each day as I entered, I was electrified by the thought of all who had gone before me . . . and terrified by those who were with me. Too many of my fellow students were good. Only one third of the class would be asked back for the second year.

On my worst days, I felt counterfeit. Everyone else had real talent. Perhaps I *had* gotten in on Father's coattails. But then there were the days when my body seemed to sing with muted power. The days when the acting teacher told me I had executed a "passable" three-quarter fall or pantomime.

It was an exciting, if crazy, time. All-night discussions of Stanislavski, Hagen, Berghof, Strassberg were followed by days of winded performances and endless criticism. I felt like a piece of metal being tempered by high flame.

Soon I realized I had miscalculated my funds. It was possible I would starve to death before I became great.

The cockroaches plodded listlessly across my cabinets and floor searching for sustenance. Easy prey. One night I contemplated eating them like Steve McQueen had done in one of his prison films. But even with a full stomach, I had never been a fan of cinema verité.

Waitressing was the time-honored solution. But as there was no shortage of hungry actors, waitressing jobs were not plentiful. Finally, I secured a part-time job at the Bo Peep Coffee Shop on West Forty-third. Part of me believed Joseph Papp would come into the Bo Peep, be enthralled with my waitressing, and offer me a job. The rest of me was too ravenous to care. My days became a demeaning scramble for sustenance. Feeling like a junkie, I stole cold grease-laden french fries from plates on their way back to the kitchen, but the busboy got all the prime garbage. I lived on parsley, fries, pickles, and toast crusts.

The manager of the Bo Peep caught me one day as I was surreptitiously sliding a prized cold fried egg down my throat.

"Gotcha!" he exclaimed.

In surprise I dropped my tray, which had been perched on my left hip. Dishes clattered to the floor. A half-eaten muffin that I'd had my eye on rolled out of sight under a booth. "Damnation!" I swore.

"You're fired," he said coolly. "Your habits are dirty."

"Do I look like a nun?" I argued.

Momentarily he was puzzled, then he said, "It isn't nice

to eat off of other people's plates." This from a man with gravy stains on his shirt.

"This food was just going to be tossed in the garbage. What's the harm?" I may have batted my lashes at him, so profound was my desperation.

"You are hungry?"

"Oh yes," I said eagerly.

"I will feed you."

"Yes?" I said, suddenly developing an affection for portly middle-aged men.

"Right after I fuck you."

My cheeks flushed. "Sorry," I replied archly. "I'm saving myself for the casting couch." I picked my way through the broken plates and strode out of the coffee shop. It was my only dramatic exit of the year.

I brooded for days after my dismissal, not so much for the lack of toast crusts as for the manager's brutish proposition. It exacerbated my concerns for my celibate state. Most of my acquaintances were screwing up a storm, sometimes in groups. Initially, I had been invited to parties but invariably I left somewhere between the grass and the orgy. Having waited so long to lose my virginity, it seemed silly to give it away to a group. After a while, I was labeled a non-player and not invited back.

There was one guy in my mime class I liked, Ben Meeks, but so far he had resisted my trivial charms. Was the Bo Peep manager the best I could do?

In one of those four a.m. sessions when your life plods hopelessly before you, I decided Mallory Delaney needed a new story line. While other girls had been developing feminine wiles, I had been tackling ring around the collar. It was time to rid myself of my family's imprint.

I started hitting the bars, nursing one draft beer until someone would spring for another. Different stories for different men. To some I became an heiress to a Fortune 500 corporation, to others a drug dealer's daughter. Often I was an orphan—the solitary status appealed to me. When I really got rolling, I would tell of being raised by wicked spinster aunts in Wyoming and long hard winters without meat. Either I was developing into a wonderful actress or men were incredibly gullible.

A month later, with still no love to call my own, I became very ill. For days I lay on my cot burning up with fever, barely making it to the toilet when necessary. On the fourth day, Ben Meeks lumbered up five flights of stairs to see me. Ben was usually stoned, because, he said, it gave him greater access to Melpomene—not, as he explained, a mind-altering chemical, but the Muse of Tragedy.

He hammered on the door and sang, "Let me in, wee-oooh, wee-ooh, oot, wee-ooh." I moaned that I was too weak to get out of bed and heard him leave.

Some minutes later the landlord, Mr. Vinnichenko, and Ben burst into the room. I groaned with apprehension.

" 'The thousand natural shocks/ That flesh is heir to,' " Ben intoned dramatically. " ' 'Tis a consummation/Devoutly to be wished. To die, to sleep. . . .' "

"NO!" objected Mr. Vinnichenko. "No die! Pay rent."

"A figure of speech," I whispered. Mr. Vinnichenko would sell my body to science before he'd allow me to stiff him for the rent.

Two men with an ambulance gurney appeared, panting, in the doorway.

"No, no, I'm all right," I lied.

"She sits at Death's door," declared Ben. I struggled to sit up and collapsed.

The doctors at Bellevue ran tests and more tests and came up with nothing. Three days later, they released me. Not, however, before I had arranged payment of my bill. The sight of the total, $896, nearly a third of my remaining assets, staggered me. How would I survive, I wondered fretfully as I plodded home. The only solace was that my tuition was paid.

A more immediate problem was how I would climb five flights without collapsing.

When at last I reached my door, the key did not fit the lock. I was kicking at the door when suddenly it opened. A blowzy woman stared out at me. In confusion I looked at the apartment number. It was mine.

"Who are you?" I asked.

"What's it to ya?"

"I live here," I replied levelly.

"No, ya dun't."

"Excuse me?" I asked, bewildered.

"See Vinnichenko," she said as she slammed the door.

"Mr. Vinnichenko!" I said, when I had flushed him from his lair in the basement. "What have you done to my apartment?"

"*My* apartment," he corrected. "No more yourze."

"But my stuff," I exclaimed.

"Cunfahskaded for monies due. Here, no sale." He tossed me a bundle of clothes in a pillowcase and slammed the door. I pounded and kicked the door to no avail.

Now I was homeless as well as penniless. It was too cold to sleep in the park. If I planned to eat anything next week,

I couldn't afford a hotel. And I'd be damned if I would call Father.

Ben was the closest thing I had to a friend. I went to his apartment and laid out the gruesome details.

"Bummer," he replied unsympathetically.

I regarded him stonily. "Look, Meeks, this is all your doing!"

"My doing?"

"If you hadn't shipped me off to the hospital, I'd be solvent. Or dead. In any case, I wouldn't be bucking for bag lady."

"I see your point," he said, viewing my pillowcase. "Well, you can bunk here for the nonce."

"How long a 'nonce'?"

"Long enough to recoup. Is your baggage being sent on?"

"In a manner of speaking. Where can I sleep?" I asked, so weary I was afraid I would faint.

"Choose your corner," he said with a sweeping gesture, which encompassed the small room.

Ben was a man who knew how to economize. While I stayed with him, he never once paid for groceries. He did his shopping in the Dempsey Dumpsters behind the supermarkets. The managers occasionally ran him off and then he would resort to garbage cans on the street. Such a man recognized the advantages of reduced rent. Ben and I came to an arrangement. I paid half his rent, and he allowed me half his double bed.

Although nothing separated us in bed, there was nothing bringing us together. Ben appeared to be a moralist in many areas. I tried different lures, from home-cooked Spam to wet

T-shirts, but handsome Ben ignored my efforts. Living with Ben, I reflected sourly, was lonelier than living alone. At least in little Ukrainia, my fantasies had been free to frolic.

I had hoped living with someone would improve my acting technique, what with high-powered discussions over breakfast, etc. But Ben was rarely in the apartment.

All too soon, the "nonce" was up. Ben told me I reminded him of his mother. I had met his mother once. My hair was not blue, I argued. And besides, I thought he wanted me to keep house. He put his hands on his hips, looked at me with his gorgeous green eyes, and said I was cramping his style. I bargained for time. We arranged a schedule. During certain evening hours the bed would be his alone. I was not fooled by the niceties of the language.

After an especially dispiriting evening, I came home early one night. I knocked before entering, but apparently they hadn't heard me over the rhythms of Santana. Never having seen homosexuals in the act, I stared, slack jawed, at the coupled figures. How could I not have known, I wondered as I continued to stare. Ben looked up.

"Jesus Christ, Mallory!"

"Oh, uh, sorry . . ." I said, backing out the door. I went down to the front stoop and waited for his guest to leave. I thought of Ben with his classically handsome features and how I had longed for him.

Eventually the friend—I recognized the wavy gray hair—left. I went upstairs.

"I'm sorry, I didn't know."

He looked at me as if I were copping an insanity plea.

"It hadn't occurred to me. I'm not offended or anything," I added hastily.

"Well, I am. That was an important trick."

"Trick?" I echoed. Ben was a whore.

"Grass doesn't grow on trees," he answered.

The image amused me. "No, I don't suppose it does. Don't throw me out. You need my rent," I reasoned.

"Hmmm . . . 'Multitudes in the valley of decision,' " he quoted bemusedly.

There would certainly be multitudes sharing my sheets, I thought unhappily. But my financial position necessitated certain sacrifices, such as privacy and pride.

"Oh, why not," he concluded. "But remember, no starch in my shirts."

In Search of a Christmas Story

I had hoped Christmas would skip a year, but soon the avenues were choked with lights and Salvation Army Santas. Without the classes to focus on, I found myself feeling glum and disoriented. Christmas always reminded me of Mother. She used to decorate the Delirium to the nines: wreaths of holly above the mantels, pine boughs laced through the stairwell, big red satin bows everywhere, large felt stockings, and a fifteen-foot tree laden with sparkling ornaments. In the years after her death, I had tried to continue the tradition. This I remembered as I placed ornaments fashioned from soup cans on the scraggly tree Ben had found.

Christmas Eve was a big night for Ben; I was hustled out early. I went to Joe Allen's bar hoping to find someone I knew. Helga Lund was there enthralling the minions. Helga was a foreign student who had not suffered in translation. Blond and buxom, she had a distinct effect on men. After a few moments of her attention, they looked as if they had been hit with a tranquilizing dart; their legs suddenly splayed, their eyes glazed, and a silly smile twisted their faces. I waved, but Helga didn't invite me to join her.

I had seven hours to kill, so I went to the bar and sat between two men. The one on the left was wearing burgundy polyester pants. I turned to the right and found a good-looking man who appeared tall even when bent. Long legs curled around the bar stool. He had thick brown hair, bushy eyebrows, and a lean face. He looked like a man who would buy an orphan story.

We talked for a while. He bought me a Campari. I learned he was Sam Morrow, a freelance writer in his mid twenties. He learned I was an actor raised by wicked spinster aunts in Wyoming.

Sam laughed aloud. "You look rather well nourished to have survived on thistles."

"It's those nuts and berries," I said. "They go straight to your hips."

"I hear boiled bark is hell on the complexion, too," he retorted.

Just as I was exalting in finding a man with a sense of the ridiculous, Helga sidled up to me and asked for a Kleenex. She did not appear to be in the throes of a violent sneeze or teary eye. She issued Sam one of her standard seductive smiles. I waited for the inevitable.

Sam looked momentarily stunned and then asked me, "Do you have any money?"

"None to speak of." Was I to outbid Helga?

"I'm tapped out. Your place or mine?" he asked, still gazing at Helga's bounty.

"Vell, our plaice is a little crowd," cooed Helga.

"Mine then, come along. It was nice to meet you," he said in dismissal. I kicked the bar. Damn the Norwegian Wonder.

"Joust let me get my furs."

Sam appeared puzzled. "Are you coming, too?"

"Tu?" Helga echoed.

"Mallory and I were just leaving, but you are welcome to join us."

"Juin you?" Helga repeated. "Bah!" She turned on her heel.

"I'm sorry if I offended your friend," he said.

"She can use the offense."

"So," he asked again, "your place or mine?"

"Mine is a homosexual brothel." The liquor had made me bold.

His bushy eyebrows arched. "Well, we all have our crosses to bear. I live in Brooklyn." Brooklyn was where you went when you got on the wrong subway.

Outside the winds were wickedly cold. The night air cut through my lightweight coat and sobered me. It was not my policy to go home with virtual strangers. Why was I going to Brooklyn? And how would I ever find my way home? "God, it's raw."

"Just a few more blocks to the subway," he encouraged.

"I may not make it. The bone marrow in my legs is congealing."

"Tsk tsk. What would your spinster aunts in Wyoming say?"

"They didn't cotton much to complaints."

"Me neither. When we get to the wilds of Brooklyn, I'll rub your legs with bear grease," he offered, as we entered the subway station.

"Oh?" I asked, uneasily. I should have known that any man who would pass up Helga Lund for Mallory Delaney could not be right in the head. Was it really the fear of being alone on Christmas Eve that put me on that subway?

Twenty minutes later, I nervously stepped into his apartment expecting to find bear rugs and moose heads. I was momentarily startled to find a large, neat room with no evidence of Davy Crockett.

"It's so . . . clean," I remarked.

"I have a bear come in every Thursday," he jested. The wilderness gambit had been mine, not his.

In the corner was a large wooden desk cluttered with piles of paper, carbons, a typewriter, and several coffee cups. It was the only sign of disorder in the room.

"Where do you sleep?" I asked, amazed at my audacity.

"In the bedroom."

"You have a *bedroom*?" I asked. No one I knew could afford such a luxury.

"And a dining room," he said with amusement.

I gasped.

"This *is* Brooklyn."

"Even so . . ."

"How big is your brothel?"

"About the size of your kitchen," I said, following him into it. "And it's not my brothel, it's my roommate's." I looked down. A large, fierce orange cat was gnawing on my shoe. "Is this domesticated?" I asked, trying to shake it off.

"Cat likes leather." He took a can of cat food from the shelf.

"Then he'll be disappointed. These are man-made uppers." I wrenched my foot from his mouth and backed out of the kitchen.

In the living room, I sat down and wondered about Sam. It was Christmas Eve yet there was no sign of tinsel, tree, or stocking. How far I had come from the caroling Christmas Eves of my childhood. I felt very alone and not a little scared.

My gaze traveled the room. At the bookcase, I saw something that made my heart tumble. I took the book from the shelf and sat on the couch turning the pages. Sam, finished with his cat chores, sat beside me clutching a salami.

"Want some?"

"No," I answered, barely registering the phallic implications.

"Aren't they great? Such a strange intensity to those photos." He took a bite off the end of the salami and chewed purposefully.

"I've seen them before. But not for a long while. They're my mother's."

Sam looked momentarily startled. "Your mother?"

"The photographer, Orin Delaney."

"I assumed Orin was a man."

"No, she's my mother."

"So much for the orphan of the windy plains," he mused.

"My mother is dead. She was trampled by a white rhino."

"Right," said Sam. He took another bite of salami.

"It's the truth."

"And I suppose your father went down with the Andrea Doria."

"No, he's alive—but not bound by reality, if you know what I mean."

"I'm afraid I don't."

"Well, never mind. It's a very long and boring story," I countered. I had already said too much.

"Yes, I can see that. Mothers being trampled by horned beasts. Fathers slipping off into Never Never Land. All the ingredients of a good yawn."

"Drop it," I warned.

"Okay," he said amiably. He munched on the salami awhile. I tried very hard to put a cap on my feelings. But it was Christmas and I missed her.

"What was she like?" he asked suddenly.

"I'm not sure." Sam looked surprised. "Oh, I mean, I remember a lot about her but I'm not sure how true it is. I was thirteen when she died, and before that she more or less breezed in and out of my life as the spirit moved her. The prototype of the liberated woman. It's silly. I know she loved me, but by dying she became a mythical figure frozen in time."

"And not your mother."

"Yeah," I said softly.

"So you can't trust your reactions to her?"

"Exactly."

"I should think you would be mad."

"Oh, I don't know. Probably on some level I am very angry with her. But after all these years," I shrugged, "what good is anger? I spend my time looking for something I'm sure she left me but I can't find."

"What?"

"I'm not sure—a sense of self or, maybe, someone to make me feel whole."

"I don't think other people can do that for you."

"You're probably right, but I can't help hoping."

"Do you think that has anything to do with your chosen profession?"

"How so?"

"You're looking for a connection, free of risk. Could that be the 'adoring public'?"

"Anyone who thinks acting is free of risk is insane," I retorted.

"Just as long as *you* realize it," he cautioned. I had the eerie feeling Mother had sanctioned Sam, that she had somehow brought me to him. But that may have been my beleaguered imagination looking for a Christmas story.

We continued to see each other through winter and spring. Sam was everything I wanted in a man—funny, kind, and intelligent. We discussed theater, literature, and the Mets. But sexually, he was as much use to me as Ben. Why had I bothered to cosset my virginity all those years? The men I wanted to give it to refused to take it.

Sam didn't seem gay, but then I'd been fooled before. It was, therefore, with relief that I learned of a girl friend, Laura, in Boston. Now that my rival was revealed, it seemed merely a matter of ousting her.

"We're good together," I argued one evening. We were in his apartment listening to early Gordon Lightfoot albums.

"We met at a bad time," he countered. Sam got up from the couch we shared and went to an arm chair, ostensibly to retrieve an album jacket.

"Why . . . because of Laura?"

"No, because of you. I can't give you what you want." Sam looked uneasy.

"Are you a eunuch?"

"No," he laughed. "But I'm not in the market for a lady love."

"Who said anything about love?" I demanded, knowing

I was about to. Sam, I was convinced, could make me "whole."

"You would sooner or later."

"The male ego should be bound at birth, like Chinese feet," I declared. He leaned over and kissed my cheek.

I was no stranger to patronization. "Look, dammit, I'm just asking a simple favor. Seven minutes of your time."

"I think not," he said simply.

"My god, you're selfish. You're not using it at the moment," I argued, gesturing at his groin. "Loan it to me."

"I beg your pardon?"

"Sam, I am a twenty-one-year-old American virgin. Otherwise known, in these heady times, as a freak of nature. You'd shoot a wounded deer, wouldn't you?" I reasoned. "Help me. No strings, honest."

"I admire your logic," he laughed.

"You'll do it?"

"Mallory, you know I am fond of you."

"Please," I begged. Sam would love me, I was certain, once we had bedded together.

"If you are absolutely sure . . ."

Mother hadn't had time for that mother-daughter talk before she died. No one had warned me that first time sex was awkward and painful. I thought I must have been doing it wrong. After all, Maude had happily slept with the entire football team.

Sam's comment was, "My god, you really are a virgin!" I couldn't tell if that pleased him or not.

When he rolled off of me, he said, "Satisfied?"

I thought not, but it would have been rude to say so. "Sam, I love you."

"Shit."

* * *

Two days later, he was gone. I called to tell him the good news. The academy had invited me back for the second year. Tangible proof that I was *good.* A disembodied voice told me the phone had been disconnected.

I was stunned. Sam had joined Mother in that wasteland where love translated into abandonment, anger, and want.

I went out and laid the first actor I could find.

Fowl Play

After two years of intensive study, I was ready to tackle Broadway. Unfortunately, Broadway had no intention of buckling to my advances. My chosen profession was a classic vicious circle with no entry points. You couldn't get an Equity show without Equity credits. You couldn't get the credits without an agent, and agents didn't want you without the credits. I was not, however, dismayed. The theater business was no more perverse than life as I had known it.

I was luckier than many new actors, I had an agent. Mort Steiner had come to a production at the academy. He signed me not for my great talent but because he needed bodies. Mort worked out of his uncle's agency and was as new to the business as I. We took each other on, each fully aware of how little the other could do for our mutual career advancement. With such low expectations, how was it possible to be disappointed?

* * *

Months passed and Mort had found me nothing. Day after day, I made the rounds of producers' offices, leaving resumes and eight-by-ten glossies. I read *Backstage* and tried to remain hopeful. To keep the juices flowing, I acted without pay in neighborhood productions staged in basements. This, I told myself, was true theater. For money, I handed out playbills and worked children's birthday parties as "Zooks the Under Clown."

Mort called me one day full of excitement. He had booked me for the American Poultry Convention.

"Poultry?" I repeated with disbelief.

"All you have to do is strut around in a chicken costume, peck at the stage, and say 'bok bok.' "

"For this I studied Chekhov?"

"Remember, 'there are no small parts, only small actors.' "

"I hardly think Stanislavski meant that to become the battle cry of agents."

"Two hundred and fifty dollars for an afternoon's work," he added. A small fortune! I thought, deliriously embracing Stanislavski's credo. "The ad agency will deliver the costume to your apartment. And they'll send a car to pick you up at two on the afternoon of the seventeenth."

When the costume arrived, I pulled off the casing and stared dumbly at the contents. If this was a chicken, where were the feathers? With horror I realized my professional debut was to be in the role of a plucked pullet.

The costume was the shape of a six-foot headless chicken. It was coated with a noxious, pale yellow, lumpy polyurethane. Touching the clammy "skin" gave me the chills.

On the breast was a large tag that read "Lickin' Chickin™." Licking seemed advisable. You certainly wouldn't want to eat it. There were small eyeholes in the breastbone but no air holes. The costume smelled like a chicken—one that had been left on the counter for several days.

It took me longer than I had anticipated to get dressed. This outfit could not have been designed for human occupancy. With my arms crooked unnaturally in the wings, it was nearly impossible to pull on the webbed feet. My toes felt like they were bound by constricting rubber bands.

Unfortunately, I was too tall for the costume. To see at all, I had to crouch down within the chicken. And even then my view was slanted, enabling me to see only the first four feet of the world.

As I lumbered to the apartment door, I heard Ben's disembodied singing from the hallway. Stoned again. I heard the apartment door open. There was a stunned silence and then, "Hail Mary, full of grace. My prayers be answered." He dropped to his knees and began ripping at my costume.

"Stop it, damn you!" I yelled.

Handfuls of polyurethane were disappearing into his mouth.

"Ben!"

That a larger-than-life plucked bird was talking did not faze Ben—nor, apparently, did the taste of polyurethane. I swung at him with my wings and missed. Kicking him with webbed feet proved more effective. I tried to skirt around his fallen body but he grabbed my drumstick and tore at it, exposing the chicken-wire foundation.

"Come back, my little chickadee," he entreated as I squeezed out the door.

By the time I got downstairs, it was close to two-thirty. There was no limo in sight. Panicked, I paced back and forth in front of my building for five minutes. Still no limo. If I expected to collect my two hundred and fifty dollars, I would have to get to the convention on my own.

New York City cab drivers apparently have an aversion to picking up fowl. The subway was out—Lickin' Chickin would never fit through the turnstile. I had to walk it. With my limited view, I was happily spared the sight of pedestrians' faces. I am a "serious actor," I told myself over and over; though it didn't drown out the laughs and jeers I was drawing from passing strangers.

I hunkered down inside the costume, whose weight seemed to be increasing with every step. With my eyes on the pavement, I counted blocks. After six my back threatened to spasm. Sixteen blocks south and five east brought me to the hotel where the American Poultry Convention was meeting. A pair of black pants rising above shiny shoes stood before me. My wing was grabbed. For an instant I feared I was being mugged, but then I heard a familiar gritty voice saying, "Where in hell have you been?" Mort Steiner propelled me into the hotel. "Well, dammit, answer me."

"Steiner, go pluck yourself."

"You're over an hour late. The agency's furious. You missed the stage show," he railed, maneuvering me through the lobby and down a corridor to a complex of doors. "The program's been changed."

"Nice of you to tell me. I spent all morning practicing my 'bok boks.' "

"I just found out an hour ago. It's very simple, just one line. They want you to mingle with the cocktail crowd and invite people to 'feel your firm flesh and meaty breasts.' "

"They what?"

"Just try to look appetizing," he paused, apparently surveying me. "Mallory, this was a very expensive costume. Why are there holes in it?"

"My roommate was hungry."

"Christ . . ."

"Listen, those holes are the only things saving me from asphyxiation!"

"Is that you?" he asked suddenly.

"No, it's Dame Mae Witty," I snapped. God, if Father could see me now.

"I mean that smell. It's awful. What have you done in there?"

"Nothing!" I protested.

"You can't go in there smelling like a dead chicken."

"I am more than willing to go home."

"No!" he said with an anguished cry. "My reputation is riding on this. Stay here."

Steiner returned a few minutes later bearing a bag with a pharmacy imprint. "Here, douse yourself with this," he said, trying to hand me the bag.

"You do it. My wing spread isn't what it should be."

He poured the contents over my stump.

"Tabu!" I shrieked as the cloyingly sweet perfume assaulted my senses. "Are you mad?" The answer was obvious. I started down the hall. Steiner grabbed a wing and pulled me back towards the complex of doors. I fought but was weakened by the noxious scent of rancid rubber steeped in Tabu.

The next thing I knew a door was opened and I was pushed through it. The door slammed behind me.

"Steiner!" I screamed, beating the door with my wings. Suddenly I was aware of an unnatural silence. Turning, I saw a crowd of male and female legs. Damn. I waddled to the nearest pair of legs and asked softly, "Excuse me, is this the convention?"

"Uh, yes," a man answered hesitantly.

"Would you care to feel my firm flesh and meaty breasts," I offered.

The legs faded into the crowd. Perhaps I had got it wrong. I turned in another direction and, using my stage projection, said to a pair of plaid pants and a pink polyester pantsuit, "I'm a Lickin' Chickin. Won't you feel my meaty flesh and firm breasts?"

The woman yelped.

"Oh hell," I swore. The hot and stuffy room was not improving matters. I smelled like an aged whore who had spent the morning eviscerating chickens. I started into the crowd hoping to find birds of a featherless. The crowd parted silently. Moses at the Red Sea. I waddled on and found a podium before me. In order to get a better view, I clambered up on it. For the first time, I could see their faces. They were struck dumb, many of them open-mouthed, by my portrayal of an American pullet.

They continued to stare. My first captive audience. As they were not inclined to feel my firm flesh, it behooved me to entertain them in another way. I could hardly shuffle off to Buffalo with webbed feet. Unfortunately, as a tragedienne, musicals were hardly my forte. I searched my memory for an appropriate song. Nothing came to me. People were still staring.

"Fly, fly," I sang, flapping my denuded wings, "where might I fly . . . ."

A door opened at the back of the room, and Steiner's stricken face appeared. He waved his arms wildly. So I wasn't a songbird. Did he expect me to entertain poultry people with snatches of *Antigone*?

I continued to sing, "Soaring over patches of green . . . ." Steiner was suddenly beside me on the podium and pushing. Why, I wondered, was my agent always pushing me? I used my full weight to oppose him and continued to sing.

"What in hell are you doing?" Mort whispered.

"Entertaining the troops, buzz off," I muttered.

"You've got the wrong regiment," he hissed, halting me midnote.

"These aren't chicken farmers?" I had thought the pink pantsuit to be irrefutable evidence. "Who are they?"

"Auto parts dealers."

"Auto parts? But I don't know any songs about auto parts."

"Mallory, out of here, NOW!"

"But they love me," I protested. How could he ask me to disappoint my public?

"Look again, lambchop, that ain't love."

And indeed, it wasn't.

The Coming Rage

"The ad agency wants you blackballed," Mort announced on the phone a few days later. "That's the good news. The bad news is Tosca's Costumes is suing you for two hundred and seventy-nine dollars in damages."

"You can't get turnips from a stone," I muttered. An uneasy silence followed. "And?" I hazarded warily.

"My uncle wants to drop you as a client."

"But you were the fool who pushed me through the wrong door!"

"I've decided to give you one more chance."

" 'The quality of mercy is not strained.' "

"Huh? Well, we've decided your best move would be to leave town . . ."

"On a rail, no doubt."

"Listen Mallory, when things die down . . ."

"Die down?" I echoed angrily. "Dead is dead, Mort."

"You're ranting."

"Fancy that. All I wanted was to act, to be someone. Now Lickin' Chickin is threatening ruination, I'm being sued for money I don't have, my body still reeks of vulcanized Tabu, and you recommend tar and feathers. Bah!"

"Are you quite through?" he asked coolly.

"I suppose," I responded glumly.

"I've got you an audition for a production in Buffalo."

"What's the play?"

"*Equus*."

"Do I speak or whinny?"

"You act, for chrissakes."

I sighed. From chickens to horses. Would I never break into human parts? "How long?"

"Four weeks of rehearsal and a three-week run."

"I meant how long an exile."

"A few months, maybe four. You build up your credits in regional theater, and we'll have you on Broadway in no time."

Six years later, I was still kicking around regional theater. The work was not steady, lucrative, or particularly rewarding.

I had had my shot at fame as the understudy in a Broadway production of *Corduroy Nights*.

When the lead called in sick, I expected to follow Shirley MacLaine in the annals of Broadway history; but if there were any critics in the audience that night, they kept mum. The play closed two days later.

I was still living in New York, but now with Maude. To be living again *en famille* was not a matter of choice but of necessity. Better to live with relatives than an ailing homosexual whore, I reasoned. One cold sore would put Ben in bed for days, as hypochondria took root and flourished. He expected me to tend to him, and I probably would have had Maude not arrived in town.

Maude and I did not get on any better than we had as teenagers. Without my occasional long stretches on the road, we never would have survived.

Maude was the agitator. She was, if anything, more beautiful than before. Men still flocked to her but Maude, having swung 180 degrees since her nights with the football team, now found them "extraneous." As the token female editor at Woolsy and Balzac, she had raised the consciousness of one of the oldest publishing houses in America. Maude claimed the senior editor actually cringed when he saw her approach. Small wonder . . . Maude took to feminism with the same relentless zeal she had applied to flying, Christ, and sex. For her, a day without diatribe was a day without sun.

My love life, with its highs and many lows, provided Maude further ammunition. While I was the first to admit that men treated me casually, rather like a favorite book, I did not take offense. This was the seventies, when commitments were anathema to all enlightened folk. Still, Maude's insistence that I was being shabbily treated reminded me of Sam. Old hurts never die, they just eat away. Soon I stopped protesting when she insisted all men were "parasitic sods."

My standard of living had slumped precipitously since my childhood. Discomfort and hunger had become the norm. That was all fine and good so long as I thought of myself as an artist committed to her craft. But lately, Doubt had been making insidious inroads. Being a good actor did not guarantee even one meal a day. I still had no New York notices, no bank account, no husband, no credibility, and no possessions. And worse, when I heard echoes of Mother asking, "What are you doing with your life?" I had no answers. To reply I was going to be a great actor was becoming painfully absurd. I began to wonder if I should look for another profession.

Maude, on the other hand, resisted self-doubt. She plowed ahead energetically while, trailing in her wake, I found myself swept back into the role of drudge. Since my hours were the most flexible and my wages the lowest, I became the housewife. Maude, who railed against men enslaving women for domestic purposes, thought nothing of selling me down the river.

Had I objected, Maude would have launched into another "dialogue" and I was bone-weary of arguing.

In the winter of 1978, changes began slapping up against us. Maude became exceedingly moody. I braced myself for yet another of her violent ideological swings. Was she considering lesbianism, politics, or returning to the womb? Her harangues at the "dinner" table were disjointed and peppered with quotations from the Bhagavadgita, Dr. Seuss, Erich Fromm, Shulamith Firestone, Nietzsche, and Marabel Morgan.

This went on for a month. Mort mortgaged my sanity with a part in a Syracuse Stage production. Seven weeks in the snowbelt numbed my ragged spirits. When I returned to the city, however, I suffered a rapid thaw. I was greeted by Maude's announcement that she was looking for sperm.

"Sperm?" I echoed, dropping in a chair.

"Not just any old sperm. It has to be high-quality, high-density sperm."

"A high-protein diet?" I guessed.

"Oh, honestly, Mallory, don't be so thick. I need sperm and it is not that easy to find."

"Really?" I said with surprise. I stood up and reached for a pack of cigarettes.

"When did you start smoking?" Maude asked.

"In Syracuse. I needed something to keep my fingers warm."

"It needs to be anonymous," she elaborated.

"Anonymous sperm?"

"Yes."

"Have you tried Bloomingdale's?"

"Bloomingdale's doesn't have a sperm bank," she said with impatience.

"Give them time."

"My child is going to . . ."

"Your child!" I interrupted. "Lord, Maude, don't tell me."

"A little girl."

I flopped down in a heap. "Why?"

"To fulfill a need."

"Dear God," I intoned dramatically, "stop her before she fulfills again. Listen Maudie, it's one thing to watch you catapult around the universe slamming into precepts, laying waste to religions and the male organ; but this is too much. You can't have a child just to play out your newest obsession."

"It's not like that," she argued.

"Right. And what's going to happen to the child six

months down the road, when you become intrigued by neo-nazism or polar ice caps?"

"That won't happen."

"It always happens. Look at your life."

She turned away. "You are hopelessly behind the times, Mallory. I am a liberated woman. Single parenthood is the coming rage."

"You haven't the faintest notion how to raise a baby!"

"Ah! But *you* do," she said calmly, turning to face me.

"So?" I asked warily.

"You'll help."

"No, I will not! I mean it, Maude."

Maude simply smiled. "Yes, you will. You always do."

"Get this straight, kid. I am an actor . . ."

"An *unemployed* actor," she stressed.

"Be that as it may, my years in the Baby Bastille are over. I am never going to take care of anybody ever again."

"We'll see," she said as she drifted out of the room.

Of Sperm and Men

Maude made an appointment with a sperm bank in midtown; but before she could keep it, a senior editor at Woolsy and Balzac died. Maude was offered the position. Editorial sway being the one inducement Maude could not resist, baby-making was postponed. I heaved a mighty sigh of relief. At the rate my dance card was being filled, I might well have ended up as Maude's nanny.

Maude inherited a number of authors from the senior editor. Most of them she classified as hacks, but she was enthusiastic about Travis Holmes.

"Sounds like a man," I ventured one night over a dinner of canned hash.

"It is a man."

"But you don't like men," I persisted.

"He's a new-woman's man."

"I beg your pardon."

"Ideologically acceptable," she answered. As I still looked blank, she added, "He's a feminist."

"Lord, not another of those men writing tracts on the super mom ethic!"

"You haven't heard of Travis Holmes?" she chastised.

I mulled the name over in my mind. "Is he the guy who writes those grisly psychological horror stories?"

"They are masterpieces," she said simply.

Over the next few months, Travis Holmes's name was often on Maude's lips. I began to suspect she had decided the sperm needn't be anonymous.

When Travis Holmes's latest oeuvre, *Heart in Hand,* came out that spring, Maude lured me to the publication party with promises of food. Protein was an item I valued more than gold. And I confess, I wanted to meet a man Maude could admire.

I arrived late because the left heel of my one good pair of shoes had fallen into a subway grating. Time spent looking for a shoe repair shop was time wasted. I limped into the party preoccupied with the knowledge that I couldn't afford a new heel.

The room was crowded with what I supposed were literati. I couldn't find Maude or anyone who fit Travis Holmes's description. Maude had spoken of Travis in ideological terms. My imagination supplied the rest: hunchbacked with slightly greasy black hair, a hawk nose, and stubby fingers.

I hailed a passing waiter. "Excuse me, is this the pub party for Travis Holmes?"

"*Yo no comprendo.*"

Sighing, I took two glasses of champagne from his tray

and went to look for protein. I was frightfully hungry. A platter of jumbo shrimp arrested my attention.

It was difficult to engulf the entire bounty without appearing indelicate. I waited twenty seconds between each sweep of the platter. "One Mississippi . . . two Mississippi . . ." I counted softly. My peripheral vision encountered a man approaching from the left.

"Are they good?" he asked, intent on poaching my preserve.

"Not especially," I lied. Licking my fingers, I turned to look at him. He was, there was no other word for it, gorgeous. Tall, blond, midthirties, with dark eyes, an assured manner, and a smile that could sell heatolaters to the Arabs. He was dressed casually but with evident taste. A male model if ever there was one, I thought disdainfully.

I had been surveying him while standing at a list, my broken shoe flat on the floor. He was regarding me oddly, trying to make sense of my deformity without appearing rude.

"Would you like a drink?" he asked.

"Why not?"

When he turned to signal a waiter, I raised up three inches on my left toes. By the time he swung back, I was level. He appeared puzzled. "A good party, no?"

"Hard to judge. I've never been to a party for a psychopath before." The waiter arrived. I returned my two empty glasses and took another.

"Just one?" teased the male model.

"Since you insist." I took another and drained it. "Cheers. Listen, would you mind moving a bit to your left. They just brought out a new tray of hors d'oeuvre." As he moved obligingly, I was most disappointed to see it was a plate of oysters.

"Ah, oysters," he said. He took a particularly large juicy one, daubed it with red sauce, opened his mouth, and slid it down his throat. I watched, aghast.

"Here," he said, offering me one.

"No, I couldn't." There are some gustatory experiences that can keep until the taste buds are dead.

"I insist," he said pleasantly. "Would you like it straight or with horseradish?"

"Straight," I mumbled. I took the oyster from his outstretched hand and stared at it with apprehension. Opening my mouth, I tilted the shell. The oyster plopped onto my tongue. Salt and slime. My throat constricted, unwilling to accept such cargo. I could hardly spit it out with the male model standing there but to swallow was inconceivable. I was drowning in juices. Finally, I held my nose, which forced me to swallow. The male model stared at me with wonderment.

"So, you like horrific literature," was all I could think to say.

"You don't, I gather."

"I've never read any. Somehow I've never felt the need to be terrified. It seems counterproductive." As did this whole conversation. My left arch was throbbing. And all for a male model who willingly ingested raw shark fodder. To hell with it, I thought, resuming my cockeyed posture.

He neatly adjusted his gaze to my lopsided stance. "Most people find horror to be cathartic."

"I'll stick to bran," I said tartly.

He laughed. It was a full, rolling laugh, tempting me to

like him. Maude appeared at my elbow as I finished my fourth glass of champagne.

"Hi Maudie, where's your friend, Insane Grey?"

"What?"

"The author. The psychopath. The intended sperm donor." I had never seen Maude blush before, even when Gerald explained menopause to her pajama party.

"Mallory, you're drunk!"

"True." And dizzy too.

"You're Mallory, Maude's sister? Well this is a pleasure." He offered his right hand and said, "I'm Travis Holmes, the psychopath."

"Dear God."

"I've been called worse—and by people who know me. Tell me, though, to whom am I donating my sperm?"

"Oh . . ." This was altogether too embarrassing. I collapsed neatly to the floor, thankful for my training. Travis knelt beside me and said, "Get a doctor."

"Don't bother," Maude countermanded. "Get up, Mallory. You never could act worth a damn."

Travis was taking my pulse, which was surely racing. "She's definitely ill."

"She's sick all right," Maude pronounced.

I opened my left eye a trace. Travis was still hovering over me. He winked. This time my swoon was involuntary.

I came to in my own bed with my head pounding and my stomach verging on upheaval. "Eraagh," I moaned.

Maude came to the door wearing the face of a sumo wrestler. She said nothing.

"We are not amused?" I hazarded. She made no reply. "It must have been the champagne. Inferior vintage."

"Yes, one who is used to the finest white Ripple should not sully her taste buds with Tattinger '73."

"I am sorry I embarrassed you."

"That is the least of it," she retorted.

"I said I was sorry. Can't the man take a joke?"

"A joke, yes. It was probably the vomit that discouraged him."

"The vomit!" I wailed. Maude smiled broadly. "Oh, Lord, I didn't . . ."

"No, you didn't," she said a little wistfully.

"He should have told me his name. How was I to know he wasn't a male model? Psychopaths are supposed to be warped and gnarled so you know to cross the street."

"Travis says Evil is most effective when cloaked in beauty."

"He should know," I said bitterly. As a person with an "interesting face," I had always resented unbridled beauty. "His looks border on the criminal."

"Thank you," said a male voice from the other room.

"Maude!" I gasped.

"It certainly wasn't my idea. He insisted on seeing us home. We're going to dinner now. Travis, come see for yourself. She lives . . ."

"No," I said hurriedly. I did not want to be viewed.

Travis joined Maude at the door. "You are better?"

For a moment, I was unable to answer. The sight of the two of them framed by the doorway was startling. A study in contrasts, dark and light, balancing to perfection. A child of this union would be something to see.

"Yin yang," I murmured.

"I beg your pardon," said Travis.

"Nothing," I said hastily.

"You are better?"

"Never worse, thanks," I said, running my fingers through my hair, attempting an impromptu coif. "I gather I was unconscionably rude this evening."

"Yes," he said flatly. So much for gracious apologies. "You dismembered a very important party."

"Then why were you wasting your time talking to me. I don't even buy your bloody books."

"Oh, for heaven sakes, be civil, Mallory," objected Maude.

"As a matter of fact, I was hungry," said Travis. "Talking to you seemed to be the only way to break your tenacious grip on what remained of the hors d'oeuvre."

I glared at him with the conviction of one caught red-handed. Unfortunately, moral certitude was on his side. He returned my glare. I forced myself to yawn indifferently. Travis surprised me by laughing.

"You are in my debt," he said with amusement.

"That is hardly a coup. I am in everyone's debt."

"With manners like that, I shouldn't wonder," he mused. "However, I am willing to settle out of court. I will forgive your debt if you eat with us."

"Why?" I asked, seeing no logic to this proposal.

"You shall entertain us."

"I am incapable of entertaining anyone but Death at the moment. You go."

Travis walked into the room and sat down in an armchair strewn with dirty clothes. "If you are ailing, we shall wait. But I warn you, I am hungry and your debt is growing."

Thus began our odd trio. For reasons I could not fathom, Travis and Maude included me in all their plans. When I begged off, citing lack of capital, they split my portion of the bill. We created a new form of social life, dutch cripple dating.

My curiosity was piqued. How could a man so outwardly charming be a professional ghoul? Maude gave me copies of his books, which I was loath to read. Why unearth the beast? I sat down one Wednesday afternoon intending to skim a chapter and stopped six books later on Friday morning. My body felt as though it had been drained through intensive electro-shock treatments.

Maude was right, his books were masterfully written. They pulled you along to a near climax of horror and then retreated slightly before pushing on to a new crest. Rather like good sex, I imagined. His characters were common folks cemented in reality. When the natural became the supernatural, it was easy to suspend disbelief and be drawn in with the characters.

Looking back on the plots, I was amazed at what I had swallowed, although it seemed perfectly plausible at the time. This led me to wonder what I was buying from Travis himself. Travis may have been engaging, generous, fun, and quick-witted. (And there was no denying he exuded sexual charm.) But from his books, I knew he was capable of masterful manipulation. I couldn't help wondering where I fit into his plans.

And Maude's plans. Travis was Maude's property. It was not like Maude to be so generous with her toys.

One night before Travis arrived, I was sitting on the bed studying lines. Maude peered in and said, "Wear that purple chemise, it looks great on you."

"Why do you want me to look great?"

"That's an odd question," Maude replied.

"Not really. Why should I look great for your boyfriend?"

"He is not my boyfriend. Travis and I are . . . twin souls."

"Spare me. Look, you two go alone, I have to study for that audition tonight."

"Travis will be unhappy if you don't join us."

"Why? Am I his triplet soul?"

"He's going through a hard time now, Mallory. Be kind."

"Hard time? What hard time?" I asked, genuinely surprised.

"Don't kid yourself, divorce is hard on a man too."

"Divorce!" I exclaimed. "He's married?"

"Not anymore." She was saying something else, but I could not hear for the noise in my head. Everything made sense now. Of course he was married. Anyone that good-looking picks up baggage along the way. And no wonder he saw us in tandem, my role was that of duenna. Maude could hardly be named as corespondent in a divorce case if Mamacita Mallory was standing guard.

"The rat bastard!"

"Mallory!"

"When was the divorce finalized?"

"In March sometime, why?"

If he was divorced before I met him, Travis had no need for a chaperone. That left Maude. What had she to gain by my presence? Maude sat down on my bed and flung her hair forward in a black glistening cascade. She brushed it with vigorous sensuality. I looked in the mirror at my own reddish mop and sighed.

"What's the problem?" she asked.

"No problem, I just don't want to be a Musketeer anymore."

"Haven't you had fun?" she asked, continuing to brush.

" 'Please, sir, I want some more,' " I mimicked in a boyish cockney accent, pushing an imaginary porridge bowl before me. " 'More?' " I thundered querulously.

Maude stopped brushing and stood up. She scowled at me.

"*Oliver*," I explained. "I feel like an orphan begging for more gruel. It's no good."

"But we need you to be a part of us," she argued. An old suspicion flowered within me.

"How could I be so stupid? You think if I come to care about you and Travis, I will want to tend to your baby!"

"Don't be absurd. Travis doesn't want any more children."

"Any *more*?" Travis was a man of subterranean depths. For three months, we had been sharing time. One drunken evening, I had told him about Sam and other romantic disasters. Yet he had never mentioned his wife and kiddies to me. What further secrets lurked beneath the surface?

If I stayed in this relationship a minute longer, I would doubtless suffer the same fate as the Titanic.

"I need some air." I grabbed my coat and script and ran out of the apartment. Travis was climbing the stairs as I descended.

"Mallory!" he exclaimed as I brushed past him. I did not stop to explain. It was time to develop mysterious depths of my own.

A week later I left town for a dinner-theater production of *Rebecca* in Wilkes-Barre, Pennsylvania. I was to play the lead, a nameless ingenue who works as a companion to the dreadful Mrs. Van Hopper. The ingenue falls for the mysterious Max de Winter. He marries her out of what she suspects is pity and takes her to his estate, Manderley. There she struggles with the memory of his first wife, the lovely Rebecca.

When I read the script, I was struck by the similarities between Max de Winter and Travis. Both were devilishly good-looking and closemouthed about their past. Max, however, was wealthy. Travis lived in the Connecticut woods.

I was glad to be away from Maude and Travis. Before leaving New York, I had spent as much time as possible away from the apartment. Maude and I came to blows as I was packing. A lot was said, none of it sisterly. Seven weeks of separation would do much to heal the lesions.

With every rehearsal, I felt more like the ingenue. Eventually I realized it was because I was in love with Travis, but this bit of intelligence didn't come to me at once. The actor playing Max was dark and arrogant beyond reason. When I did make the connection, it hit me like a sudden fever. I became at once chilled and sweaty—not an attractive condition and not one I could have hidden from knowing eyes in New York.

I didn't want to be in love. I had loved Sam and he had vanished. I had loved Mother and she had died. Clearly love required sterner stuff than I was made of.

By the time I returned, Travis and Maude would be married (Maude had intimated as much). I threw myself into my part and tried not to think what would happen when the play was over.

The reviews were mixed. One critic said my performance was "adequate but not distinguished." Much like my life, I mused dispiritedly.

Backstage after the final performance, I was scrubbing my makeup off with a vengeance when I saw Travis's face in my mirror. It seemed natural enough: my life was in crisis,

I was hallucinating. Pretty soon other specters of my past would crowd the mirror. Mother and Sam could lead the inquisition.

"You'll hurt yourself," said the vision.

I whirled around and sure enough, there was Travis in the flesh. I couldn't think what to say, so I continued to scrub my face.

"You'll be down to the subcutaneous tissue soon."

"What are you doing here?"

"Lecturing you on the evils of home-style dermabrasion."

"Actors are like snakes, we have many skins to shed." I patted my raw face with a towel. It stung like mad.

"You were admirable out there."

"You are too kind, according to the local critics."

"Take my word for it, you were good. I've always found *Rebecca* to be overwritten and fussy. But through you, I saw it differently. The girl's distress was palpable."

I laughed. "So, Art *does* imitate Life."

"Are you distressed?" asked Travis.

"No more than your average unemployment statistic," I answered glibly. "What are you doing here anyway?"

"Research," he replied.

"You need a map. This is Pennsylvania not Transylvania."

He smiled and my heart seized up. "I'm going to tour the Civil War battlefields for my next book, *Civil Souls*."

"Oh. How's Maudie?" I asked, as I smeared moisturizer onto my face.

"You know Maude."

"Barely. Every time I think I've got her pegged, she flies off on another tangent. Not to speak ill of your beloved, but she is the most easily obsessed person I know."

Travis was frowning. He picked up a jar of cold cream and idly tossed it from hand to hand. "You left rather abruptly. Maude said you were running from us."

"Maude is liable to say many things."

"She thinks you are in love with me."

I laughed hollowly and hoped my performance was adequate if not distinguished.

"Are you?" he asked, putting down the cold cream and gazing at me.

"No. As Maude says, 'Love is an invalid seizure.' "

He stood up. "Where are you headed from here?"

"California. Or maybe Omaha. No one is clamoring for me at the moment."

"Why not come with me, then?" he offered.

"Why not leap onto a whirring buzz saw?" The end result would be about the same.

"What are you talking about?"

I shrugged my shoulders.

"Look, I'm trying to help," he said, sitting down again.

"Who appointed you good Samaritan? Oh, Maude, of course."

"I haven't seen Maude in a month." That snapped me to attention.

"Why not?" I demanded.

"I hadn't the urge," he said with sarcasm.

"Dear me . . . *And Then There Were None.*"

"Now will you consider my invitation?"

"Certainly not. You are far too devious for a simple sod like me. Hell, I only discovered by accident that you had a wife and kids. I am willing to assume you are a necrophiliac, but I fear there's more I haven't even guessed at."

"I am not hiding anything. I was married to Sarah, whom I loved very much. She left me and took our three children, one in utero. There was a very nasty court battle and I lost. It is not a part of my life I enjoy talking about. Maude was aware of the situation because it affected my work. If you want the details, read the scandal sheets." Such cool anger.

"Where's Sarah now?"

"In Boston. I don't like to talk about this." He leaned forward in a challenging manner. "Marry me."

I stared at him dumbfounded. "Why should you want to marry me?"

"I want you."

"You can have me. And it won't cost you a marriage license either."

"Don't you want to get married?" he asked, astounded.

"No," I said. "You know my history. I've not had great success with love. Six months at the outside, that's what I'd give our marriage. So let's just keep it simple."

"No. I want to marry you, Mallory."

He had not mentioned love. All things were possible, declared my heart. My head, however, knew that Travis ought to be marrying the bright and beautiful Maude. Travis was Byzantine by nature. I might never know his reasons. But dear God, I wanted him.

To marry Travis would require a leap of faith, and there was a good chance I would end up face first in the dirt.

"Sounds good. Where do I sign?"

He laughed that rich, rolling laugh and kissed me. I realized with a start it was the first time he had ever touched me.

"Let's find a justice of the peace," he said.

"Shouldn't we date first?"

He laughed again.

"Not that it seems to matter to you, Travis, but I do love you."

"I know that. I knew it when you denied it."

"Christ! Another bad notice," I joked, but I couldn't help noticing he didn't return my declaration.

Leger de Main

In bed Travis was artful, obliging, and energetic . . . all night. By first light I was thoroughly limp, but not Travis. While I struggled to recoup with a nap, he jogged. Eight miles later, he returned, showered, read the papers, worked on his notes, ordered breakfast, and then roused me.

Struggling with cumulative exhaustion, I dogtrotted after Travis as he strode around the battlefields. Through Gettysburg, Antietam, Bull Run, and Manassas we marched.

From Virginia I called Father to tell him I had married. He asked where we were spending our honeymoon.

Bermuda, I lied. To be honeymooning on battlefields seemed an evil omen, a portent of the wars Travis and I would someday wage.

The land was verdant and peaceful now. I saw no telltale signs of carnage. But Travis would stare at the bend in a creek or a copse of trees and suddenly start scribbling notes, almost as if the ghosts were parading for him. This gave me no great sense of ease.

One night in bed, I asked him about his books. Why did he want to terrify people?

"Do you want the real answer or what I tell the magazines?"

"Both." I curled up tightly against him.

"It is an art form that affords me a twisted pleasure. I like finding people's phobic pressure points and hitting them at their most primitive level.

"*Or*, I create horror to help people cope with the real horror of the world."

"Which is which?" I asked. As he said nothing, I turned to face him. He was smiling slyly. "Well?"

"Whatever you choose to believe."

When our tour was done, we hopped into Travis's old Toyota station wagon and headed north to his home in Redding, Connecticut. I had no idea what to expect. Maude had once told me that only five percent of writers in America could support themselves on their royalties. Certainly Sam's lifestyle had been minimal. And Travis's earnings had been winnowed away by alimony and child support. I resolved to forget acting and find a job that paid. After all, as a feminist, Travis would surely expect me to shoulder some of the financial burden.

We stopped by the New York apartment so I could get my things. Maude was at work. I left a note asking her to forward my mail to Travis's house and fled.

Travis was waiting, double-parked. He looked doubtfully at the one box of belongings and battered suitcase it had taken me six years to accumulate. Hurriedly, I shoved them in the trunk and climbed in front.

"That's it?" he asked incredulously.

"Well, half the couch is mine. Will we need it?"

"The one that smells like cat semen?"

"Is that what that was? We wondered why anyone would leave a perfectly good couch on the sidewalk. The smell didn't hit us until the third floor landing, and by then it was too late. Let's go, I feel ridiculously guilty about Maude."

"Why? You didn't take the couch."

"I took you."

"She didn't want me," he said as he rammed the Toyota into first and pulled out into traffic. I considered the ambiguity of his statement. Had Travis wanted Maude?

An hour and ten minutes later, we turned off Route 53 onto Gallows Hill Road, Redding.

"Almost home," he said. The road was tortuously twisted and steep.

At last he turned the car into a driveway on the left. Hanging over the stone wall was a green wooden sign. In small letters it read, "Leger de Main." The driveway wound through deep woods and up yet another hill. I was prepared for anything but what I saw.

A magnificent white house with dark green shutters sat on the hill. From the circular drive, a wide manicured lawn stretched down the hill to the woods.

"Damn you!" I cursed. "Did you have to be rich, too?"

"Too?"

"Isn't there anything wrong with you?" I asked with exasperation.

"Let me count the flaws."

"I'm serious, Travis."

"What about that mansion you grew up in?"

"The Delirium? That's back in the mists of time. I wouldn't know how to live with all this grace and comfort."

"Well, then, we'll build you a squalid hut on the back hill and hire someone to come flog you twice a week."

"Very funny. Where did you get all this money?"

"It's not my fault people like to be scared shitless."

"All this comes from writing?" I railed. I couldn't help thinking of the inequity of our professions.

"That and my grandparents, who left me a tidy bundle."

Before I could argue further a bent old man in a dark suit emerged from the house. I smiled my Lady Bountiful Meets the Manservant Smile but he ignored me and went around to Travis's door.

"Hello, Father," greeted Travis.

I stared dumbly at my newly acquired relative. He was mostly bald but for a fringe of white hair of uneven length. The patch of hair behind his right ear was black. He did not share his son's good looks.

Mr. Holmes looked at me. His eyes darkened and narrowed. Turning to Travis, he said in a low voice, "Clara was acting up again, Teddy. But don't you worry. I taught her a lesson she won't soon forget! Stripped her down and reemed her out good this time."

"Who's Clara?" I whispered nervously.

"Dad, I want you to meet Mallory. She's going to be living here."

"Why?"

Why indeed?

"Because I asked her to, Father," Travis explained gently.

"Women are no good, Teddy."

"This one is."

"Trouble is coming, I see it," Mr. Holmes muttered ominously.

I smiled with forced gaiety. "What marriage is complete without a soothsayer?"

"Marriage?" Mr. Holmes bellowed.

"Dad, would you like to drive?" Travis asked as he hurriedly got out of the car.

"With *her*?" I took my cue and got out the other side. With surprising agility, Mr. Holmes jumped behind the wheel. I had time only to remove one suitcase from the trunk before the Toyota lurched away.

Under Mr. Holmes's direction, the Toyota seemed to be having a Grand Mal seizure. It moved in fits and starts around the drive. The rear hatch door swung up and down, the windshield wipers slapped back and forth, and the emergency lights flashed rhythmically.

I turned to my husband of eleven days and said, "Is there something you would like to tell me?"

"Such as?"

"You're adopted?"

He laughed. "And not ten minutes ago you were begging me for a flaw. Dad's been a little queer since Mother departed, but he's quite harmless."

"I doubt Clara would agree."

"Clara is an Oldsmobile."

"He disemboweled an Oldsmobile?"

"So it would seem."

"Why?" I asked flatly.

"Maybe she asked for it," he said with amusement. We watched the Toyota lumber haltingly around the back of the house. Mr. Holmes was playing "Camptown Races" on the horn.

"Shall we go in?" offered Travis. Inside there was a lovely front entrance hall.

"I'll take this upstairs," said Travis of the suitcase. "You explore down here."

"I'll wait for you."

"No. Leger de Main is best seen alone. I'll catch up. Start in there," he said, pointing to a door under the curved staircase.

It was soon evident I would need to leave a trail of bread crumbs if I intended to explore at any length. Some rooms seemed to go on forever, and others were scarcely the size of a large closet. Something else was strange. It looked as though an unseen force had randomly removed the house's furnishings. In the music room, there was a piano bench but no piano. Clumps of books were missing from the library shelves. One room had half a set of drapes. The dining room contained eight Hitchcock chairs grouped around an empty space.

Apparently, Travis was not much on entertaining. The living room was an ocean of space surrounding one wing chair. Perhaps Sarah had perched there while Travis sat adoringly at her feet.

From the living room, I was able to see the side lawn where Mr. Holmes was beating the ground with a tennis racquet.

I leaned against the wall, which opened. Suddenly I found myself in another lit room. There were no windows or visible doors, just a fireplace and the portrait of a blond woman in a riding habit. There were several darts embedded in the painting.

Feeling like I had stumbled into a Nancy Drew mystery, I pounded on the walls and screamed for Travis. It was a good fifteen minutes before he suddenly materialized through the same hidden panel.

"Thank God."

"Sorry it took so long to find you. I had to make some calls, and you were in the last secret room I checked."

"There are others?"

"I've found only four, but legend has it there are seven."

"What if I had disappeared in one of the unknown three," I quarreled nervously.

"I was rather hoping you had."

"I could have died."

"Possibly," he laughed. "Come on then . . ." He pounded on a corner panel three times and kicked the baseboard once. A doorway slid open, revealing a darkened space. He picked up a broom and tapped the center of the ceiling twice. Another door opened, this time onto a hallway. I pushed Travis aside and darted for the open space.

"Does this place come with an instruction manual?"

"The only thing you need to know is that they are all one-way mechanisms."

"In other words, just because I found my way in, doesn't mean I can find my way out."

"Exactly."

"I am not budging another foot until you show me all the other secret rooms."

Travis shook his head. "You'll have to find them as I did, in the course of everyday life."

"But . . ."

"It will give you a sense of adventure. That is my wedding

present to you." He kissed me on the head. "Now, what do you think of Sarah's decorating?"

"Quite . . . original."

"Yes. I call it 'Belated Revenge.' The house was furnished when I left two weeks ago. Sarah seems to have collected a few things in my absence."

"Can she do that?"

"Not legally. That's what the calls were about. Let's get something to eat."

How could he act so calm when his house had been pillaged? "What are you going to do about Sarah?"

"Do? Nothing. You'll probably want to decorate Leger de Main in your own style anyway."

"Decorate?" I repeated dully. My experience was limited. And somehow I didn't think Deprivation Chic would be appropriate here.

The kitchen was the size of a tennis court with utility islands strategically positioned across the tiled floor. There was a huge professional cooking range, a microwave oven, several recessed refrigeration units, and acres of cabinets. This was not the place to confess to Travis that I liked my canned hash medium rare.

"What would you like for dinner?" he asked, opening one of the refrigerators.

"Whatever . . ." My attention was caught by a pool with cerulean blue water. It shimmered temptingly in the late afternoon heat. I wished I knew how to swim, but everytime Mother had tried to teach me I had sunk like a stone. Next to the pool was an off-scale two-story house. "Is that a cabana?"

"Hmmm?" he said, looking up. "No. Nell's playhouse."

My stepdaughter owned her own real estate. "What's that behind the trees?"

"An old carriage house. I write there."

"Why not here?" Surely there was enough room.

"I like the distance. There are no phones, and it still smells of old hay."

"Is that what you like about me?" I asked. His eyebrows arched in question. "Well, sometimes I feel like old hay." Used and useless, and out of my element.

"I have never thought of you as old hay," he said levelly and then turned back to the refrigerator. Proclamations of love were doled out sparingly and only when coupling.

"Well," I said with strained joviality. "What's it to be? Rack of Ham or Lobster Newport?" Travis seemed lost in a decision. I joined him at the refrigerator and said, "Then again, what I really hunger for is a vat of unflavored yogurt." The shelves were stocked with dozens of cartons of plain yogurt. Nothing else.

Surely the cabinets held something. They did, two chipped mugs and some mismatched plates. I opened a closet and found four fifty-pound sacks of dry dog food and a case of canned dog food.

"I didn't know you had a dog," I commented.

"I don't," he answered distractedly, still studying the yogurt.

I went to the refrigerator on the far wall and opened it. My scream was involuntary. A dead woodchuck lay on the top shelf. Its glazed eyes appeared to stare up at me. Travis hurried over and peered in.

"Oh," he said calmly. "That's for Mozart."

"Mozart is dead," I snapped.

"Not the composer," he said, "the wolf."

"I may be a city slicker," I argued, "but that is no wolf!"

"You've got it wrong."

"Lord, I hope so."

"Mozart is *my* wolf."

After a moment's silence, I found my voice. "Travis, this day has not been what I would call encouraging." I sat down and glared at him expectantly, defying him to make it right.

"Wolves need meat. Whenever we find a stunned animal on the road, we bring it home for Mozart. You understand?" I took his tone to mean that my new wifely duties would include foraging the highways for fresh kills.

"In other words, when Mozart claws at back door, I'm supposed to lob the woodchuck out to him, and then maybe he'll allow me safe passage to the cars."

"Mozart is in a three-acre pen surrounded by a ten-foot fence. He's a sly one though. Sometimes he manages to break loose. I'll have to ask you not to roughhouse with him just yet."

I studied my husband in silence. Clearly, he had no idea whom he had married. "I hardly ever force myself on fanged beasts," I said dryly. "Where did you two meet?"

"He was a gift."

"But of course, perfect for the man who has everything."

"When *Wolf's Down* became a best-seller, Sarah bought him from a breeder in Vermont."

I hadn't the stomach to ask what she had given him when *The Ghouling* was published. No doubt I would stumble on it sooner or later.

"Mozart is actually a crossbreed, five-eighths wolf and three-eighths malamute."

"Practically a lap dog," I commented.

Travis went to the closet and poured a good ten pounds

of dog food into a bucket and then took the woodchuck from its resting place. "Come meet Mozart," he invited.

"Silly me, I forgot to pack my chain-mail suit."

"Mallory, he's only a wolf." Travis sounded just like Mother.

"So you say. You run along, I'll catch up with you later."

"All right," he said with evident disappointment.

Several minutes after Travis left, Father Holmes came in through the kitchen door carrying a large metal bucket. He looked at me but said nothing. He went to the refrigerator, opened it, and emptied eight containers of yogurt into the bucket. Without a word, he left.

The phone rang.

"Hello," I answered.

"Are you mad?" bellowed a familiar voice.

"Yes, Maude, I do believe I am."

Warts and All

Travis returned to the kitchen an hour later, looking winded and flushed. "Mozart needed a workout," he explained.

I resolved not to mention the long tear in his shirt. It might be misconstrued as irrational female interference between a man and his wolf.

"Your editor called," I reported.

"Oh?" he said, dropping into a chair and running a hand through his damp blond hair. "What did 'my editor' want?"

"Blood," I answered, spying several beads of it under the rip in his shirt.

"Maude?" he asked incredulously.

"Ummm. She seems to have taken umbrage at our recent union. She rained doom, gloom, and if I heard her right, entrails down about our heads."

"She won't stay angry for long."

"Would that it were so simple. Maude has issued alarums to the entire Delaney tribe."

"Meaning?" he asked with amusement.

"You may expect several curious bodies prowling about the estate this weekend. And by 'curious' I mean peculiar, though they are no slouches at inquisition either."

"Good, I want to meet your family."

"No," I stated emphatically. The very last thing I needed in my life right now was my blood relatives.

"How bad can they be? You raised most of them."

"Next you'll be congratulating Dr. Frankenstein."

"I am no stranger to aberrant behavior. I daresay I can handle it," he boasted.

"It had occurred to me that a horror writer who lives in a carnivorous house could fend for himself." I smiled. "It wasn't you I was protecting."

"Then I shall protect you," he avowed. "Now, how many Delaneys are we talking about?"

"I think we'll be spared the full brunt of the spectacle. Most of them can't afford bus fare to the airport. But Maude will be here. I don't know what Ned does when he's not icing the puck in Buffalo. Lord, I hope there is a plague in New Mexico."

"Might I ask why?"

"That would keep Gerald out of our hair." Travis arched his brows. "Gerald is a county coroner," I explained.

"Really?" he exclaimed with excitement. "But why didn't you tell me?"

"Gerald is not something we brag about. Listen, are we going out to dinner or should I fix some dog food?"

"Dog food?"

"Well, it wouldn't be the first time." My husband's face filled with wonderment. Travis, it seemed, was not a member of the Ken-L Ration Generation.

"Mallory, you are simply amazing."

"There is nothing amazing about it. Poor people do it all the time. I prefer Kal Kan with oregano and freshly ground pepper, though it is more expensive. I used to eat Alpo, but now it is riddled with tubular things. I can't decide if they're intestines or arteries."

"Well, you've certainly whetted my appetite, let me get my coat and make a phone call." He disappeared behind a hinged bookcase. When he returned some minutes later, he thrust a handful of bills at me. While he wriggled into a sports coat, I counted the bills.

"Five hundred dollars!" I exclaimed.

"Isn't it enough?" he asked, adjusting his collar.

"That depends. Do you want me to throw it in a salad bowl with a little viniagrette or spend it?"

"The cupboards are bare. Hell, Sarah used to spend at least three hundred a week."

"How does gold bullion taste?"

"We entertained a lot," he said, shrugging his shoulders.

"Oh," I replied uneasily. "Is that a job requirement?"

"Don't you like to give parties?"

The last party I had given was in 1977. A bag of Fritos, a Mexican bean dip, and a case of Old Milwaukee beer. "Certainly."

"Sarah was famous for her parties. It will be good to have people in the house again. We'll wait until you've redecorated, of course."

"Of course." Redding was slightly more than an hour from the city. But my new life was light years away from my old. I had thought myself a competent person until I hit Connecticut five hours ago. Now it seemed I lacked every essential skill. I couldn't decorate, or cook, or entertain, or swim, or wrestle with wolves, or find my way from pillar to post. Travis was gazing at me expectantly.

"I'm sorry. Did you say something?"

"Yes, I said if you hurried I'd treat you to a box of Milk Bones."

That night we ferried four shopping carts through the aisles of a supermarket in Ridgefield. When one basket was filled, we delivered it to the manager's office to await the final tally.

Travis was a laborious shopper. He inspected each package, comparing ingredients and unit prices. He asked my opinion of several name brands. I had no opinions but had learned enough to know this to be unacceptable. Products I had never tasted were condemned for being too dry, too seasoned, or too bland. Travis followed my specious advice unquestioningly. I felt like a thorough fraud.

At the deli counter, he ordered provolone, prosciutto, pastrami, roast beef, smoked turkey breast, cappocola, hard salami, swiss cheese, antipasto salad, pickled peppers, liverwurst, and imported baked ham. Somewhere between the salami and the swiss cheese, the woman behind us in line abandoned her subtle groans and sneered, "Don't forget the olive loaf." Whereupon Travis ordered some olive loaf.

In the produce section, he took at least one of every vegetable, many of which looked like they had sprung from an alien soil. I had no idea how to cook them. But it was in the fruit section that Travis really let himself go wild. One whole shopping cart was devoted to pineapples, ugli fruit, bananas, kiwis, strawberries, imported raspberries, black grapes, green grapes, oranges, nectarines, mangoes, lemons, limes, plums, apples, and grapefruit. I stood by in stunned silence wondering if I would ever get the hang of conspicuous consumption.

At the checkout counter, I tried to stifle my cry when the register rang up $462.57. "My family is coming," I said weakly. The checker paid me no attention. This was Fairfield County.

Buying the food was the easy part. When we got home, I realized it would have to be put away. I was not equal to the task, but Travis was still running in high gear. Numbly I followed the flash. I stuffed detergent next to the cans of tomato sauce, peanut butter next to the toothpaste, figuring I had a lifetime to sort it out.

The produce went into the refrigerators. We would have to open a soup kitchen to use all the food before it rotted. When we were done, Travis looked very pleased with himself. I gathered he was one of those people who like to know the larder is full—to bursting.

"What can I get you to eat?" he asked genially.

The thought of eating anything made me gag. Travis made himself a thick sandwich and ate it purposefully. I could see the muscles of his jaw working as he chewed. I loved this man.

Funny I should feel like screaming.

I awoke disoriented. The nightmare was still fresh. I had been clinging to a log in a thrashing sea.

Drenched with sweat, I looked around and realized I didn't know where I was. Travis's sports coat anchored me. But Travis was not to be seen.

Downstairs, I made several wrong turns before I found my way to the kitchen. Would Travis object to a few discreet hatchet trail marks on the door frames?

Father Holmes was sitting at the breakfast table. I noticed the black patch of hair was now white. He was spooning a mixture of something red and green from a bowl.

"You can't have any," he declared, clutching the bowl to his stomach.

"Good morning to you, too, Father Holmes." Spying a pot of drip coffee on the stove, I went to pour myself a cup. But both of the mugs I had seen yesterday were gone. Father Holmes had one by his side. I found a bowl and poured coffee and cream in it.

Father Holmes was watching me. "You're a late sleeper."

I looked at the clock, prepared to apologize. "It is barely seven-fifteen!"

"Teddy's been working for hours."

"Oh. What are you eating?"

"Breakfast," he snapped.

"You don't like me much, do you?" I asked pleasantly.

"Can't say as I do. But it is of little consequence."

"Why?"

"Your days are numbered," he said with a hint of glee.

"In a manner of speaking, everyone's days are numbered," I responded calmly.

"I am not talking semantics. When Teddy's got them, you'll be gone."

"When Teddy . . . I mean Travis has got what?"

Father Holmes smiled broadly but would say no more. I picked up my bowl of coffee and went out through the french doors to the flagstone patio. Although early it was already warm. I sat on one of the chairs by the pool and took three deep breaths. Father Holmes was a demented old coot. I would just stay out of his way until he died.

As I took a large sip of coffee, I heard a rustle and then a growl in the bushes. Mozart! I dropped the bowl of coffee and ran for the french doors. They were locked. Panicked, I headed for the safety of the diving board. Did wolves swim? Did it matter? If I stood my ground, I would be mauled. If I backed up I would drown. "Travis!" I wailed.

Father Holmes peered out through the french doors and then turned away.

I edged further out on the diving board while keeping one eye on the bushes. There was more rustling and cracking. Part of a head emerged from the bushes. It was musty brown with an eerie eye.

"Travis!" I squalled. The head disappeared. Make it go away, I prayed. When ten minutes passed without a further sighting, I inched my way off the diving board and collapsed into the lawn chair. My imagination, fueled by Father Holmes's dark hints, must have produced the beast. I would have to learn to relax.

The sun was warm on my face. I closed my eyes and dozed a bit. Something cold and wet on the side of my neck snapped me from my reverie. The beast was back. It was not a wolf, but it didn't look like a member of the Welcome Wagon either. It had a squarish, blunt, canine head, yellow eyes, a bony torso, and a short thick stick of a tail. We eyeballed one another. He opened his mouth to reveal discolored teeth and unspeakable breath.

Too terrified to move, I lay there. For an instant I wondered if this were a bizarre game, if Travis was probing my phobic pressure points. But that was absurd.

The creature moaned. It was the most pitiful sound I had

ever heard. He dropped his head on the arm of the chair and looked up with soulful yellow eyes.

Edging my way out of the chair, I backed away from the pool. The dog started after me with a hobbled gait. The bottom of his left hind foot bent at an odd angle. There was a gash on his thigh.

"Why you poor thing," I said as I went to stroke his head. He looked friendless, which struck a chord. I picked him up and nearly dropped him. For a dog whose ribs were prominent, he was very heavy. I lowered him onto a lawn chair and told him to wait.

Father Holmes said Travis had been working for hours. I hated to interrupt his eerie trance, but the dog needed medical attention. Maybe Travis took opium breaks, à la Edgar Allan Poe.

At the door at the top of the stairs to the carriage house, I knocked tentatively.

"Not now, Father," barked Travis's voice.

"It's me," I said apologetically.

The door opened. My visions of Travis as Poe faded abruptly. If Travis smelled old hay here, it was a tribute to his remarkable imaginative powers.

The walls were white, the floor was white, the Wang Computer and the Xerox copier were white. The desk, the chair, and the file cabinets were black. No color anywhere except the luminous green letters on the console of the Wang.

"This is it?" I said with annoyance.

"Ah, you'll be wanting the 'Inner Sanctum.' " He took my hand and led me through a door into another room paneled with a deep rich wood. One wall was lined with books, another with photos and illustrations. There were several Gahan Wilson prints, a Booth cartoon, and an Edward

Gorey lithograph. A big desk was covered with clutter and piles of manuscripts.

But it was the far wall that commanded my attention. There, a large picture window looked out on a clearing in the woods. In the field were several large white statues of naked women. One was seated in a rocker with her head thrown back and a hand on her brow. Others appeared to be dancing. The statues were whimsical, not erotic.

"Did they come with the house?" I asked.

"No, I bought them. They are Maleys. Aren't they magnificent."

"Yes," I said, for I did admire the artistry. But I had to wonder what these statues said about my husband's view of womankind. I turned back to the room. "So, this is where you write."

"It looks like a perfect spot, doesn't it? Photographers always take my picture here, usually pressed up against one of Gahan's drawings. But the truth is I've never written a decent sentence in this place. I need the cold emptiness of the other room. By the way, I write until one. I'll see you for lunch," he said, clearly a dismissal.

"Oh, I'm sorry." I started away and then remembered. "Travis, there's a wounded beast by the pool."

"Anyone we know? A Delaney perhaps?"

"It's a dog. I think it may know Mozart."

"Why?"

"It has a broken foot and a deep gash on its leg."

"We'd better get him to the vet then," Travis responded. "Did you call its owners?"

"No . . ." I said, feeling stupid.

"Well, come on then."

* * *

By the time we got back to the pool, the dog was gone. We looked in the woods but found nothing.

"Well, what are your plans for the day?" asked Travis, eager to return to his work.

"We need dishes."

"Have Father take you to town."

"I'd rather not."

"Oh, he was just showing off yesterday. He's all right on the road, though he tends to straddle the middle line."

"I thought I might explore."

"Good idea." He dug into his pocket and produced a wallet. "Take these," he said, handing me a sheaf of credit cards.

"Should I take the Toyota?"

"Whatever runs today," he said cryptically and was gone.

When I approached the garage, I understood. Four cars sat before me with their hoods up and their mechanical guts splayed out on the ground. There was an old blue Mercedes, the Toyota wagon, Clara the Oldsmobile, and an old black Karmann Ghia. Father Holmes was kneeling on the ground tinkering with a mass of wires attached to an engine part. All means of transportation had been deactivated. No wonder Travis bought out the store last night.

By my feet was a familiar galvanized bucket. I peered into it. Last night's yogurt was now mottled.

"Keep away from my yogurt."

"Why is it black?" I asked.

Walking over he reached into the bucket and fished out an engine piece.

"Most people eat it with fruit," I commented.

"Shows what you know. It's the best engine cleaner in the world. It eats the grease."

"If you say so. Listen, do you expect to have any vehicles operational in the next week or so?"

"That depends," he said, looking at me slyly.

"Travis has asked me to go to town for him." He said nothing. "Perhaps there's a donkey cart?"

"Take Emma."

"Is that a beast or an automobile?"

"She's around the side, I just finished with her." He led me around to where Emma lay. Definitely beast, I thought. Emma was an aged Plymouth station wagon with a hitched-up rear and a manual shift. The doors were hanging open.

"I was airing her out," explained Father Holmes. "Let me help you." He pushed me into the driver's seat and went around slamming all the doors. Standing twenty feet away, he smiled at me mischievously and waved.

Contrary to my expectations, the car did not explode when I turned the ignition. With a great gnashing of gears, I found reverse and backed out into the drive. I tested the brakes on flat ground and then headed for Gallows Hill Road. Emma filled the majority of the narrow road. I prayed no one was attempting to come up as I was plunging down. Like many of my prayers of late, it went unanswered. I avoided the oncoming Mercedes only by plowing through two feet of foliage on the right.

With the Volvo, we weren't so lucky. Emma sheered a tree and a large rock. By the time I reached Route 53, I was shaking. I pulled over on the shoulder of the road and took a deep breath.

It was then I understood the need to "air" Emma. She smelled of disease, foul and rotting. I wrenched around to roll down the back windows and found the wounded beast from the pool gazing up from the floor.

"You!" He looked at me limply and then closed his eyes. "Oh Lord. Don't die on me." I sped off up Route 53.

The arresting officer was very helpful. As he handed me the ticket, he gave me directions to a veterinarian.

Getting "Wart," as I had dubbed the wounded hound, out of the car proved to be a problem. Finally, I maneuvered him into my arms and staggered towards the door. I had no hands free to turn the knob. Kicking repeatedly brought the receptionist.

She opened the door, looked at us and said, "All animals must be on a leash."

"I haven't got a leash."

"How can you not have a leash. There *is* a leash law in this town!"

"It is not my dog," I said, struggling not to collapse under Wart's unwieldy weight.

"Have you got an appointment?" she asked officiously.

As she did not appear to be impressed by mangled limbs, I announced, "Trooper DiMatteo sent me."

"Oh, very well then," she conceded unhappily. She went back to her desk and fiddled with a rolodex. The waiting room was full. There was one chair without a pet owner. It was filled by a fat gray cat who was hissing at Wart. The other animals were straining at their leashes trying to get a good sniff or bite of the newest arrival. Wart appeared thoroughly undone. Trying to recoil further in my arms, he emitted pathetic whimpers.

I lumbered over to the seated cat, who was now showing teeth. "Do you suppose we could sit here?" I asked politely. The cat's owner stared at me in annoyance. Wart was about to slip from my grasp. He felt it and tried to claw his way back up.

"Please!" I boomed. The cat owner swiftly removed her charge. Wart and I collapsed in the chair. All eyes were trained on us. "He isn't mine," I said lamely to the crowd.

"You ran him over," assumed a man with an asthmatic Pekingese.

"No, I did not. I found him." No one believed me. I tried to assume a St. Francis of Assisi aura.

Attention was diverted by the arrival of a German shepherd. He looked to me to be in strapping good health—and very nasty too. He snarled pretentiously. Wart bucked at the sight of the shepherd and then loosed a stream of diarrhea down my leg.

"Oh God, Wart!" I exclaimed. I pushed him to the floor where he stood on three legs quivering.

"Your dog!" accused a cat owner.

"I told you he's not my dog."

Wart began to yelp. His quivers turned to convulsions. "Help us!" I pleaded. The receptionist disappeared through a door. An awful din was loosed, howls and screeches and toenails clattering on the linoleum floor. The pet owners pulled their animals close. Wart was on the ground shaking wildly. I took off my sandal and stuffed it between his teeth.

The vet and his assistant appeared and hoisted Wart up into their arms. I followed them into an examining room.

"Has he eaten any poison?" demanded the vet. His back was to me, and I couldn't see what they were doing to Wart.

"I don't know. He's not my dog," I said again, although I was beginning to suspect he was. "I think he had a run in with our wolf."

"Wolf?" he said testily.

"Yes, well, I found him this morning with a broken leg, and I was going to bring him in but he disappeared."

"Has he been hanging around before today?"

"I don't know. I just moved in yesterday."

"You and your wolf," he said levelly.

"No, it's my husband's wolf. He's been there a while. I'm the newlywed."

The vet turned to look at me. "This animal is frightfully malnourished."

"I just met him," I said helplessly.

"Wait outside, please."

Back in the reception area, pets and owners alike stared at me reproachfully. I retreated to a bathroom, where I scrubbed my legs with brown utility-paper towels. When I returned, the receptionist said the vet wanted to see me.

Wart lay on the table, sedated. His lower leg was bound and his upper leg stitched. His ribs stood at attention.

"We'll need to keep him for tests."

"Well . . .uh . . . as I said, he isn't my dog."

"You want us to release him as is?" the vet asked angrily.

"No, but I don't know if it's all right for me to assume responsibility. Someone may be looking for him."

"He has no tags. From his state of health, I'd say he was abandoned. A lot of families move on and leave their animals to fend for themselves."

"That's obscene!"

"I quite agree." He looked at me expectantly.

Damn. I was barely holding my own in this marriage as it was. What would Travis say to an additional weak sister? "What kind of dog is he?" I asked, as if it made a difference.

"Weimaraner. This one's got jaundice. Fatten him up and he'll do you proud."

* * *

By the time I got the Plymouth back up Gallows Hill Road with the crates of dishes and glasses, it was the late afternoon and I was too strung out for explanations.

Father Holmes came around from the garage as I pulled into the driveway. His face went pasty.

"What did you do to my Emma?"

"Help me carry in these boxes, please."

"What about Emma?" he demanded as he gently fingered her scraped side. "You can't molest my girls!" he hollered.

"It wasn't me. She had a few cross words with a rock and an elm."

Travis came out of the house. He glanced at his watch. "Where have you been? I was about to send out a search party."

"You'd never have found me. How can one state be so green and twisted?"

"Miss the avenues?"

"A straight road would be a pleasant novelty. The occasional street sign wouldn't hurt, either."

"She violated Emma, Teddy," Father Holmes accused.

"Nonsense, Father. Mallory is a very prudent woman." Father Holmes stalked off toward the garage. "I have a surprise for you," Travis said.

"And I have a surprise for you," I replied.

"Really, what?"

"I found the wounded beast."

"Oh, good. Now . . ."

"That isn't all of the surprise," I interrupted.

"Oh?" he said quizzically.

"I adopted him," I announced in upbeat tones. I didn't want Wart to become an issue.

"Oh," he said flatly.

"Well, he's dreadfully sick not to mention mangled. It seems he was abandoned."

"Probably with good reason," Travis surmised. He looked in the back of Emma and asked, "Where is the cur?"

"At the vet's," I said defensively.

"If you had told me you wanted a dog, I'd have bought you one—a healthy one."

"I didn't want a dog," I argued.

Travis ran his hand through his blond hair and sighed.

"I couldn't just let him die." Travis said nothing. "Don't you like dogs?"

"Not especially."

"But Mozart . . ."

"Mozart is a wolf—a noble creature," he said staunchly.

"Your noble creature tried to eat my dog."

Travis laughed. "Good point."

"Here, take this crate. I hope you like the china pattern."

"Does it have doggies frolicking around the rims?"

"Certainly not!"

"Then I shall love it. Come see your surprise."

How could I have forgotten? "What is it?" I asked excitedly.

"Gerald. And a dwarf."

The Newlywed Game: Hide and Go Seek

Gerald was but the first of my relatives to arrive. His once wild red hair was now streaked with premature gray. He looked almost respectable. But I was still not pleased to see him. The next day my family assembled like a flock of carping geese. Some of them brought friends. Gerald was the only one who thought to bring a dwarf.

When Father arrived by private airport limo with a middle-aged woman swaddled in yards of Indian print, I was so surprised I ignored the nagging suspicion that an unseen hand was at work. But by the time penniless Claire and her mystic boyfriend blew in from Oregon, I could no longer ignore the obvious. Travis was having a party.

When confronted in his office, Travis did not deny responsibility for the gathering. In fact he seemed puzzled by my reaction.

"I thought you'd be grateful, Mallory."

"Grateful?" I bellowed. "I'm working on 'civil.' What got into you? You knew I didn't want to see my family."

"I assumed you were being modest. Family ties are important. Take Gerald. You haven't seen him for ten years and look what an entertaining fellow he turned out to be." Gerald, Travis, and Edgar, the dwarf, had spent the evening discussing the clinical effects of putrescence.

"But *everyone's* here!" I argued. Father and his friend, Althea. Gerald and the dwarf, Edgar. Ned and his wife, Toni, tethered to their three children by an elaborate complex of harnesses. Claire and the Thing that Smoked Portland. And Maude.

"Of course," he said with a touch of pride. "Maude said you would give anything to see them all."

"I'd like to see Mother again, too. Were you thinking of having her body exhumed for the day?"

"I don't see why you are so bitter," he said, cracking his knuckles. "Is it too much? Perhaps I should have flown them in separately so you might get reacquainted in a one-on-one situation?"

"Maude and I have never gotten on in any ratio," I snapped. Travis would never understand my quandary. I honestly loved my family, I just didn't want to see them.

"It's time you got to know them as adults," he said paternally. "And I suspect they feel the same way."

"Don't count on it."

"They were all delighted to come for the week."

"The week?" I gasped. Custer's Last Stand had only lasted a day.

I would drown in my husband's thoughtfulness. Travis had assumed we were a family like any other. But we were not. Mother's death had broken our natural symmetry. And my attempts to redress the loss just set me further apart. Seeing my family en masse reminded me how I had failed Mother's memory. She had had such definite ideas. Surely we would have turned out differently if she had been in charge.

I had been in enough off-off-Broadway plays where the family gathers at a loved one's funeral to know we were about to witness a rehashing of the past. Who wanted to sit through a week of emotional fireworks, watching all those unpleasant truths take shape?

I had more pressing matters to attend to. Wedded less than two weeks, my marriage was already floundering. My husband thought I was someone I most definitely was not and doubted I could ever be. And now in the name of family unity, he was parading past failures before me. How could I concentrate on my marriage with all these reproaches lounging about the property?

"It'll be fun, you'll see. I'm just about done here for the day. I'll meet you at the house for dinner."

"Ah yes, dinner. What do you suggest I serve fifteen people?"

"Let's see . . . how about a butterflied leg of lamb with a parmesan crust, garlic potatoes, arugula salad, and a pear tart."

Dispiritedly, I walked past the pool towards the kitchen. The bodies draped decorously on lounge chairs looked like mannequins in a Bloomingdale's window. The only sign of life was in the pool where Toni and her children were splashing frantically. Father was lying stone-faced with his arms spread across two strategically placed tables. His body glistened with oil. He did not look like the father I remembered.

If anyone noticed me, they didn't acknowledge it. I went into the kitchen. Maude was on the phone. She had one hand on her hip and was pacing as she spoke, "I don't care what he says, tell him clause seventeen is a no-go." I heard the phone hit the phone cradle with force.

I opened the refrigerator. My family members were no strangers to my unappetizing meals; could they deal with root salad for dinner? And even if I had the nerve to serve it, where would they eat it? There were only eight chairs in the dining room and no table. We would have to eat in shifts or squat on the floor.

"Anything I can do?" Maude purred as she strode across the kitchen.

"I think you've done enough," I said with determined gaiety. If Maude won this round, I was done for.

"It's such a treat having everyone together again," she said dryly.

"Umm . . . all that's missing are the boys from the football team."

"What?" she asked with surprise. In her radicalism, she had clearly forgotten the bedrock of her rebellion.

"*Your* ghosts," I explained.

"Oh," she said flatly.

"No one is immune to the past."

Maude laughed, "Well, certainly not you."

It was time to change tacks. "Since this is your party, Maude, why don't you prepare the meals and the beds."

"I don't do drudgery."

"Then how about explaining the guest list," I said,

carrying assorted roots and vegetables to the sink.

"I suppose I could do that," she allowed.

"Are Gerald and Edgar an item?"

"Heavens no. Travis happened to ask Gerald if he knew any little people and, if so, to bring them along. Edgar works at the coroner's lab with Gerald, so he was ideal."

Ideal for what? I wondered. I had put Gerald and Edgar in adjoining rooms last night but was now running out of beds. "What about Althea. How long has Father been seeing her?"

"About seven hours. He picked her up on the plane."

"Christ. Well, I suppose I should be grateful. I'm running out of bedrooms."

"Have you heard her talk?" Maude demanded.

"I caught something about 'mind/body zonations' but thought I was hallucinating. She's too old to be a hippie."

"She's stuck in a sixties time warp. Father's taste in women is abysmal."

"Why are you still surprised?" I asked.

"I don't know, everywhere I look there are vapid females. Look at Toni," she said, gesturing out to the pool area where our sister-in-law was struggling to restrap our dripping niece into a harness.

"Maybe it's a new method of bonding," I suggested.

"Hardly. I mean, what is she afraid of? This is Connecticut."

"Well, Ned is useless as a parent, a chip off the old block. Look at him out there, so self-absorbed he might as well be bronzed. But this harnessing can't be healthy to their spirits. When I tripped over Joshua's leash earlier, I asked her if it was really necessary to keep them bound. She replied it was the only way she could save them from 'electrocution, strangulation, poisonous ingestion, and/or concussion.' "

"My God! What did you say?" Maude pressed.

"What could I say? I offered her the use of Mozart's penned run."

Maude laughed, "At least you have a sense of humor."

"Even though I'm vapid?" I hazarded.

"I'll admit I don't know what Travis sees in you," she said.

"As opposed to you?"

"Yes," she answered firmly.

We were getting too close to the raw. Another minute and we would be climaxing in act two. I bit my lip and ran some turnips under a spray of water. Maude's lower lip was pouted, a sure sign she was spoiling for a fight.

I withdrew another armload of vegetables from the refrigerator.

"Are you opening a root cellar?"

"Dinner," I said flatly.

"Oh, no Mallory, please."

"Unless you would like to bone a leg of lamb and knead a pie crust, it's root salad for dinner."

"Let me get Gowf."

"What?"

"Not what, who. Claire's mystic is a cook." Maude strode out to the pool area where leggy thirteen-year-old Claire, tangled in a strange knot that was either sexual or religious, shared a padded lounge with Gowf. I had not paid any attention to this blond creature, assuming him to be just another airhead doper with dilated pupils and a ponytail. Claire was rebelling against boarding school. I had been disturbed by her lack of originality, but now it seemed she was the only family member who had thought to bring someone useful.

Maude tapped on a shoulder and received no response. With a surprisingly accurate chop, she sliced between the bodies, pulled Gowf off the lounge and propelled him into the kitchen. Claire, stunned, collapsed through the dead air and onto the lounge.

Gowf's body was surprisingly well muscled, I noticed, and at least ten years older than Claire's. I fought down my maternal complaint.

Dinner was surprisingly good. Travis supplied several magnums of champagne, and there were rich brownies for dessert. Gowf must have known they would be popular, he had made three trays. We sat out by the pool listening to the tree frogs and ate every last one.

Strangely enough, it felt good to be sitting with my family in Connecticut. I looked over at them and felt happily reassured. Perhaps this was a good idea after all. With Toni upstairs putting the kiddies to bed, everything seemed peaceful. The fact that Father Holmes had not emerged from the garage didn't hurt either.

My own father had stopped sulking. When he wasn't ignoring his children he wanted to be idolized by them. (Or perhaps we were to adore him even while he was ignoring us.) Before dinner "the fruit of his loins," as he referred to us, had not delivered sufficient hosannas. But now, Althea was stroking his cheek and singing softly.

Maude was talking earnestly to Travis. She had her arm slung proprietarily over his shoulder. Let her try, I thought dreamily. Travis was mine.

I awoke to bright sunshine and was startled to find that I was still by the pool. Ned, Edgar, Claire, and Gowf were still here, too. My watch said it was almost nine o'clock. Why did I still feel groggy?

Travis would be working by now. I heard a scratch at the french doors and turned to see three little faces pressed up against the glass.

As I opened the doors, my nieces and nephew lurched out onto the patio. Toni had apparently tied their reins to the door handle. I looked around quickly and saw no sign of her. "Come on, kids." I would take them to the woods and set them free. But before I got the reins untangled, Toni reappeared.

"Oh, I hope they didn't wake you."

"Can we go swimming now, Mrs. Holmes?" asked the boy.

For a moment, I did not realize he was addressing me. "Hmmm? Oh certainly."

"No, no Joshers, mustn't wake Daddy." The children's faces fell.

"Why don't I take them for a walk," I offered.

"Where will you be going?"

"I thought we might explore."

"In that case, I think it better we stay here."

"Whatever," I said. My stomach felt funny. I had to lie down. Upstairs I crawled into our bed, noted that it hadn't been slept in, and fell deeply asleep.

It was late afternoon when I awoke. The cicadas were humming at fever pitch. I was ravenous. Downstairs, I made it to the kitchen with only one wrong turn. Claire was atop the marble pastry table swaying to unheard music. Ned was juggling cantaloupes. Gowf was whacking a small hammer at the bottom of a raw rib roast.

"Why are you hurting that nice piece of beef?" I asked.

"Getting at the marrow," he said with a dazed laugh.

One of Ned's cantaloupes crashed to the floor.

"Sumbitch," Ned said, letting the others follow suit. Toni came down the back stairs, gasped at the mess, and shook her finger at Ned. "Naughty boy."

"Where's Gerald?" I asked.

"Playing the piano."

"Travis doesn't have a piano. And even if he did, Gerald does not play."

Claire slid off her perch and said, "All I know is he said he was going to do something with Mowsart."

"Ah, Mozart is Travis's . . ." I stopped in time. Toni was busily cleaning up Ned's cantaloupes. If she suspected there was a wolf within forty miles, she'd call in the Texas Rangers.

"And Maude?"

"Haven't seen her," Edgar said. I hadn't noticed him before. He was reading *Wolf's Down* in the corner. Claire giggled.

"Am I missing the joke?"

"You missed Gowf's stew."

"Is there any left? I'm starving."

"There's some on the stove," Edgar pointed. "Do you have any Vaseline?"

"No why?"

"Althea was looking for some. She said Mazola would do."

"That answers my next question." The stew was delicious. There was a predominant flavor that I couldn't place.

"What's in this," I asked. Maybe Gowf would leave me the recipe.

"Veal, carrots, onions, hash, tomatoes . . ."

"Hash?" I exclaimed. Then I groaned. I put down the bowl.

"Roast beef hash?" Toni queried, standing up with a dust-pan of smashed melons.

"The brownies?" I asked. Gowf nodded. "Can't you cook any other way?"

"Why bother?"

"I thought dope was passé," I argued.

"Dope," Toni squeaked. Her face drained of color. "Oh, my babies, my poor babies." She dropped the dustpan and rushed out of the room.

"Please tell me you haven't been doping the children."

"The Mama hen feeds them," answered Gowf.

"Maybe I had better resume cooking duties."

"You never were much fun," Ned commented.

"We can't spend the whole week stoned," I argued.

"I'm just about out," Gowf admitted. "I hadn't realized there would be such a demand."

Gerald came in. He looked surprisingly well-kempt for someone who had been wrestling with a wolf.

"How's Mozart?" I asked.

"I didn't see him. I just left the food. Where's Travis?"

"In the carriage house," I supplied.

"No, he's not," Edgar responded.

"That's funny," I said, looking at my watch. "He usually works until six. Did he say anything at lunch?" I looked around the room. No one answered. "Well?"

"We haven't seen him all day," Ned answered.

"Maude is sure to know," I reasoned.

"We haven't seen her all day either."

I felt dizzy. I clutched a chair rung and sat down.

"Maybe they eloped," Claire offered.

"We have to find them," I stated.

"Ah, let 'em be. More ribs for us," Gowf reasoned.

"You don't understand. They could be in danger."

"Of your wrath," Ned joked.

"No, this house. It's swallowed them," I said.

"Right," laughed Ned. "Face it Mallory, Mauda-Hari has aced you out again."

"This house has seven secret rooms," I retorted. "Travis knew where four of them were. I only know one of them. It's possible he and Maude found one of the other three and can't get out."

"Isn't it also possible they deliberately went into one?" Ned asked.

A rush of hot pain spread through my gut. "No, of course it's not possible."

Gerald was my only hope. He might be devious enough to unfold the secret corners of Leger de Main. "Gerald, are you stoned?"

"Don't be ridiculous. I'm clean."

"Did you eat the stew?"

"Yes, Mommy, I licked my bowl clean."

"Damnation," I swore. It was hopeless. I couldn't even find my own way around the house; how was I supposed to find hidden rooms? If Travis had been kidnapped we could have paid ransom, but what did you offer a carnivorous house?

"We have to look." While various people voiced agreement, no one moved. "Please." A few of them got up and shuffled around the kitchen. Claire looked in the sugar canister.

"For Christ sakes, fan out—and watch out. The house could easily swallow you, too." I knew it was a mistake the moment I said it. Claire dropped the lid on the jar and went back to her seat.

"I'll let you know if I see them," Ned announced, sitting down.

Several hours later, Gerald, Edgar, and I were still looking. I was desperate to find Travis, yet terrified of what I would discover. Part of me couldn't help believing that they had deliberately disappeared. Edgar and Gerald searched Maude's room, sparing me the humiliation. I kicked at panels, tapped cornices, and twisted fixtures. In the process, I found two secret rooms, one in the basement and one off the music room, but no Travis.

I did find Father and Althea, slicked down with oil, in the tub. Why couldn't they have been the ones to disappear?

When I went to ask Toni to help with the search, I found her quoting scripture to a squirming Ned. Soon thereafter, a cab arrived and Toni the Tetherer and her three charges decamped for Buffalo.

At nine I went to get something to drink. My guests were still having a good time. No one could say I was not a good hostess. I thoughtlessly dampened the party spirit with another plea for help.

"Frankly, sis," Ned opined, "Travis seemed like a nice enough guy. But Maude, well . . . don't tempt the fates. They took her, let 'em have her."

I looked at Ned's complacent face. Yes, Mother, I

thought, here he is, your wonderful caring, sharing child. Haven't I done a good job with him?

"Here's the deal," I said, putting down my drained glass. "Either help or haul ass out of here."

I left the kitchen before I could be disheartened by their inactivity.

The night was deathly hot, with no trace of a breeze. About one in the morning, I broke down in tears. Gerald had already gone to bed. Edgar came to say he was calling it quits for the night. The poor man was drenched with sweat. His shirt stuck to matted chest hair.

"We'll find them."

"Before or after . . ." I didn't want to say "dead" aloud.

"Before," Edgar said emphatically.

"I can't thank you enough."

He reached up and patted my shoulder consolingly. "Get some sleep, you look like one of my clients."

I went back to my bedroom and opened Travis's closet. His clothes were all I had left. I buried my face in his shirts, smelling his scent, and cried.

Crawling into bed with an armful of shirts, I fell asleep.

I awoke feeling strangely calm. Travis and Maude had been missing for thirty-six hours. Surely, no one could screw that long. Their disappearance had to have been an accident.

Downstairs, Edgar was drinking coffee. No one else was about.

"They are not in this house," he said, scratching his oversized head. His brown hair looked as if it had a life of its own.

"Who knows?" I said wearily. "We've been so haphazard." I poured myself a cup of coffee and looked at some tempting brown muffins in a baking tin. I fingered one gently wondering if it were laced with PCP.

"Go ahead, I made them," Edgar said. I took two muffins and spread them with butter. "I think we should broaden our base. Gerald is checking the playhouse."

"Who's going to canvas Mozart's den? For all we know," I said, sinking my teeth into a muffin, "the pen may be littered with human femurs."

"No, we'd have heard screams," he said with unpleasant logic. "What about the carriage house?"

"Two rooms over a large garage."

"I believe they are there," Edgar said.

"Why?"

"We've missed something. Just because your sister was exuding sexual heat, we assumed they were trysting. We did not fully consider Travis. My guess is that they were doing business."

"Let's go," I said, through a mouthful of muffin.

Outside, we ran into Gerald. He was frowning. "I've measured the inside and the outside of the playhouse, there's no unaccounted for space."

"Edgar thinks they're in the carriage house," I blurted. "Come on."

Gerald and Edgar hurriedly paced off the length and width of the carriage house, while I ran up the stairs. Inside the sterile office and in the inner sanctum, there were no traces of them. I had hoped to find two glasses with flat champagne. The air felt stale and hot. I turned on the air conditioning.

Gerald and Edgar came in. "Don't forget to account for the stairwell."

Gerald began measuring. Before he reached the wall he exclaimed, "Eureka, three paces short." He was about to probe the wall.

"Back up," I shouted. "We'd better form a human chain. That way if one of us finds it and is swallowed the others can block the mechanism."

"Right." Gerald and Edgar massaged the wall with their skilled coroner's fingers. I grabbed a ponderous book, *Maleficia,* from beside the Wang.

Twenty minutes of skillful prodding brought no success in the outer office. We went into the inner sanctum. They began again. A panel gave way. It wasn't that wide a space. They must have been huddling together when they hit the pressure point.

A gust of intensely hot fetid air rushed out at us. I threw the volume onto the floor of the opening just as the panel was snapping shut. Gerald started to go in, I pulled him back. I had to see for myself.

They were dead. The smell of heated urine was oppressive. Maude was naked but for flowered underpants. Her head was on Travis's stomach, her black hair covering much of his bare golden body. I screamed. Edgar squirmed in behind me.

Travis groaned and rolled partially over. I was ridiculously elated to see he was still wearing his briefs. Then I realized he was still alive.

House of the Living Deadbeats

Neither Travis nor Maude was seriously harmed. The doctor confirmed Gerald's diagnosis of heat exhaustion. He treated them with liquids and ordered bed rest.

Ned expressed his relief that Maude had been found . . . from the pool. He then sniggered loudly about the couple's state of undress. From his life in the locker room, Ned was armed with many bad jokes. He regaled the poolside crowd for hours. Father's jangling laugh filtered up to our bedroom where I wrestled with my doubts as I watched Travis sleep.

Did I trust him or not? I did. He had married me, not Maude. But why had Maude seemed victorious even when prostrate?

As soon as Travis awoke that afternoon, I blurted, "Why were you in your underwear?"

He stretched his arms, yawned, focused on me, and smiled. "I knew you'd find me."

"Yes, well you certainly provided an impetus." He frowned. "Maude," I elaborated.

"You were more concerned for your sister than me?"

"Hardly. The general assumption hereabouts was that you two had snuck off for a quickee."

"Some quickee," he mused.

"My sentiments exactly. Now, why were you undressed?"

"It was hot."

"What were you doing there in the first place?"

"Maude wanted me to make some changes in chapter seven." He sat up and ran his left hand through his hair. He reminded me of the man in the Paco Rabanne ads. I wanted to jump him. "Was there something strange in our dinner?"

"Hashish," I said, drumming my fingers on my knee.

"Ah. Well, one moment we were standing together looking at the manuscript, and the next we were crumpled on the floor of that hell hole. It was sort of funny, actually."

"You're the hotshot. Why couldn't you get out?"

"From the way you're carrying on one would think it had been you stuck in the pressure cooker."

"Things weren't exactly copacetic on the outside," I snapped. Why did he have to look so appetizing?

"Maude said you probably had everyone scouring the house in organized drills."

"Hardly. Only two of your houseguests gave a rat's ass whether you and Maude lived or died. The rest were too busy eating your food and drinking your booze."

"Didn't Father help?"

"Father was too busy dealing with his priapism."

"I meant my father."

I laughed with astonishment. "I completely forgot about him. And you still haven't explained why you didn't Harry Houdini your way out of there."

"Believe me, I tried." He swung his legs out of bed. "Nothing worked." He sounded earnest enough, but I wasn't convinced. "How's Maude doing?" he asked.

"Do you love Maude?"

"What a bizarre question." He started to stand up. I pushed him back down and had my way with him.

The vet called a few days later to say the dog was ready to resume life. I asked Gerald to go with me—knowing that if anyone could bully a car out of Father Holmes and negotiate the tortuous roadways, it was he. And Gerald was the one relative I did not actively hate at the moment.

Father Holmes readily relinquished the Karman Ghia. Too readily. I lifted the hood.

"What do you think you are doing?" Father Holmes barked. He slammed the hood down before I could check for dynamite. "Have you no sense of decency? Exposing Mary Elizabeth's private parts! You should be ashamed!"

Gerald sluiced the Ghia down Gallows Hill Road like a kayak in white water. "I like him," said Gerald.

"Father Holmes?"

"Him too, but I meant your husband."

"Watch out for that truck."

"He's not your type," he said swerving neatly.

"What do you know of 'my type'? We've hardly spoken in ten years."

"I've watched you this week."

I laughed. "Imagine yourself an unarmed guard in among

the prisoners, each of whom is wielding a grievance. Even Father seems sour, though Lord knows why. As he has pointed out repeatedly, he was right and I was wrong. My being a failed actor gives him great satisfaction."

"Edgar thinks Father is unwell."

"He looks fit enough, though he is chain-smoking again. Gerald, why did Travis ask you to bring a 'little person'?"

"Research, he said."

"How many dwarves fought in the Civil War?" I wondered aloud.

"Is that a question or a joke?"

"Oh I don't know," I said with exasperation. "I thought his new book was about an uprising of Civil War dead."

"*Civil Souls* is. The other one has something to do with the special powers of dwarves."

"I wasn't aware they had special powers." Nor was I aware Travis was working on two novels.

"As Mother and Shakespeare used to say, 'There are more things in heaven and earth, Horatio, than are dreamt of in your philosophy.' I suspect Mother would have liked Travis enormously." Gerald sounded rather wistful. "I miss the East."

"So move."

"I might. Travis has invited me to stay at Leger de Main."

"Oh," I said uneasily.

Wart bounded out of the vet's back room on three legs with his teeth bared and his tail pumping. In his enthusiasm, he nearly sheared off my left kneecap. His color had changed from yellowish gray to silver brown in just five days. His ribs were now concealed. Wart licked my thighs and then jumped up on me.

Gerald slipped the choke leash we'd brought over Wart's head. Wart whipped around and snarled at my brother.

"Whoa," said Gerald, yanking on the leash.

"Stop!" commanded the vet. Gerald stared at him defiantly. "You cannot use a choke collar on this animal. He has a collapsed trachea."

Gerald groaned and dropped the leash.

"A what?" I asked warily.

"A collapsed trachea," Gerald answered. "Genetic defect most likely. He can't take any pressure on his throat."

"Nor," added the vet, "much strenuous exercise. He also has asthma, hip dysplasia, and a weak heart."

"I thought you said he was ready to 'resume life'!" I argued.

"A limited life. Treat him as you would a retired executive."

"How old is this sorry excuse for a dog?" Gerald asked.

"My guess," said the vet, "is four years."

"One of nature's little lemons," Gerald commented as he hoisted Wart into his arms. Wart growled menacingly. Gerald put him down in a hurry. I realized with a start that Gerald was afraid of live animals.

"You've hurt his feelings," said the vet, stroking Wart's head. Wart whipped around and snapped at the vet's hand.

"Well! I guess we'll be saying good-bye. You can pay at the receptionist." He turned and retreated to the safety of his lab.

Gerald said he would wait in the car. I was still wondering how I was going to get the dog to the car when the receptionist handed me the bill. Three hundred and twenty-seven dollars. Numbly I wrote a check, knowing full well it would bounce all the way to the city. I certainly couldn't expect Travis to pay for a dog he didn't want. Maybe I could borrow some money from Ned.

I looked down at Wart, who was staring at me expectantly. His pink tongue hung loosely out of the side of his mouth. "I'm going. If you want to come, fine. Otherwise, you're free to seek your fortune."

I was hoping he would bolt when we got outside, but he trotted close by my side. I opened the car door and he leapt into the passenger seat. No amount of cajoling would move him. Gerald tried to push him and was bitten for his trouble. Priding myself in being able to recognize an immovable object, I climbed into the cramped area behind the seats. Even Edgar couldn't have sat there comfortably. Wart turned and licked me hotly on the cheek.

We bounced homeward. Wart stuck his head out the window and sniffed the air. Bits of his spittle were carried back on the rush of hot air to where I was contorted.

When we arrived at Leger de Main, Travis was with a group of white rabbits on the grass. Wart was out the open window in flash. On three legs, he tore over to the rabbits, howling, his hackles raised. The rabbits scattered in all directions. Travis charged at Wart, grabbed him by the scruff of the neck, and wrestled him to the ground.

I pried myself from the back of the Ghia. Gerald remained rooted to the driver's seat. "Aren't you coming?" I asked.

"The view is fine from here."

Travis seemed to be enjoying himself in this battle of wills. Wart growled angrily but was trapped in a hammerlock.

"Where did the rabbits come from?"

"I ordered them for your nieces and nephew," he grunted

as Wart threatened to wriggle out of his grasp. "Forgot to cancel them," he added.

"Watch out for his neck," I cautioned. "He's a retired executive." With that I went into the house.

I found Ned; but before I could hit him up for a loan, he began whining about his "depressing financial picture." He wondered if Travis could lend him "a few grand" to tide him over. I sighed at the inevitability of it all.

Everywhere I turned there was more family. Would I ever be able to rout them from Leger de Main? Or start a life with Travis? I went to the living room. Claire and Gowf were sharing a joint. I slipped past them unnoticed and leaned against the far wall.

Quickly the wall released and I was in the Nancy Drew room. It was cool and quiet. I lay down and dozed. Wild and weird dreams visited me—sirens and holocausts.

I awoke feeling odd. Looking around, I saw the blond lady in the portrait staring down at me. Was it the darts embedded in the painting or her peculiar smile that made me so ill at ease?

Emerging through the broom closet, I was met by heavy silence. I walked through the house and could find no one but Wart, who was on the screened porch. Most of the furniture there had been overturned. There was a large tear in the screen. Wart limped over, his tail between his legs.

"What've you done, Wart?" He sheepishly lowered his head and moaned softly. "Oh, come on, no theatrics. Where is everyone?" He wagged his stump of a tail. We went round to the back.

The pool area was deserted. A remarkable fact given the weather. Over at the garage, the Ghia stood alone. Father Holmes came out of the garage holding a wrench.

"Haven't you done enough damage?" he accused.

"I beg your pardon? Wart, stop that hissing."

"You knew my girls haven't been well. I said you'd be trouble."

"Where is everyone?" I asked, hoping to forestall another harangue.

"At the hospital, if they didn't kill my girls first."

"What?" I asked alarmed.

"That hound of yours," he said stabbing the wrench in Wart's direction. I looked at Wart. He couldn't have bitten everyone, could he?

"Is Travis hurt?" I asked, alarmed.

"Grazed is all, which is more than I can say for your father."

"Wart bit Father?"

"A direct hit on the pecker," Father Holmes chuckled. "Didn't you hear the ambulance?"

The dog I saved had deballed my father. Surely this was a joke, but then where was everyone? "What hospital?" I asked frantically.

"Norwalk. But don't think I'm giving you Mary Elizabeth so you can follow the pack. Your brother stripped her gears this morning."

"Give me the keys."

"I will not."

"Give them to me," I insisted. Wart growled obligingly. Father Holmes rubbed his groin thoughtfully and then handed me the keys.

Forgive Us Our Debts . . .

Wart and I got lost several times on the way to the hospital. I might never have found it but for the car stranded on the shoulder of Route 7. Claire and Gowf were sitting on the hood of the Mercedes. Ned sat inside. When I pulled over in front of them, Ned emerged from the Mercedes and trotted over.

"Bloody heap of a car," he cursed.

"What happened?"

"I dunno. Something 'mechanical,' " he said disgustedly.

"I meant to Father."

"Oh . . . we were out by the pool catching some bennies when this fat orange cat came out of the woods." He took off his sunglasses and wiped them on the hem of his Ralph Lauren shirt. I looked at him with mounting anger. Ned put his glasses back on and said, "Can you give me a lift home? The others can wait for the tow truck."

"Dammit, what about Father?"

"Hmmmh? Oh yeah, it was great, like a Harold Lloyd movie but in color. Your dog there jumped through the screened porch and chased the cat. The cat springboarded off of Althea's tits and onto Dad. The dog lunged for the cat but missed. He got Dad—in a most peculiar place. I think," he said in confidential tones, "Wart may be a homosexual."

"How badly was he bitten?"

"Barely a puncture wound, from what I heard."

"Then why the ambulance?"

"He kept falling down. Travis got bit dragging the dog away from Dad." He started to chuckle but then sighed, "I suppose you'll want to go to the hospital."

"Good guess."

"There's no real need. Everybody else went, it was like a bloody parade."

"Do you have directions?"

"Yeah, here," he said, handing me a piece of paper. "But, like, there's no rush, so stop and call a tow truck first, okay?"

"Get in the car, Ned."

"What, with him?" Ned said, pointing to Wart.

"He's already had a taste of the family jewels. I doubt he's interested. Get in."

Edgar, Maude, and Althea were milling about the waiting area of the Emergency Room, reading magazines, smoking cigarettes, or sipping soda. In the corner, Gerald and Travis were consulting with a doctor. Ned and I arrived in time to hear that Father had suffered a massive stroke.

The excitement of the afternoon had tilted his high blood pressure into overdrive and ruptured an artery. The CAT

Scan indicated a clot "the size of a muffin" on the left hemisphere of his brain.

Father was paralyzed on the right side of his body, the doctor said.

I looked guiltily around the room. Was I imagining the accusatory stares?

Dr. Benutis went on to say recovery was certainly possible, if the swelling went down. Otherwise Father would slip into a coma. Medically speaking, they were doing all they could for him. It was a question of time and family support. Dr. Benutis recommended hand-holding and massage. One of us could go in now.

No one leapt down the hall.

"Well? What are you waiting for?" Maude demanded of me. "This is your doing, go undo it." My houseguests stared at me with varying degrees of self-righteousness.

"Would you like me to come with you?" asked Travis.

Lord, yes. But this was my father, however distant. I went alone.

Father looked absurdly healthy, tanned and rested, against the white bedsheets. I half expected him to rail at me about the service he was receiving. But his eyes did not move in tandem. The left one followed me as I crossed the room to his bed. The other remained stationary.

"Oh, Daddy . . ." I said, fighting the tears.

"Etgh mahuft," he said quietly. His speech was gone.

Suddenly, everyone had pressing business elsewhere. Father's stroke emptied the house in less than twenty-four hours. Gerald's defection hurt the most. I had just begun to like him.

They moved Father out of Intensive Care. Travis and I

took shifts at the hospital. I would have preferred having Travis with me as a buffer, but he said this wasn't "time efficient."

One afternoon when our hours overlapped, I arrived to find Travis talking intently to Father. I lingered by the door. Father's eyes rolled slowly closed then opened with a jerk. When he came to suddenly like that, Father looked very frightened. It frightened me as well, that weak hold on consciousness. It was one of the things I dreaded most about our afternoons together. Travis continued to massage Father's good arm and talk softly.

My husband was better with Father than I was. I found it difficult to rub his hand and arm for hours at a time. I ran out of things to tell him ten minutes into the visit. And I had so many mixed feelings about the man.

I thought about Mother a lot during those visits. I could see her striding into the hospital room carrying a pot of azaleas, full of brisk cheer. My cheer was decidedly false. When I spoon fed him like a baby, I had to bite my lip to stop from crying.

Travis never expressed any qualms about our task. Many days I wanted to flee the country rather than face Father again. But I went. If Travis wasn't complaining, how on earth could I?

Maude checked on his progress through periodic phone calls to Travis. Perhaps she resented the time he was spending with Father. Travis said she was nagging him about deadlines. Gerald also called. Brief, dispassionate inquiries, as though he were wondering about the crop reports.

After two weeks, Father had regained some feeling on his right side and was talking, or more accurately, snapping. All his responses were negative. Did he want green beans? "No!" he'd holler. Ice cream? "Never!" Despite his progress, he was very depressed.

I, too, was depressed. I saw myself saddled with an infirm, incontinent old man for the rest of my life. My brothers and sisters had shown no willingness to shoulder any part of the burden. Could I legally force them to care?

Travis said nursing homes were out of the question, he'd seen too many Geraldo Rivera exposés. It was my husband's intention to install round-the-clock nurses at Leger de Main.

With two fathers-in-law in residence, one unhinged and the other bedridden, my marriage was clearly doomed. But I bit my tongue. Someone had to care for Father.

After four weeks, Father was walking with a walker. I was astounded by the miracles of medicine. Travis felt vindicated for the time and effort we'd put forth. Father spoke to him in actual sentences—often totally irrelevant, but sentences. Sometimes he got words confused, saying "yes" when he meant "no." The doctor said this would be corrected in time.

To me, Father still spoke in negatives. His imperious manner had returned. When I misunderstood him, he hurled things at me. He didn't like my wardrobe, my hairstyle, or my manners. And where did I get off thinking I could be an astronaut? I tried to be patient, but the bit was chafing in my mouth.

After six weeks, the doctors wanted to release him to a rehabilitation center that would make him self-sufficient. *That* would be a neat trick, I told the doctor. He misunderstood and said Father would be back to his old self within the year.

Travis and I went to the hospital together on the day of

Father's release. I was to ride with him in the ambulance to the rehabilitation center. Travis went to the business office and told me to go on ahead. Waiting for the elevator, I was struck with terror. I wheeled around and went into the office. Travis was seated at a desk, surveying a thick sheaf of papers. He pulled out a checkbook and began to write.

"Doesn't insurance cover this?" I asked the woman seated across the desk from Travis.

"Ah, Mrs. Barlow, this is my wife Mallory, Mr. Delaney's daughter."

"Pleased to meet you," Mrs. Barlow said, rising. "I so enjoyed him in *Mission to Marnes*."

"How much is covered by insurance?" I repeated.

"Your father did not carry insurance."

I felt like I'd been kicked. "What about Medicare?"

"Your father is only fifty-nine."

"How much is the bill?" I asked, hoarse with fear.

"Eight thousand or so," Travis said, tearing a check from his book.

"You can't pay this," I said tonelessly.

"Someone has to," he replied.

"But it's not your debt," I argued.

"We'll discuss this later. Thank you, Mrs. Barlow." He escorted me out of the room.

Travis and I sat at the kitchen table that evening with some take-out Chinese food. While he masterfully wielded his chopsticks through "Tinkling Bells" and "Eight Precious Treasures," I stared suspiciously at my plate. How could anyone eat such a jumble of unrecognizable meat and fungi? The longer I peered at the food the more I became convinced there was a severed pinky finger poking out from under what Travis called a "tree ear." And what was that thing next to the bamboo shoot? Travis claimed it was a straw mushroom, but it looked alarmingly like a withered penis.

Even if the food had been American, I wouldn't have been able to eat. I was too distraught by my growing debt to this man across the table. I did not want Travis to pay my father's medical bills, but I was hardly in a position to be noble. I was furious at Father for having no insurance and more furious at Travis for being so good-hearted. What had I done as a wife to warrant such generosity?

And the bills had just begun. Father would be in the rehabilitation center for many weeks. A Busby Berkeley Production of dollar bills danced frenetically in my mind's eye. Was Travis planning on funding Father's entire recuperation?

"I will never be able to pay you back," I protested hopelessly.

"Sure you will," he said amiably, unaware that the hospital bill was more money than I had made in three years.

"How?" I asked with mounting desperation.

"You know, Mallory, most people would just accept the money and be happy."

"I can't. I'm too indebted to you as it is." All those hours he had selflessly given Father.

"All right," he said, dropping his chopsticks and running his hand through his blond hair. "I can see we're back to square one. What do you propose to do about the hospital bill."

"I'll get a job and pay it off—a little at a time."

"Fine."

"Fine?" I echoed nervously.

"If that's what you're determined to do, do it."

"Maybe I'm being too hasty," I argued.

Travis rolled his eyes heavenward. "Mallory, you agonize too much. It is only money."

"Maybe to you, but not to me."

"But that's the point!"

Father Holmes came into the kitchen and surveyed our cartons of food. "Chinese!" he said excitedly.

"Would you like some, Father?" I asked.

"In a pig's eye!"

"I think I saw one floating in that carton there," I said.

"Hrumph." He went to the refrigerator and pulled out an economy-size bottle of ketchup, a carton of cottage cheese, and some old tunafish salad. Next he went to the cabinets and got a bowl and the box of Rice Krispies. Father Holmes mixed the tunafish and the cottage cheese with the Rice Krispies, threw in some sugar, and then covered it all with a layer of Hunt's Ketchup. He sat down at the table, said "Haile Selassie," and began to eat.

"Well, Father, we've good news tonight. Sean has moved to the rehabilitation center."

"Does this mean she won't be tearing up Route 7 with Mary Elizabeth anymore?" Father Holmes asked, jerking his elbow in my direction.

"No. That is not what it means."

"Mary Elizabeth needs rest. Her clutch is fairly seized up. I can't bear to think what she's done to the fuel line."

"Then let Mallory drive Clara or Emma," Travis suggested.

"Never!"

"Very well, Father, but remember our bargain." So Travis had struck a deal with the Mad Mechanic. I had wondered why I'd been able to pry the Karmann Ghia from his grasp every day without a fight. I had thought Father Holmes was mellowing towards me.

Father Holmes growled. I thought for a moment it was Wart, but he was outside. Father Holmes got up, held his bowl in one hand, and with the other dragged his chair across the room. He sat down at a butcher block and continued to eat, hunched over his bowl.

"So," Travis said quietly, "back to the matter at hand."

"Oh, Jesus, Travis, I wouldn't mind if I thought there was a way I could pay you back."

"There is."

"How?"

"Just stick around. I'll think of something," he smiled.

It wasn't likely he would get equal measure, I thought.

Father Holmes choked on a mouthful of his mush. He sputtered and lunged into a coughing fit.

Had I been a dog, I would have smelled the danger.

Privileged Information

Fall closed in around us with a sudden snap. The foliage turned, blazed, and dropped; and still I was visiting the rehabilitation center. Father's progress had slowed. He wanted to go back to the hospital where his needs were capably met by an army of women in white. Fending for himself was what Sean Delaney would have considered a spectator sport.

Father's daily audience had shrunk to one. Travis could no longer ignore his business affairs. Maude had lodged a formal complaint: I was disrupting the creative process. Her accusation was laughable. Travis and I saw precious little of one another. When we weren't driving in opposite directions on Route 7, he was either holed up in his sterile office, wrestling with Mozart, or on the phone with lawyers. He was very preoccupied of late. As a matter of pride, I could not and would not tell this to Maude.

I told Father, however, when he accused me of keeping his only son from him. The stroke had swept through Father's memory, upending facts and fantasy and making Travis a blood son. He had no idea where I fit into the puzzle. He would squint his eyes at me, trying to make a determination. Each day I reintroduced myself as his daughter Mallory, but either he didn't want to believe me or he couldn't. Ten minutes later, he'd ask what I was doing there. I was beginning to wonder myself.

One day I came home weary from trying to convince Father that I was not his first wife Ellen (all the more unsettling because I didn't know if Ellen was real or fictional). I pulled into Leger de Main and spotted a white Mercedes in the driveway. Once inside, I followed voices.

I must have looked a curious sight standing at the entrance of the living room with my eyes wide and my mouth gaping. The room, which had been all but empty a few hours ago, was now fully furnished with matching sofas, loveseats and arm chairs. There were paintings on the walls—dunes and seascapes mostly. A woman with thick blond hair wearing a white silk blouse and black leather pants sat curled on the sofa near Travis. She had one arm resting on the back of the couch just centimeters from his outstretched hand. For a moment, I feared I had stumbled upon a tryst, but then I saw the man standing against the windows. A camera hung from his neck. He was fiddling with a light meter.

"Mallory, at last," Travis said, rising. "How's Sean today?"

"Fine," I said. "He asked for you." The blond woman smiled but did not change position.

"Darling, this is Kerra Kenilworth, from *People.*"

"How do you do?" I asked, though it was evident she was doing just fine.

"Trav has told me so much about you," she purred.

I looked at "Trav." "Oh, really?"

"Yes, please join us." I went over to the loveseat facing them and sat. I looked down at the fabric, blues and greens on a white background. I felt its nubby texture. Where had all of this furniture come from? When I looked up, everyone was staring at me.

"I was just complimenting Trav on your taste. Are these Rico Vermi's?"

Nervously, I looked at Travis. He gave me no clue. "Possibly," I said.

Kerra laughed. In doing so, she threw back her mane of hair exposing a long, sensuous neck. "Trav *said* you had a tart sense of humor. In fact," she said, reaching over and tapping his hand playfully, "he credits you for the humorous subtext of his newest oeuvre."

Travis smiled disarmingly. I sneezed violently. I had been sneezing since the end of August. Hay fever, I had told Travis. Nerves, he had accused. Travis was one of those creatures who never sneezed. His elegant nose remained unviolated even when I taunted it with a meatloaf redolent with black pepper.

"Trav has such a genial nature," Kerra sighed. "He says you complement one another well," and here she looked at her notepad. " 'Mallory's wit is a whetstone against which I sharpen my writing tool.' How delightfully phallic," mused Kerra. I smiled weakly. "I understand you are an actress."

"On the rare occasion."

"Ah, modest!" Kerra condescended.

"No, honest," I replied. I realized then I no longer thought of myself as an actress. I didn't know what I was.

"Well, we'll just say you're an actress whose time is coming, shall we?" She turned her attention and her dark brown eyes back to my husband. "Are you still a hopeless insomniac?"

"Well, I do sleep but only from midnight to three."

I regarded my husband with astonishment. "What do you do the rest of the time?" I blurted.

Kerra laughed. "How long have you been married—four months? Perhaps I should loan you some back issues." Kerra smiled broadly. I wanted to dig a hole in the couch.

"Mallory is a sound sleeper," Travis explained, as I sneezed again.

"Does she snore?" Kerra asked lightly. It seemed to me then that my entire marriage hinged on his answer.

Travis gracefully deflected her curiosity. "Mallory, I write from three in the morning until lunch."

"Those weird hours help him commune with the dark forces," Kerra added.

"Oh, well, there are plenty of those around here," I said.

Kerra raised her left brow. She looked at Travis with the commiseration due a man who had married someone unwise to the ways of the muse. "And how are your children, Trav?"

"Fine," he said, rather abruptly.

"Isn't Nell delectable?" Kerra said to me. "Tell me honestly, Trav, our readers all want to know . . ."

"On the advice of my lawyer, I cannot discuss my children," Travis replied.

"Oh, then the custody battle is still on," assumed Kerra.

What custody battle? I bit my lip so as to not say something stupid in front of The Press. It was at this inopportune moment that the photographer started snapping pictures. He crouched over me, the camera clicking and whirring. I smiled grimly. Dropping to the floor, he shot photos in which my kneecaps and reddened nostrils were predominant. I wanted to swat him but was afraid such an action would pre-empt Travis's answer.

"On the advice of my lawyer," Travis repeated, "I cannot discuss my children."

"Even with an old friend?" she asked winsomely. I found myself hoping he would answer. Travis smiled one of his most alluring smiles but said nothing.

"All right then," she said, miffed, "on to a lighter subject. Are you planning any more gala costume balls?"

"We haven't done much entertaining. Mallory is still getting established. She wants to redecorate the place with her own stamp first."

"Ah, well, that is certainly understandable. I love the artwork. Are those Kip Bramhall's?"

"Yes," I answered boldly, for I could see the artist's signature.

"As you probably know, Kerra, I spent my childhood summers on the Vineyard. That painting there," he said, pointing to a picture, "is of a marsh near my home."

"Do you ever go back?"

"No. Mother still goes though." I stifled my surprise.

"How's Phil these days?" Who was Phil? I wondered.

"Oh, he's fine. He spends his time working on the cars." It was hard to think of Father Holmes as "Phil."

"Does he keep a hand in at the agency?" Kerra questioned. Could Father Holmes ever have lived a real life?

"Not so you'd notice," Travis replied.

"A pity. He was a great agent in his day. I was talking to Saul the other day. He credits Phil with his escape from Morrow."

The Mad Mechanic was a literary agent? I was dizzy with facts. I wanted this woman with her knowing questions gone. Given the time, Travis might just as casually disclose fratricide or political ambitions.

"Well, do give him my best," she said, standing. Kerra latched on to Travis's hand and pulled him to his feet.

"I will," he promised. "When do you expect the article to appear?"

"We'll hook it into the movie release of *Wolf's Down* next month. I think those photos we took with Mozart will be just the ticket." Kerra did not seem inclined to relinquish Travis's hand.

"Goodbye," I said firmly.

"Hmmh? Oh. Awfully nice to have met you, Valerie."

"Mallory," I corrected.

"Yes, of course. Thank you for the lovely lunch, Trav. We'll have to do it again. Soon. Come along, Rolf," she said to the photographer.

"Here, let me walk you out," Travis offered.

Travis returned moments later, whistling. He looked at me and stopped midtune. "Is something the matter?"

"Matter? What could be the matter?" I said angrily.

"Is it Sean?" he asked.

"It's us! No, damn it, it's you," I answered. "Life with you is a continual sleight of hand. Sometimes I think if I blink three times and click my heels, I'll wake up in Kansas."

"Kansas?" he repeated dully.

"Where did the furniture come from?" I asked with exasperation.

"Ah, you don't like it."

"I love it. That's hardly the point."

"Four months ago, I invited you to do what you wanted with the house. You did nothing. In principle I accepted that aesthetic decision. But with the media about to descend . . ."

"The media is going to descend?" I asked, barely able to breathe.

"There is always a certain amount of publicity involved when a movie is released. I thought it sensible to have one room where they could sit. I ordered it last week. Happily it arrived today or *People* would have been sure to write something cute about our empty rooms, like 'the bride has been so happily engaged upstairs she hasn't had time to decorate.' If you don't like the furniture . . ."

"Forget the bloody furniture," I stormed.

Travis looked surprised. "The paintings? Well, we'll have to keep them. They are from my mother."

"Ah yes, your mother. You said she was 'departed.' Imagine my surprise on learning the corpse summers on the Vineyard."

"Departed? Oh, I meant she left us. We don't see her anymore, a bit of bad blood." How readily people were severed from his life. "Is that what this stink is about? Why didn't you ask?"

"An incurious mind, obviously, or it would have occurred to me to ask what you did between three and seven in the morning. Funny that a purring stranger knows more about your nocturnal habits than I do.

"And 'Phil,'" I continued. "How could I not have guessed he was a literary agent? He's a natural. Deals sealed with a wrench over a three-yogurt lunch."

"I hardly think your sarcasm is merited."

"Don't you?" I was up and pacing now. "Just when were you going to tell me about the custody suit?"

"On the advice of my lawyer . . ."

"Don't you dare try to fob me off with that bushwa!"

"As I was saying, on the advice of my lawyer I am trying to obtain custody of my children. He thinks I have a chance."

"I repeat, when were you going to tell me?"

"I didn't want to get your hopes up," he said quietly.

I stopped in my tracks. "That *is* rich!"

"I beg your pardon?"

"What makes you think I want to take care of your children?"

"You love children," he said matter-of-factly.

"Says who?"

"But . . . Maude. Your brothers . . ."

Slowly, with measured emphasis, so there could be no doubt, I said, "What we do out of duty is not necessarily what we'd do given half a chance."

"You don't want my children?" he asked, astounded.

"I haven't *met* your children."

Travis put his arm on my shoulder. "You will love my children," he said, as though it were the Eleventh Commandment.

Suddenly I flashed back on a conversation with Father Holmes. What was it he had said? "When Teddy's got them, you'll be gone." My stomach knotted.

I had long suspected Travis had married me for a reason.

As a husband he was attentive and warm, but something was a little "off." For a while I reasoned it was my insecurity standing between us. Why should a man of such wealth, intelligence, and good looks love me? But sometimes I told myself I had charms I knew not of. Those were generally the days I sang Cole Porter tunes while I burned dinner. Travis had always seemed amused by my efforts, however misguided.

Until this moment, I could deny the unsettling suspicions. Now the truth rolled over me like a diesel on a downgrade. Travis had married me as a matter of judicial expedience. He wanted his children back. To get them, he needed a new wife with credentials. I had raised several kids. The courts would love it.

And how could I say no? Travis knew I adored him. And if that wasn't enough to buy my compliance, he had an ace in the hole: my Father's debt.

I looked at my husband. His blond hair darkened in the fall, his tan surprisingly remained. Although his expression was neutral, his dark green eyes had the look of a man who enjoyed watching the trap snap. He smiled.

Surely this was how Mother had felt when she was gored by an animal she loved.

Back in Harness

Under the old custody agreement, the children were to spend Christmas vacation with Travis. The court date for the new custody hearing was set for February 3rd. Jess's fifth birthday would fall near the end of their two-week visit. Travis calculated that between birthday balloons and Christmas stockings I would have ample opportunity to win the children over.

For days, I stewed over my possible courses of action. I could actively resist or pretend to accede to Travis's plan. At no point did I consider enduring another life sentence of motherhood by proxy.

Travis's lawyer interviewed me shortly after I had learned of the custody trial. Edmund Trehune was a fat man who bore his weight as if it were a privilege of the bar. I took an instant dislike to him.

"As Travis has told you," he said with oily license, "we will be putting you on the witness stand. Is there anything I should know about your past?"

I wished then that I had been a gun runner. "No," I answered sourly.

"But surely . . ." he said with disbelief. "You were an actress." (I noted his use of the past tense with resentment.) "It is well known that people in the arts have fewer . . . uh, shall we say, moral strictures . . . than the rest of us."

"Really? I hadn't heard that," I said, smiling coyly.

"Whom have you slept with?" he asked, leaning forward in a challenging manner.

"That is none of your damned business," I snapped.

"But I'm afraid it is," he purred.

"My own husband has never asked me such an obnoxious question!"

"But Sarah's lawyer will. They will use anything to assail your credibility as a maternal figure. So please," he said, straightening up, "a list of the concerned parties." His complacency was enraging.

"George Kaufman," I brazened . . . he smiled, "Arthur Miller, William Inge, Clifford Odets, John Synge, Christopher Fry, Bernard Shaw, Bill Shakespeare . . ."

Greedily, he made notes.

His odious questions continued. Finally, he shuffled some papers and said, "One last thing. How would you sum up your theory of child rearing?"

I looked him straight in his piggy eyes and said, "I have it down to a science. You put children in a box at birth. You drill air holes. When the children turn eighteen, you fill in the holes."

* * *

When I got home from the interview, Travis was pacing in the hallway. "Why didn't you tell me you'd slept with the Manhattan phonebook?" he demanded, as I was removing my coat.

"I can understand why that whore of a lawyer would believe such slander, but I had expected better from you."

"I knew it," he said with a relief that belied his statement. "Trehune doesn't think we should put you on the stand."

"Okey dokey."

"Mallory. You will help me, won't you?"

At the lawyer's, I had decided on open rebellion. Now looking at the pain in my husband's eyes, I felt subversion the better course. "I expect so," I said, lightly.

"Good news!" Travis announced, coming into the living room where I was sorting through Christmas decorations. "That was the doctor on the phone. He has agreed to let your father come home for the holidays!"

"All of the holidays?" I knew it had been a mistake to tell Travis Father missed him.

"No, just Christmas Eve and Day."

"Will we be able to care for him?" Despite the doctor's prognosis, Father had not improved appreciably in the past month. "Really, Travis, there'll be so much confusion with the children here."

"Just the tonic he needs," Travis assured me.

"Frankly, I'm surprised he wants to come after his last visit."

"Well, I promised him Wart wouldn't be here."

I put down the knotted strand of lights. "Oh? And where did you say Wart would be?"

"A kennel. You knew he couldn't be here, with the children and all."

"No, I didn't know that." I had planned to train Wart to herd the children. "And I object. I can't send him away at Christmas."

"I don't believe Wart can read a calendar."

"But I can. If Wart goes, so do I." If I didn't fight this now, there would be no stopping Travis from ousting Wart after he had won the custody battle. And Wart was my only friend in Connecticut.

"For heaven sakes, Mallory. Be reasonable. Schuyler is just a toddler. For all we know, Wart eats toddlers."

"Dammit Travis, I am doing everything you want, allow me my dog."

He picked up an ornament and looked at it unhappily. "Since you insist," he conceded. "But you'll have to keep him penned in the north wing."

Better than bunking with Mozart. "Fine."

"There's one other thing. I sort of invited Maude for Christmas."

"Why?" I protested.

"We haven't seen her since this summer. She can help with your father."

"Be serious. Maude's help is worth about as much as a pound of red pepper on an open wound."

"Nell asked that she be here."

"They know one another?" I asked uneasily.

"I took the kids into the city a few times last year. It was before I met you," he said apologetically.

What was I going to do for two weeks with three children I'd never met? I didn't even know what kids liked these days. I sat down in front of the television one afternoon to do research and was appalled. No more Crusader Rabbit and Rags the Tiger cartoons, it was all space invaders and some insidious creature called Strawberry Shortcake.

Redding was not exactly a cornucopia of amusements. If you didn't like trees, hills, and more trees, you were out of luck. There were no cinemas, toy stores, bookstores, no cable television, video arcades, or even a McDonalds. I suggested to Travis that we take them to New York City. He vetoed the idea as we would need a court order to take them out of the state.

And there was the damned birthday party to worry about. I remembered Claire's parties as the longest two hours of the year. Birthday parties for young children are supposed to be fun; but look closely at party pictures and you'll notice that most children are discouraged or bored. At least two will be bawling, and one will have suffered an allergic reaction to the cake.

In my professional capacity as "Zooks the Under Clown," I had tried to bring money to my bank account and merriment to children's birthday parties. I knew both to be an uphill battle, even when one was willing.

Assuming I could provide the entertainment, where was I to find playmates for the party? Could one rent-a-child in Connecticut? Travis said none of Jess's old friends were still in town. He suggested I approach children at the elementary school.

"Don't they have laws against that sort of thing?" I asked.

"I suppose they do. Why don't you canvass the neighbors."

"Why don't *you*?"

"Because this is a perfect opportunity for you to meet

other women. Once the children come to live with us, you'll need to meet them anyway."

"Right." I'd be damned if I would go from house to house borrowing a cup of child. I wandered into the kitchen where Wart was lying on a dog bed. "Wart, what should I do?" He looked at me with soulful eyes. A solution presented itself.

Two days before the children were to arrive, Travis handed me a sheaf of papers as I came in the door from visiting Father.

"What's this?"

"Bios of the kids." I looked at the top page. It read, "Cornelia Holmes: Nickname, Nell; born 11/8/72. Sweet, sensitive, tends to be a bit too serious. Special interest, lower animal orders; food likes: belgian waffles, praline cream, chocolate mousse . . . ."

I flipped to the next sheet: "Jessica Holmes: Nickname, Jess; born 12/30/75. Quite the athlete, enjoys all outdoor activities, suggest sledding, ice skating, cross-country skiing . . . ."

Did he expect me to become Nanook of the North for the sake of his children?

My anger evaporated when I looked at the last sheet of paper. "Schuyler Holmes; born 9/4/78."

That was all. Travis hadn't seen enough of his two-year-old son to know anything about him. The lost connection echoed in my past. Whatever resistance I had felt towards this project melted away. Schuyler should know his father.

Nell, Jess, and Schuyler arrived a day early but with a nanny. My spirits soared. With any luck I wouldn't have to do anything but smile benevolently for two weeks.

The children were little jewels. Blond, fair, and polite. The girls were dressed in matching blue wool outfits. The little boy was in a pair of lederhosen with red knee socks. Nell and Jess curtsied. Schuyler stared at me with wide-eyed wonder.

"I'm awfully glad you could be here," I greeted. "We weren't expecting you until tomorrow."

The nanny, Mrs. Carstairs, replied, "Madame wished to see them off before she sailed."

"Well, why don't I take you up to get settled, and then I'll fetch the children's father."

"I know my way around," Mrs. Carstairs replied.

"I wish I did," I laughed. Mrs. Carstairs leveled me with an icy glare.

Wart rounded the corner at that moment in full gallop. He slid to a stop inches from the girls. Schuyler clawed his way up Mrs. Carstairs's hem. I grabbed onto Wart's halter collar to prevent a lunge.

The girls stood stock still. "What kind of canine is he?" asked Nell politely.

"*Canis non grata,*" I joked. She turned her head slightly and issued a small laugh. This child was eight? "He's a Weimaraner," I explained. "His name is Wart." The object in question was staring intently at the children. He began to wag his stump of a tail vigorously.

"Mother says dogs carry worms and ticks," said Nell.

"And mice," added Jess.

"Lice," Nell corrected.

"Well . . ." I stalled. We had to keep the battle lines clear. I was not the natural mother, just an import. Mrs. Carstairs eyed me carefully, leaving little doubt that she would report any and all infractions.

"Can we touch him?" Jess asked.

"If you would like," I said—nanny's eyes darkened, "but wash your hands afterwards." Timidly, the girls stepped forward and patted his head. Schuyler cooed and struggled to get out of Mrs. Carstairs's arms. Wart showed every sign of loving children. I took this to be an unexpected good omen and went off happily to find Travis.

When Travis and I came back, Mrs. Carstairs was standing alone in the foyer with her coat, muffler, and gloves on.

"Hello, Nanny Car," Travis said warmly.

"Mr. Holmes," she said, nodding curtly. "I'll be on my way now."

"You aren't going!" I exclaimed.

"Yes. Madame was quite firm on that point."

"Travis . . ." I implored.

"Have a safe trip," replied Travis.

There was a certain logic to Travis's meanness. I would have to get to know them sometime, why not now when I could bribe them legitimately.

Never had I met children such as these. They were pleasant, intelligent, and congenitally courteous. Even Schuyler was a model of good behavior. Where were the "Terrible Twos" I remembered with such dread? Claire's tantrums in the supermarket had left me weak-kneed and nauseated. Schuyler said "please" and "thank you."

Travis literally shone in his children's company. It was hard to believe such a happy and contented man could summon up ghouls at whim. He rearranged his work schedule so as to cook the children's meals, attend to their bathtime rituals, and sing them to sleep.

The rest, he said, was my job. Panic descended like an iron-clad balloon. Travis expected me to ignite his children's sense of wonder.

There are two schools of mothering: nurture the soul or attend to the body. Some women, I suppose, managed to combine both, but it had never been accomplished in the Delaney family. Where my mother had been a master of nurturing the spirit, all of my experience had fallen in the second, pedestrian category. I had kept my brothers' and sisters' bodies fueled, cleaned, and clothed. But I had neither the experience nor the imagination to fill their heads with dreams and ideas.

When I explained it was my mother he wanted, Travis was furious.

"Look, I'll cook, clean, whatever . . ." I offered.

"Had I wanted a caretaker, I could have hired one."

"But I'm no good at stirring imaginations," I confessed.

"You're an actor, for chrissakes. What else does an actor do but 'stir imaginations'?" he asked with damnable logic.

"If I had known I was signing up to play Mother Goose, I'd have never married you." There. I'd said it. Travis ignored it.

"You said you'd help."

"And I will. They are good kids. I like them. But let me do what I know how to do." We were coming to blows with feminist ideology. Travis was willing to do the dirty work in child care, but so was I.

"You're just afraid to do battle with the almighty legend of Orin Delaney," accused Travis.

I hadn't thought of it in those terms. But of course, he was dead on target.

* * *

"We're going to play a game," I announced to Nell after Jess and Schuyler had been tucked into bed. "It's called 'Name that Beast.' " I was amazed how readily it came back to me.

Nell was a formidable opponent. A half hour into the game, she had depleted my inventory of obscure data and turned the tables.

"What is so special about a male flatworm?" she asked me.

"Aren't they the ones that reproduce segments when they are chopped in half?" I guessed.

"The male flatworm has a multifunctional penis," Nell stated.

"Well . . ." I said, unhappy to be discussing penises with an eight-year-old. "Aren't most penises multifunctional?"

"No, most just have two functions, ejaculation and urination," she said clinically. "The flatworm's penis comes out of its mouth and is equipped with spikes and poison glands."

"How . . . handy."

"Do you know what is interesting about the Indian cobra's penis?"

"I think I hear Schuyler," I said, beating a hasty retreat.

With Jess I made angels in the snow, hiked through the woods, and hurled snowballs. She told me she thought dolls were "dippy." I agreed. That night after they were all in bed, I drove fifteen miles to return the dolls I had bought her for Christmas.

Schuyler and I played with Matchbox cars for hours at a stretch. I had not realized there were so many subtle variations to the word "vroom."

If the children missed their mother, they didn't tell me. I

respected their tact, it enabled us to look like a television family.

One day, I found Nell slipping out of the broom closet.

"Oh! Mallory, hi. I was just, uh, sweeping up some spilled cereal." She hurried away. I went around to the Nancy Drew room and pushed the panel. The darts were still in the portrait, but they were now embedded in the eyes. Still waters run deep, I mused.

With deep pleasure, I confessed to Travis that I enjoyed his children. They had taught me it was the day to day maintenance that ruined motherhood. I almost said I wanted a child of my own, but I didn't.

Travis cheered my enthusiasm. And by the way, now that we were all friends, he wanted to spend quality time with his kids. Could I resume kitchen detail?

I was in the kitchen cursing Fanny Farmer and her "simple" flaky pie crust when I heard a commotion from another part of the house. Wart was yowling like his tail was caught in a door. I was covered with pastry flour and little gobs of dough but knew Wart to have unfailing good instincts. Reluctantly, I followed the noise. In the front hallway, I found Wart whirling in circles on his hind legs.

There stood Maude, shaking the snow from her boots while clutching a manuscript bag. Father Holmes hovered subserviently by the front door, bearing Bloomingdale's Big Brown Bags filled with presents.

"Hello," I said with forced cheer. "Wart! Calm down, sweetie."

"I thought the beast was taking a holiday," Maude said coolly. Wart's velocity increased.

"And miss your visit? He wouldn't think of it. Wart, sit!"

"Aunt Maude!" Nell and Jess said happily, arriving behind me. I noted their glee with more than a twinge of jealousy.

"Hey, how are my favorite kidlets?" The phrase abducted me from the present and dropped me down in the hallway of the Delaney Delirium. Surely, Travis's children would be able to see through this ruse as we had seen through Father's indifference. Not yet, apparently. They clamored around Maude. Wart continued his aggravated twirling.

Schuyler and Travis arrived. "Mallory, get that dog out of here."

Returning from my mission, I found Father Holmes carrying in more Big Brown Bags.

"Bring them in here, Philip," Maude directed from the living room. "Philip and I had the most enchanting drive. We hardly noticed the traffic for our conversation." I looked at Father Holmes. He hadn't spoken a civil word to me in five months. And if Travis wasn't in the room, he spoke not at all.

But I was missing the point.

All attention was focused on Maude. Unwillingly, my eyes followed suit. I gasped.

"Isn't it wonderful? Maude's pregnant," Travis explained unnecessarily.

The Road to Hell . . .

"Who's the father?" I asked when I found my breath.

Maude's feet were up on the coffee table. "Does it matter?" she said airily.

It mattered. "When is the baby due?" My voice refused to remain flat.

"April ninth," Travis supplied. "She was just telling us," he added somewhat lamely.

I counted backwards. The child was conceived in August. Maude had been here in August. "Excuse me," I said abruptly. "I smell something burning." It was my marriage, going up in flames.

Maude's condition poisoned Christmas. Even my favorite Christmas carols made me flinch with their many references to the newborn child. Travis and I did not speak of Maude's pregnancy in private. Any allusion to it would have prompted me to beat him senseless.

Realistically, I should not have been surprised that Maude had slept with my husband. The fact was that Travis had always been Maude's property; she had merely loaned him to me for her own amusement.

Travis had betrayed me—but perhaps unwittingly. They had been trapped together. Perhaps they had just been fighting boredom or panic. I would have been willing to believe even the most ludicrous story. But Travis offered no explanation.

It galled me that I still loved him. How was it possible, I wondered, fearing for my emotional health.

Would Travis acknowledge paternity? Or was he still opposed to bearing more children? And if so, would I get my walking papers before or after the custody hearing? My only hope was the children. They liked me. Travis would appreciate that. If I did a good job, maybe he would let me stay . . . and adore him.

Father arrived Christmas Eve wearing the new Chesterfield coat Travis had given him. He looked surprisingly dapper for a man who had spent the last five months in institutions. Father parked himself in the living room with a bell that he rang whenever he required attention. For a while, it sounded like the bells of St. Mary's chiming on the quarter hour.

Christmas morning I was up at dawn expecting to hear the excited babble of children wanting to get at their presents.

The children arose at eight-thirty and respectfully requested that they might be allowed to see if Saint Nick had been in the neighborhood.

They were pleased with their bounty. The girls opened

each present carefully, smoothing the paper and saving the bows. They expressed admiration for the gifts but little more. I looked at Travis with apprehension. He seemed to find nothing untoward in their reaction.

If it hadn't been for Schuyler, I might have screamed with frustration. He giggled and "vroomed" delightedly over his new Hot Wheels Service Station and fleet of Matchbox cars. He loved the cloth floor map I had made.

Maude came down claiming she had overslept, but her entrance had all the timing of a professional actor. Whereas Nell had "appreciated" the microscope we gave her, she "loved" Maude's gift—a pink sweater with silver heart-shaped buttons.

When Jess opened her doll, I smiled inwardly. But Jess squealed with delight and threw her arms around Maude. I stalked off to the kitchen to work on Christmas dinner. Travis followed.

"What's the matter?" he asked.

"Nothing."

"You're hurt."

"Bleeding," I snapped.

"They're confused."

"There's a lot of that going around." I hoisted the stuffed turkey from the refrigerator onto the counter. "Do you know how hard I worked to get their presents just right?"

"You have to understand. The kids are afraid to show you affection. They don't want to be disloyal to their mother."

Of course, he was right. But it didn't stop the hurt. "When are we going to exchange gifts?"

"After the children are in bed," he replied.

Right, I thought. Mustn't let the children think Daddy is giving gifts to the impostor.

* * *

I had never looked at a cookbook before I met Travis. All of my "recipes" had been from the back of the can. But for Christmas dinner, I had spent days consulting cookbooks and setting a time schedule. There were so many different dishes to coordinate.

As dinner time approached, I realized I had forgotten the vegetables. Thank god for microwaves. I rinsed and cut up the broccoli and arranged it on a white platter. It needed a festive touch. I peeled some carrots and placed them decoratively around the broccoli. Then I popped it all in the microwave.

I went to check the table. The holly centerpiece and red candles on the white tablecloth put me in the spirit for the first time that day.

Travis came to carve the turkey. I began ferrying platters into the dining room, where Maude was buckling Schuyler into his youth chair. Nell and Jess stood solemnly by their places. Father Holmes and Father Delaney were arguing spiritedly about the career of Basil Rathbone. I dropped off the broccoli and the homemade cranberry relish and went back for the mashed potatoes.

When I returned, Jess was shrieking. Schuyler said, "Werms, Mauwawee, werms." And Nell was peering at the platter of broccoli.

"What!"

Travis hurried into the dining room. "What is the matter?"

"Dead worms," announced Nell, pointing to the platter. My stomach dropped.

"Jesus, Mallory," he cursed, grabbing the platter. There,

inescapably, were dozens of curled gray worms atop the broccoli. "Did you soak the broccoli in salt water?"

"I rinsed it."

He marched back to the kitchen with the offending dish. Everyone at the table regarded me stonily.

Except Maude. She smiled a Cheshire grin.

Father went back to the rehabilitation center that night—and not a moment too soon. Upset by recent events, I was in no mood to pander to his continual whining. I just wanted to clear the house and beg Travis for forgiveness while the spirit of Christianity was still abroad in the land.

Maude was scheduled to leave the next day but was delayed by a severe case of diarrhea. I might have gloated, but I too was bivouacked in the john—as were Travis and the children. (Father Holmes had refused to eat any of my dinner after the broccoli episode and was thus spared.)

Travis, when he learned that I had stuffed the turkey two hours before cooking it, said we were lucky the food poisoning had been so mild.

Everything now hinged on Jessica's birthday party. That my marriage rested in the hands of ten whining, fretful children was not a happy thought. I redoubled my efforts. This had to be the best birthday party ever.

The sky was gun-metal gray and vaguely threatening the morning of Jess's party. There was already a foot of accumulated snow on the ground, but the roads were clear as I drove to Ridgefield to pick up the birthday cake. Travis had insisted that I order a cake, fearing, I suppose, that I would serve chocolate botulism if left to my own devices. His faith in my judgment had plummeted since Christmas. And it was not only my dinner that had caused him concern.

After careful consideration of Travis's needs, I had given him a raven for Christmas. Travis made polite noises, much like his daughters. But then the raven had escaped from his cage and shat all over Travis's manuscripts and his Wang. Travis's sense of humor was not what it might be.

Travis's present to me was a new car—not a sporty coupe or luxurious Jaguar, but a wood-paneled station wagon. A testament to passion, I reflected sourly.

There was a long wait at the bakery. Driving home with "Miss Berries," the bakery's three-layer salute to Strawberry Shortcake, I noticed the road had turned slick. If I did the week's grocery shopping now, I wouldn't have time to inflate the four dozen balloons for the entrance way. I could shop after the party. And if the roads turned nasty, we still had enough food until morning.

A light snow was falling by the time I reached home.

I found Travis playing Tickle Monster with the children. Travis lay on the rug making growling noises while the kids jumped on him and tried to tickle him to death.

"It's snowing again. Do you think we should cancel?" I asked, trying to be prudent.

"Mallory, this is Connecticut. People are used to driving in snow. What time did you say?"

"One to three."

"The sun will be out by then."

"But . . ."

"If it gets bad, we can always take them home by sled."

Travis still assumed the guest list was composed of neighbors. There was no sense in spoiling the children's surprise.

The Merry Moppet Mob Scene

At five minutes to one, I was dressed in my clown costume and waiting by the front door. Travis came into the hallway and laughed. "Very effective," he said, tweaking my green rubber nose.

The van from the Robleigh Children's Home pulled up in front of the house. "Ah, good, right on time."

"What's that?" Travis said, peering out at the van.

"The children for the party," I explained.

Travis read the sign on the van and grabbed my arm. "Is this some sort of joke?"

"No, I thought it would be nice for the orphans to come to a party."

"Orphans!" he exclaimed. "And what about Jess. Did you think of her?"

"Of course. Kids are kids. She'll have a fine time."

"With orphans!" he said with bewilderment.

"They aren't contaminated," I said, shaking off his grip. "What's wrong with bringing a little joy to underprivileged children?"

"Is this some latent crap you're dredging up from your motherless past?" he snapped. "A compulsion to take in strays. Christ, Mallory, do you see what you've done? You've arranged a party of human Warts."

There was a knock at the door. "I hadn't realized you were such a snob," I replied angrily.

"I'm thinking of my daughter."

"So was I." Shouldn't he be pleased by my ingenuity and social conscience?

There was another knock. "Just don't tell Jess they are orphans."

"Why the hell not?"

"I want her to have fun, not to think she's embarking on a social crusade." With that, Travis opened the door wide and was all smiles.

The snow had stopped. A uniformed man stood in the doorway. "Merry Christmas. Here they are. See you at three."

The children filed in solemnly. Some looked up at the balloons with awe and suspicion, others stared at the floor. I had asked for nine children between the ages of four and six. What I got was a racially mixed group of boys and girls between three and five feet tall. One had a five o'clock shadow.

Travis looked at the children, then at me. "Woof woof," he said.

"You get Jess, I'll get things rolling." He turned to go. "Hello gang. I'm Zooks the Under Clown, and I've lost my smile. It's in the living room somewhere. Could you help me find it?" Children at this point are supposed to dive into the party spirit and help the bereft clown. The orphans stood rooted in the hallway.

"Where's the food?" demanded one.

"Soon. Let's give everyone a name tag so Zooks knows who you are." The boy with the whiskers told me his name was "Boss."

"Ross?" I queried.

"Boss!" he responded emphatically.

Travis returned with Jess, Nell, and Schuyler. As meetings go, it was awkward. I checked my watch—an hour and fifty-three minutes to go.

Since no one seemed to care if Zooks ever smiled again, I moved on to a traditional icebreaker, the balloon stomp. Balloons were tied to each child's ankle. Children were to break each other's balloons while keeping their own intact. The winner was the child with the last unpopped balloon.

We attached the balloons, stood back, and said "go." All hell broke loose. Boss and two cohorts mowed down the younger children. Schuyler's balloons popped under his own weight as he buckled to the floor.

"Great, Mallory," Travis muttered, as he went to Schuyler's aid. "I want Mommy. Where's Mommy?" wailed Schuyler.

I ran after Boss, who was pushing an Oriental girl's face into the sofa cushion. Taking a chunk of his hair, I dragged him to a corner. "Pull that stunt again, and Zooks is going to put out your lights."

"Try it, clownie," he challenged. I took a fold of skin under his left ear and twisted it sharply. He yelped in surprise.

I couldn't tell if anyone was having fun. Jess looked dazzled, but that was not necessarily a good sign. One little girl said she was tired and lay down on the couch. Another cried for her rag doll, which had been left at the orphanage. Boss and his friends played the games with an enthusiasm bordering on the rabid. They thrashed and swung and twirled mindlessly, sending a lamp and a Steuben ashtray to premature death.

It felt like we'd been together for a week by the time the games were done. I was horrified to see there was still an hour and six minutes left.

The cake and the ice cream, which were expected to last twenty minutes, were devoured in a flash—fifty-four minutes to go.

Fresh air was important for orphans. Let them play outside, Travis suggested. I looked out the window. It was raining.

Slowly, Zooks the Under Clown emptied her repertoire of jokes and riddles before the unsmiling crowd.

All that remained were the goodie bags. I doled them out. The prizes were what every normal four- to six-year-old boy and girl wanted, according to the man in the Bethel toy store. The operative word, apparently, was "normal." Boss jeered at the contents and set off a wave of general discontent.

"Where's Mommy," Schuyler asked plaintively, tugging at my clown suit.

"For the eightieth time, Mommy is in Europe. Now have fun."

Travis came over, wiping his brow and said, "How much longer?"

"Forty-two minutes."

"Right. You take the younger ones upstairs to play. I'll take the punks."

"What are you going to do?" I asked, too relieved to be alarmed.

"Tell a few stories," he said with a sly smile.

At two minutes to three, feeling a good decade older, I brought the younger children back downstairs and put on their coats. Travis's charges were slightly dazed. Travis must have pulled out the stops.

By ten after three, the bundled children were hot and antsy. Schuyler was in the living room with his sisters asking them where Mommy was. Travis kept looking at his watch and muttering, leaving little doubt there would be hell to pay as soon as the guests were gone.

Where was the damned van? Could it be stuck in the driveway? Stepping outside, I fell flat on my ass on the slate steps. The children laughed for the first time. I struggled to stand in my oversized clown shoes but kept slipping. Travis came to the doorway and joined the laughter. "You should have tried this earlier."

On my hands and knees, I crawled back into the house afraid to look Travis in the face. "I have to make a call," I said, unnerved.

In the kitchen, I dialed the Robleigh Children's Home.

"Ah, Mrs. Holmes, I was about to ring you," said the directress.

"Where is the van?" I asked with little hope.

"He just called in. He can't get up your road."

"Tell him to stay put. I'll bring the children down to him."

"I'm afraid he's left."

"LEFT!" I bellowed into the receiver.

"Well, with the ice storm . . ."

"Ice storm!"

"Yes. Haven't you heard? It looks like it could be a bad one. I hope you have enough provisions for the night . . . Mrs. Holmes? Are you there? Mrs. Holmes?"

The power went out late that afternoon, plunging us into an eerie half-light. I could do nothing. The lack of electricity exacerbated my sense of powerlessness. Travis sensibly brought out candles and lit the fire.

The orphans, no strangers to hard times, did not seem cheered to learn that even the rich must suffer. After the initial fear wore off, they complained loudly. And who could blame them? The temperature had dropped drastically in a short time. Travis tried to tell them they were having an adventure. They didn't buy it. He told them stories about children in the South Seas. When even his vivid imagery failed to warm them, Travis passed out his cashmere sweaters.

"We're going to die," I stated.

"Nonsense. This is Connecticut," he said.

Why did people keep saying that as if it were a magic incantation? From what I could see, Connecticut was little better than the Northwest Territories.

"This is a nightmare," I protested, looking at the children huddled by the fire. Boss and his cronies were smoking cigarettes.

"What did you expect?" Travis quarreled.

"Well, certainly not this!"

"Orphans are orphans," he said obscurely.

"I didn't adopt them," I said defensively.

"It appears you didn't need to. See if you can get Boss and the boys to slither out to the wood pile. We may have trouble with nothing but wet wood."

* * *

As the dark gathered force, we sat in groups around the fireplace looking like aberrant pods. Travis's sweaters hung oddly on the shivering, coated children.

Nell, Jess, and Schuyler were lost souls. "I want my mommy," Schuyler wailed. I went to comfort him, which just set off a new round of complaints.

"You're not our mommy," Nell accused sternly. I had been waiting for that comment from the moment they arrived. It seemed to pop up in every movie, novel, and play ever written about step-parents. Wisdom dictated ignoring it.

"I want my mommy!"

"Schuyler, we *all* want our mommies. I want my mommy. These poor little boys and girls haven't seen their mommy for years. Try to be a good boy," I soothed as I stroked his head nervously.

"Where's Mommy? I want my mommy."

My reserves of patience were depleted.

"Where's Mommy?" he demanded.

"Mommy went on an intergalactic mission," I said icily. "She left Pluto yesterday, hit an asteroid field but is fast approaching the Blagerian Galaxy. If all goes well, she should be back in Boston on Tuesday."

"Where's Mommy?"

"Schuyler!"

Travis handed me a flashlight and suggested I go make dinner.

"What would you like?" As if he had a choice.

"Anything. Damned good thing you did the shopping today."

"Ummmh," I muttered. Please God, let me get to the store before Travis discovers I screwed up again.

My fingers were too numb to spread the cold unwieldy peanut butter. I heard a wail in the distance and remembered Wart, who had been sequestered in the north wing since noon. We were long overdue for our nightly ordeal.

Braced for the onslaught, I cautiously opened his door. Wart was whirling in circles. The room looked like an earthquake had hit a paleontology lab. Gnawed shin bones were strewn everywhere. Wart ate the marrow from dozens each week and "buried" them in the rug, the bedspread, and the chair.

Attached to his halter-leash, Wart barreled down the stairs, dragging me behind. As he finished his dinner, I opened the back door. Wart turned tail and rushed for the kitchen stairs, knocking the flashlight from my hand. I grabbed his halter and dragged him back towards the door. The freezing rain blew in on us. Wart dug his claws into the floor and whined piteously. Wart did not like winter. The back stoop boasted a three-foot ring of yellow snow. I hoisted his rear up and out and slammed the door.

By the time I returned with the sandwiches, the last of the milk, and a bottle of wine, Travis and the gang were down to the twenty-third bottle of beer on the wall.

"You want some wine?" I asked Travis.

"I just had one hundred and seventy-seven bottles of beer. All flat."

"Is that a yes or a no?"

"That's a plea for hemlock," he snapped.

The sandwiches took longer to eat than the ice cream and cake had. Either the children had lost their appetites or the peanut butter and honey on four-grain bread was gumming up the works. The silence, with just the frozen rain pelting the windows, was quite lovely.

Travis motioned me to follow him into the hallway. Out of the children's earshot, he said, "I don't want to alarm you, but we may have some problems."

"Oh?" I said, marveling at his gift for understatement.

"The well . . ." he replied confidentially.

"Surely the water isn't frozen," I objected.

"Might as well be. The pump won't work without electricity."

"There's no water?" I asked with alarm. "How am I going to do the dishes?"

"Dishes are not my concern."

"But there are only a few clean ones left."

"Screw the dishes. Where are our 'guests' going to piss?"

I did some quick calculations: twelve children, two adults, and no working toilet. Maybe we could join Wart at the back stoop.

Boss was singing "Great Green Gobs of Greasy Grimy Gopher Guts" when we returned to the living room. Thus inspired, the older children told one disgusting story after another. Nell corrected some of the anatomical details. Jess seemed too cowed to say anything. Schuyler continued his "where's-Mommy" chant.

The little girl who had lain on the couch during the party came to say she had to vomit. Travis picked her up and ran her to the upstairs toilet. That seemed as good a time as any to explain the bathroom situation to the children. Boss countered with an obscene remark.

Travis brought the girl, Jeanne, back down. "She's very flushed."

"Too much excitement."

"If you say so," he said dubiously.

* * *

I brought blankets and pillows downstairs. We camped in a circle and pretended to sleep. The nightmares started around ten. Travis and I spent the night lying to frightened children. Things, I knew, would not "work out fine." We would survive the storm, but their own private nightmares awaited them at the orphanage. And mine wouldn't be far behind.

Two more children became feverish and chilled during the night. We gave them Tylenol and moved them away from the others.

At some point, the freezing rain turned to snow. By morning, there was a thick layer of snow on top of the ice. When I awoke, Travis was staring balefully out the window. The children were still asleep.

"I'll work on breakfast," I whispered. Travis nodded.

With dread, I reconnoitered supplies.

Travis was no fool. After a breakfast of crackers, dry cereal, Dr Pepper, and peanuts, he motioned me out in the hall. "Is this it?"

"Just about," I said, braced for his recriminations.

Travis's laughter filled the room.

We broke down the division of labor. I tended the sick, whose numbers were growing, and Travis handled the rest of them. The healthy gathered snow to melt over the fire, played cowboys and Indians, and made a great deal of ruckus. If we could have let them roam the house, it would have helped matters. But we couldn't risk it. The house might be hungry.

By noon, Jeanne began scratching through her many layers of clothing. I ignored it. Three hours later, the others in sick bay were squirming. I intended to ignore them as well, but they had caught Travis's attention.

"Lice?" he inquired pleasantly.

"We should be so lucky," I responded dourly.

"What do you mean?" he asked, panic edging in his voice.

"If memory serves . . . what we have here is chicken pox."

Mother Teresa Takes the Stand

Travis's first wife looked less life-like in person than she did in her dart-laden portrait. Sarah Bentley Holmes was an icy beauty. Her white-blond hair was pulled back sleekly into a chignon, emphasizing her high cheekbones and enormous green eyes. She wore a triple strand of pearls on her sea-green ultrasuede dress. The green, of course, matched her eyes.

I took all this in as Sarah flung her sable at a minion and strode across the lobby of the courthouse.

"Hello Sarah," greeted Travis.

"I thought we had settled this last time," she said abruptly.

"Things change," he said mildly.

At this Sarah turned her gaze to me and laughed smugly. "Philip said you'd married a troll, but this . . ." she said, waving her left index finger at me. I considered biting it off at the knuckle.

"When did you speak with Father?" Travis asked with a start.

"We keep in touch," she said lightly. "I do hope this is the last of your dreary appeals, Teddy. It is devilishly difficult. Because of you, I am missing two of the best parties of the season."

Travis laughed. "And to think I once accused you of being selfish."

Sarah reddened, turned on her heel, and went to join her lawyers.

"There is something evil about that woman," I observed uneasily.

"Quite a bit, actually," he replied.

"Why would Schuyler miss her so much?"

"If there's one thing I've learned, it's that you can't help who you love."

Piggy Trehune had decided to put me on the stand. This after he had shown the list of my alleged men to Travis, who had laughed aloud. Travis supervised my wardrobe. On the day of my testimony, he had me wear a blue-and-white striped dress. My red hair completed the wholesome image. Next to the elegant Sarah, I looked like the old tried and true American flag.

There I was in the limelight getting the best reviews of my life. At one point the court might have been forgiven for thinking Trehune was describing Mother Teresa. He painted me as a dutiful daughter to my ailing father and a loving mother to my younger brothers and sisters. A girl who had sacrificed her career to care for the needy. For a moment, I feared he would introduce Claire as an article of evidence. But happily he swept past specifics.

"Now, Mrs. Holmes. Would you tell the court of your views on motherhood?"

Well rehearsed, I spouted, "Children need a mother at home, full time—not a nanny but a mother. I will gladly put aside my career ambitions, for the children's sake." Privately, however, I was musing about something quite different. In preparation for the custody trial, I had looked up the word "mother" in the dictionary. It came right after the word "moth-eaten." Surely there was a message there.

Mr. Trehune was staring at me. "I'm sorry, did you say something?"

"Yes, I asked if you felt confident assuming the role of stepmother."

"Certainly," I smiled.

Sarah's dapper lawyer, Mr. Bristol, was not quite so flattering in his cross-examination.

"You are an actress, are you not?"

"I was."

Mr. Bristol turned to Judge Beckman and raised his eyebrow knowingly. "Isn't it possible you are acting now?"

"I beg your pardon," I said disdainfully. How dare he question my integrity. Hadn't he been listening to Piggy Trehune?

"I suggest, Mrs. Holmes, that this show of motherly concern is but another role for you. That far from being a wholesome caring person, you are . . . Medea incarnate."

"What?" I gasped.

"A woman so contemptible that you would feed dead worms to unsuspecting children." Damn it! The children had promised Travis to keep mum.

"Travis," I pleaded. But my husband's eyes were glazed.

Trehune seemed absorbed in a sheaf of papers. "No one ate the worms. It was a mistake."

"Like the food poisoning?" Mr. Bristol pressed.

"That was an accident." Wasn't Piggy supposed to object?

"An 'accident'?" questioned Bristol with a false laugh. "I suppose it was an accident that you had a known man-eater in the house."

"What are you talking about?" With my brown thumb, we had no plants at all in the house.

"A vicious cur, an animal who had bitten your own father and sent him into Intensive Care. You think such an animal is a suitable companion for defenseless young children?"

"But the children loved him."

"Surely you could not have known that in advance. I suggest you were not only risking an attack but banking on it."

"Objection." Finally.

"Overruled."

Bristol smiled warmly at the judge. "Do you feel, in your role as temporary custodian of the children, it is your duty to teach them sex education?"

What was he getting at? "Eventually. I mean, if the subject came up, I would deal with it."

"Isn't it true you subjected little Cornelia, an eight-year-old girl, to a prolonged discussion of penises?" Judge Beckman's whole body jerked. Travis and Trehune gasped in unison.

"And isn't it true," Bristol continued, "that you told her penises were equipped with spikes and poison glands." Travis's face bulged with alarm.

"No!" I wailed.

"And came out of the mouth."

"No. She told me that."

"And you did not feel obliged to correct her?"

"We were talking about flatworms. It was a game."

"A game?" he repeated, theatrically. "Do you consider penises a suitable topic for little girls?"

"I . . . it was a very clinical discussion. It wasn't dirty or anything. We had been playing 'Name that Beast' . . ."

" 'Name that Beast,' " he interjected, savoring the implications.

"It's educational. My mother used to play it with me."

"Educational, indeed."

"But Nell was the one who brought up the damned penises."

"Oh? Do you have something against penises, Mrs. Holmes?" Sarah smiled broadly at that question.

"Objection."

"Your Honor," Mr. Bristol argued, "I think the court should know if this woman harbors any resentment toward the male organ. It is possible it would affect her care of the impressionable young boy, Schuyler."

"Overruled," the judge obliged.

"I repeat my question, do you harbor animosity toward the male member?"

"No! I love . . ." The look on Travis's face stopped me in time. "No," I repeated solemnly.

"I see. Tell me, Mrs. Holmes, what is it that qualifies you to be a good parent to these children?"

My mind blanked. Trehune had coached me on this point. I looked to him, hoping for cue cards. He mouthed something, but I couldn't understand.

"Mrs. Holmes?" repeated Bristol.

"I love their father very much."

"That's not what I asked."

"But that is why I'd be a good mother to them."

"You would look out for their welfare?"

"Certainly."

"Care for their emotional and social needs?"

"Yes."

"See to their nutritional requirements?"

"Yes," I said impatiently.

"Would you say peanuts, dry cereal, cookies, and Dr Pepper constitute a balanced breakfast?"

The chickens had come home to roost. Travis looked as miserable as I felt.

"There were extenuating circumstances," I said softly.

"By 'extenuating circumstances,' do you mean the arrival of nine diseased orphans?"

"No," I snapped. "I meant the ice storm."

"Why *did* you have nine diseased orphans in your house, Mrs. Holmes?"

"It was a birthday party," I answered sourly.

"I see. You hired them as entertainment."

"No, dammit. It was Christmas."

"Is that supposed to be an explanation?"

"Jessica needed playmates for a birthday party. At the time, it seemed a good idea to invite a group of less fortunate children, so I contacted the Robleigh Children's Home. I just wanted everyone to have a good time."

"A good time." He went to his table and picked up a note pad. "Tell me, Mrs. Holmes, what, in your judgment, constitutes a good time?"

I stared at him sullenly.

"Games?" he asked. "We know you like games, Mrs. Holmes. Noisemakers? Cake? Ice cream?"

"Yes."

"And how long should this fun last?"

"I don't understand."

"How long did you open your house to the 'guests'?"

"The party was from one to three."

"I see. And then they left?"

"No," I mumbled.

"When did they leave, Mrs. Holmes?"

"Three days later."

"Three days later? My, you must have been having fun."

"Not especially."

"Oh?"

"Look," I said angrily. "I can hardly be held accountable for power outages and icy roads . . ."

"No, I suppose not. And who should be held accountable for a brute by the name of Boss? Did you think of him as a suitable companion for your five-year-old stepdaughter?"

"He was unexpected."

"Are you saying he crashed the party?"

"I left it to the directress to pick the children. I asked for a mixture of boys and girls between the ages of four and six."

"Don't you think you should have previewed the selection?"

"They were only supposed to stay for two hours. I didn't feel it necessary to grill them on their party manners."

"Might you, in the light of what followed, have inquired about their health, Mrs. Holmes?"

"They were party guests! Would you have me roll back their lips to get a good look at their gums as they came in the house?"

"How many children became ill while at your party?" he persisted.

"No one got ill *at* the party," I argued. "Later, *after* they should have been home, five of them, through no fault of my own, broke out with chicken pox."

"After exposing Cornelia, Jessica, and little Schuyler to a virulent strain, causing them to be ill for weeks."

I bent my head in shame. "I tried my best. That's all I can say. I wanted Jess to have a nice party. I really tried." I said this more to Travis than to the lawyer or the judge. Travis was looking intently at his shoes.

"I am flabbergasted," remarked Mr. Bristol. "Are you actually admitting this is the best you can do?"

I looked hopelessly at Travis.

"That is all, your Honor."

Awaiting Sentence

After my testimony, Edmund Trehune sat dazed in his chair. Prompted by the judge, he half-heartedly rose to present Travis's case against Sarah. Trehune introduced evidence from a private investigator. The charges against Sarah sounded so wild I wondered if Piggy had trumped them up. Alain "Big Stick" Dufaut, Enrico Mendoza, Count D'Urbanville, Boss Jeffries, and someone named Prince Turgenev figured prominently in Trehune's account of her illicit connections.

Judge Beckman peered thoughtfully over his half glasses. He looked at Sarah and then at Piggy. Judge Beckman would not believe Sarah was a drug-crazed nymphomaniac. She was clearly too imperial to have such human appetites.

To no one's great surprise, Travis lost the custody case. As we rode home in silence, I could feel the storm of his anger gathering force.

Despite my best efforts, I had lost his children. Would I ever be able to convince him that I hadn't done it intentionally?

While he drove, I glanced surreptitiously at his face. The jaw muscles strained and rippled as if they were working on a piece of tough meat.

Marshaling my defenses and assorted pleas, I braced myself for his inevitable rage.

But it never came. The first day I stayed out of his way. The second day, he made polite conversation. After two more days of his courteous treatment, I was nearly hysterical. When would he yell at me? Why hadn't he thrown me out?

His silence was more effective than if he had ordered me to a public stoning. Every time I looked at him my guilt and craziness multiplied. But still I did not dare broach the subject myself. For I was sure the fury was there, merely hidden.

So we lived in precarious harmony. Travis worked all day. When he came in for meals, he was pleasant. In bed we had sex. No endearments, just, "Thank you, Mallory," when we were done.

Time hung heavy on my hands. Now that the children and my father were gone, I had little to do. Father had insisted he be allowed to return to California. The local climate, he complained, was "stifling his notions."

Travis financed the move and the new nursing home. His unending generosity exasperated me. Hadn't I already proved I could not repay him in any capacity?

I had made no friends in Connecticut other than Wart. There was no one with whom I could discuss my predicament. Travis had assigned me to limbo. The next move was clearly his.

* * *

Kerra Kennilworth returned for an interview when *Civil Souls* hit the stands. The book was receiving critical acclaim unusual for a horror story.

When I came into the living room, Kerra said, "Hello, Valerie, how nice to see you again. I don't want to keep you, as I'm sure you have more pressing matters at hand."

I waited for Travis to correct her but he didn't, so I left the room and hovered out of sight by the door.

"She doesn't look well," Kerra said with false concern.

"It's been a rough year for her," Travis answered simply.

"Now," she said, changing gears. "*Small Packages* comes out later this year, correct?" Travis nodded. "What is that one about?"

He laughed. "Originally it was to be about dwarves, but I changed it one night after I went to the bathroom."

"Oh?" she said coyly.

"Since you are not a parent, you probably won't appreciate this book."

"I'm sorry?"

"One night in the dark, on my way to the john, I stepped on one of those little Fisher-Price people. Only two inches high, but they're deadly on bare feet—and they're everywhere. Any house with children must have at least fifty of the damn things. From that experience, *Small Packages* was born. The Fisher-Price people come to life and take over the world. Very nasty creatures."

"Can a child's toy be so ominous?"

"Certainly. Anything can be used to horror's purpose."

"Is horror different from terror?"

"The best terror comes from a pervasive sense of disestablishment . . ."

I reeled away from the door and ran gasping to my room.

A master of the dark corners of the human mind, Travis knew just how to punish me. Every act of unearned kindness was designed to torment me. My suspended status was intentional. He wanted me dangling and disoriented. It would have been simpler to banish me, but Travis enjoyed the game.

Well, damn him, I thought. Two could play at this sport.

No longer did I quail under his cheerfulness but returned it in full false measure. I signed up for Chinese cooking classes, decoupage lessons, aerobic exercise, and the League of Women Voters. We had the neighbors in for cocktails and sushi.

Travis did not seem surprised by my reformation, which was irritating. But I pressed on.

Maude called early in March. I answered the phone, winded after a half-set of exercises.

"Who is this?" she asked.

"Your sister."

"Are you still there?" she inquired abruptly.

"Actually, Maude, I live here."

"I must say, I admire your gall."

"Sorry," I snapped, "but I can't return the compliment."

"After that debacle in court, one would have thought you'd have the good sense to leave Travis to his misery."

"Travis isn't miserable," I stated. "What do you want, Maude?"

"Aren't you going to ask how I am?"

"How are you?" I asked without enthusiasm.

"Marvelous, according to my doctor. She thinks I may deliver early. She wants me to take my leave of absence now, but I'm going to wait until the very last moment."

"Typical. What did you call about?" I asked with impatience, trying to forestall another of her Wonder Woman Gives Birth sagas.

"I wanted to tell Travis that he left his underwear at my apartment."

I hadn't realized until then how much I still loved Travis. "Why don't you just press it in your memory book?" I slammed the phone into its cradle.

The guilty party wandered into the kitchen moments later, while I was dry heaving over the sink.

"Are you all right?" he asked with concern.

"Your editor called."

"Maude? About the galleys?"

"No, about your undies."

"Oh good. She found them. I couldn't remember where I'd left them."

I whirled around to gape at him. How many women was he sleeping with?

The look on my face prompted him to explain, "I bought a new supply of socks and U-trou at Saks the other day when I was in the city."

"Oh! I thought . . ."

"You thought what?" he asked quizzically.

"Nothing." That still didn't explain what he was doing in Maude's apartment. "How is old Maude?"

"You just talked to her."

"Yeah, but I haven't seen her. Is she grossly swollen?" I asked with a tinge of excitement.

"No, she looks quite well. Pregnant women generally look

glorious." He picked a large red apple from the basket. "By the way, has she told you who the father is, yet?"

I looked at him cautiously. "No. Has she told you?"

"Nope," he said, biting into the apple.

There was but one way out of this dilemma. I, too, would bear Travis's child. He would love the baby, and then maybe me. Perhaps it would even make up for my losing the custody battle.

I would have to work fast in order to be pregnant by the time Maude gave birth. In the true fashion of soap operas (which I had lately begun to watch as I exercised), I would present Travis with a fait accompli. Otherwise, he might get it into his head to object.

In the bathroom, I watched my birth control pills swirl down the toilet. My memories of Claire's infancy departed with the pills. Having a little Travis would be wonderful, I told myself.

With any luck, I would be with child before I regained my senses.

Mother Maude

Maude called from the recovery room to announce she'd had a baby girl. There was no need to ask what the baby looked like. It would bear as little resemblance to a wrinkled, squally, newborn as a grackle to a peacock. Maude's and Travis's daughter would be a state-of-the-art baby.

"That's wonderful. I'll tell Travis."

"No need, he assisted at the delivery."

"What?" I demanded, unable to mask my outrage. Wasn't his assistance in the conception enough for her?

"Well, you knew he was in the city today."

"At his agent's."

"Yes, well, happily, I was able to track him down. My Lamaze partner was suddenly unavailable. And Travis is such an old hand in these matters, it seemed natural to press him into service."

"Naturally," I replied sourly. "What's her name?"

"Oh, we haven't decided. Everything I suggest Travis vetoes as too strident."

"I suppose you'll be heading straight to the office from the recovery room."

"Not quite," she laughed. "I'm going to take a month off. You'll come visit."

"Not if you expect me to come armed with a burp cloth. I told you, I will not be sucked into your nursery."

"Oh, there's no need for that. Esperanza will handle everything."

"Esperanza?"

"A girl from El Salvador. She'll care for the baby."

"I realize Hispanics do not get paid on a scale with British nannies, but I'm surprised you can even afford a wetback."

"I can't."

"Are you paying for Maude's wetback?" I demanded of Travis the instant he walked in the door that night. I had meant to sound casual.

"Certainly. She needs help," he replied, shaking snow from his blond hair. The baby was his, not mine. He had no right to sound so noble.

"So does Nigeria, but I don't see you shipping bushels of wheat."

"She's your sister. I thought you would be pleased."

"Have I *ever* asked for your help—for me or my family?"

"No. It's one of the things I admire about you."

Damn. More unjustifiable praise. We both knew Travis never gave me a chance to ask for anything.

"Wait till you meet Oriana."

"Oriana? I thought her name was Esperanza."

"Your niece. Do you like the name? I thought of it, it's for your mother, Orin. She's a real beauty."

"Dark curly ringlets?" I guessed.

"No, surprisingly, she seems to be a blond."

"That's a big surprise, all right."

Travis thought the time had come for me to resume my career. I hadn't the nerve to tell him the only role I was interested in playing was Connecticut wife and mother. Instead, I told him I would never be good enough to be viewed, much less reviewed, by the New York drama critics. Travis refused to let me entertain such defeatism. With little enthusiasm, I contacted Mort Steiner and started the rounds again.

Once, after a depressing day spent in producers' outer offices, I was mugged on the way to my car. Not only was I grazed with a knife, but I hadn't enough money left to pay the Triborough Bridge toll. Groveling before an indifferent toll attendant had reduced me to tears.

Travis said it was the law of averages, but I knew better. I had never been mugged when I lived in New York. My street smarts had molted in the country air.

The next day he showed me a camouflaged coin holder he had installed in the car (so I could "always come home") and prodded me back to work. It was important, he said, that I be someone in my own right. Echoes of Mother were not appreciated.

Maude went back to work and became one of those women expressing milk by the water cooler. Esperanza ferried little Oriana to the office daily for a noon-time suck and to pick up the morning's milk. It was all too dismal to contemplate.

Maude invited me to lunch. I declined. She persisted. "We've so much to talk about."

"Like hell," I muttered.

"Please," she said, for the first time in my memory.

I had an audition that morning, but I was so skittish that I flubbed two lines. The perfunctory "Thank you," rang out sooner than usual.

Oriana was nursing contentedly when I walked into Maude's office. Esperanza stood by the window picking at the dead leaves of a ficus tree.

"Are we going out or did you save some milk for me?" I asked.

"Ah, humor. And so early in the day." Maude looked radiant.

I threw down my purse and sat in a chair by the desk. Despite my best efforts, I still was not pregnant. Now I wondered as I observed Oriana if it would be wise to put a child in competition with this little beauty. At three months she had golden curls, a defined nose, and delicate coloring. Her eyes were closed, but no doubt they were enormous and dark.

"We can talk," Maude said, dismissing with a gesture Esperanza's linguistic competence. "Isn't it amazing? I never thought I would have a child after what Mother did to me."

"Did to you?" I said, astounded. Somehow I had never thought Mother's death affected Maude. She seemed impervious to sentiment. But perhaps, I realized with a start, that was what Mother's death had done to Maude.

"Families should share resources," she said casually.

"I've shared all I intend to," I stated flatly. Christ! What more did she want?

"I meant I wanted to share with you," she replied sweetly.

"You don't have anything I want," I retorted.

"We all know that is not true," she answered, stroking Oriana's curls.

Here it comes, the long-awaited paternity announcement. "You can't have Travis," I said angrily.

"Don't be silly. I have all I want of Travis," she said, gently prying Oriana away from her breast. "He's a good friend who is capable of remarkable work. Hand me that burp cloth." The phone buzzed. "Get that, Mallory."

Annoyed, I tossed her the cloth and lifted the receiver. The secretary announced Ms. Delaney's lunch date was in the reception area. I hung up. "I thought I was your lunch date."

"We'll have to make it a threesome. It's an author I'm thinking of signing. He's quite talented."

"Why didn't you just call and cancel our date?"

"I tried, but Travis said you had already left." She handed Oriana to Esperanza and buttoned her blouse. Maude scrutinized my appearance and said brusquely, "Mallory, try not to disgrace me."

What was I, a mongoloid relative fresh from the attic? I resolved to froth at the mouth throughout the meal. Screwing my face into an idiot's grin, I followed Maude into the reception room. I trailed behind her, face down, and dragged my right foot through the carpet. But Maude wasn't paying attention to me. I made snuffling noises. She shook hands with the lunch date. I chirped and mewed.

"Mallory, what *are* you doing?" she said, turning. I swayed my head and revved my chirp into a whine.

"Mallory Holmes," she said, disowning me, "this is Sam Morrow."

It couldn't be. I slid my glance upwards and there he was. He looked wonderful—a bit of distinguished gray at the temples and a few lines in his face, but wonderful nonetheless. I used to fantasize about running into him. I would be worldly wise and we would laugh at that girl he had known in the early seventies. And then I would beat him senseless.

Crouching down further, I duckwalked toward the elevator.

"Mallory?" he said with puzzlement. "Mallory! Mallory Delaney! Well, I'll be." I waddled faster. There was no way I was going to own up to this.

"You two know each other?" Maude asked.

"Certainly. Is she all right?"

"You're the Sam Morrow that seduced and abandoned Mallory! I should have made the connection," exclaimed Maude. I pushed repeatedly at the elevator button. Maude strutted over to block my exit. She spun me around and pulled me up by my french braid.

Shamefacedly, I went over to Sam. "Hello, Sam." I extended a hand. He pulled me towards him and embraced me heartily.

"Damn! It's good to see you. I've often wondered what had become of you." He continued to hug me.

"Clearly, she went round the bend," Maude supplied.

I pulled myself away from Sam. He still wore the same cologne. It was dredging up memories faster than a back hoe.

"This is so strange," said Sam. "I've been thinking about you all week. When Ms. Delaney called, the name triggered a reaction. But it never occurred to me that you two were related. You never mentioned you had a sister."

"You can't always get what you want," I muttered.

"But this is *unbelievable*!" he exclaimed, drawing me into

another hug. I didn't remember him as being such an enthusiast.

"Our reservation is for 12:30," Maude said unsubtlely.

Struggling to break free of Sam, I said, "I've got to run. It was good to see you again."

"Don't be ridiculous," Maude countered. "You've got the whole afternoon yawning ahead of you." Esperanza walked by with Oriana asleep in her arms. Maude did not even glance at them.

"Travis expects me home early," I fibbed.

"Who's Travis?" Sam inquired.

"Travis Holmes, my husband," I supplied.

"The author?"

"My author," Maude said, before I could answer. Sam would soon be "her" author as well. Maude was systematically acquiring the men in my life. Well, let her have him, he was of no use to me.

"You two have business to discuss. It was lovely seeing you again, Sam."

"Call me, will you? I'm in the book."

"Sure thing," I lied and went to stand with Esperanza at the elevator.

Sam mumbled something. Maude roared with laughter and said, "Mallory? You must be joking!"

My cheeks burned all the way home. I could not dispel the sound of Maude's triumphant laughter. What had Sam said to her?

I did not want to think about Sam, but he kept crowding my mind. By the time I reached Redding, I knew he was not going to vacate the premises without a struggle. How could he when I was swamped by unresolved anger? Stopping at the Mark Twain library, I looked him up in the card catalog. There were two novels.

They looked like they had never been cracked. Please God, let them be dreadful.

At home I got a bottle of wine and some crackers and went out by the pool to read. Some time later Travis appeared from the path to the carriage house. Startled by his intrusion into my private thoughts, I jumped.

"I thought you were lunching with Maude." Travis sneezed.

"I got bumped for a better date." I shrugged my shoulders. "How did you know I was here?"

"I followed the sound of maniacal laughter."

"Oh, it's this book," I said.

He took it from my hand, losing my place. "*The Witch's Teat?*"

"It's very funny."

"So I gathered. Is it new?" Travis sneezed again.

"No, just unused." Travis looked again at the cover. "Sam Morrow," he said reflectively. "Have I heard of him?"

"He's Maude's latest hot pick," I said with irony.

"Maybe I should read it if I'm being pre-empted."

"No, don't bother," I said too fast.

He looked at me questioningly but let it drop. He sneezed for a third time.

"Travis, you're sneezing."

"I am aware of that."

"But you never sneeze."

"Apparently, I am ill." He let loose a monster sneeze. "I'm glad you're home," he said. Then he turned and went back to the carriage house.

Watching his retreating back, I wondered what his reaction would be if he knew I was the heroine of another man's novel.

"What took you so long?" Sam said on the telephone the next day.

"You're not in the Brooklyn directory."

"Possibly because I live in Manhattan."

"If you're going to be sarcastic, I can hang up now."

"No, please. When can I see you?"

"You can't. I'm only calling because I said I would."

"That's not true," he countered.

"Oh, but it is," I lied.

"I can't let you disappear again," he declared.

"As I recall, I wasn't the one who disappeared the last time," I answered, striving for a light tone.

"I would like to explain."

"Don't bother. It's hardly relevant." What could be more relevant? Sam's abrupt disappearance was solely responsible for my guarded attitude toward the entire male species.

"Maude brought me up to datc."

"I'll bet."

"She's quite a woman."

"Hosannas to Maude," I snapped.

"Ah, a family squall? I gather it's mutual. I asked her for your number, but she wouldn't give it to me."

"Really?" I said, intrigued. I would have expected Maude to promote the drama.

"She said it wouldn't do for you to be reminded of 'yet another failure.' "

"Did she now?" I said levelly.

"Is your marriage really on the rocks?"

"I love my husband," I stated.

"Oh."

"Have you signed with Maude?"

"There's not much money up front, but I understand she's a damned good editor. After the sales of my first three novels, I'm grateful she's even interested."

"Three? I thought there were just two." Damn. I hadn't meant to say that. "Maude says you're very good. You can trust her editorial judgment. But little else."

"She seemed very intent on keeping us apart."

"She's an acquisitions editor," I said wryly.

"Meaning?"

"You have been acquired."

"I want to see you, Mallory."

"I want to see you, Sam."

"Tomorrow, at one, the Apthorp, apartment 512."

Open Season on Marriage

For the next nineteen hours, I concentrated on one thought —bedding Sam. I loved Travis, but I had once loved Sam. And those feelings predated and colored everything else.

The next morning I told Travis I had an audition. At the car, he checked my coin holder and kissed me good-bye. He looked, for the first time since I had known him, defeated. It was as if all the colds he had missed had massed together for a single appearance. His nose was red, his eyes slightly sagged and pink. His posture was that of a New York bag lady.

"I could stay home," I offered.

He shook his head. "Take care of yourself for once." He sneezed. "Do you have a Kleenex?"

I opened my pocketbook and pulled one out. "Here. Are you sure you want me to go?" I asked guiltily.

"With my blessing."

* * *

Sam was waiting for me in the courtyard of the Apthorp. We shook hands and walked to the elevator. I couldn't even look at him, much less make small talk.

He opened the door to his apartment. The living room was done in blues and greens and bookcases. I followed a hallway past a small kitchen, past a dining room that was strewn with manuscripts, to the bedroom. Sam stayed in the living room. "Very nice," I said, coming back to join him.

"Maude told me you live in a mansion."

"More of a fun house, really."

"Still, it's a long way from the homosexual brothel." He handed me a glass of wine and gestured me to sit. "Damn, but it's good to see you. Do you really love your husband?" So much for small talk.

"Yes, I'm afraid I do."

"Why does Maude think your marriage is on the rocks?"

"Possibly because my husband fathered her child."

"What?" he asked with astonishment.

"Maude believes in sharing family resources," I said wryly.

"What does your husband say?"

"The subject hasn't come up. Which," I said, taking a large gulp of wine, "is very handy as it allows us to continue in a civilized fashion. Travis is basically a very decent, if twisted, person."

Sam shook his head disbelievingly. "How can you still love him?"

"Unfortunately, I am quite tenacious in my attachments. I hang on long after the fact." How good it was to talk about this to someone who didn't bark. I had missed male friendship. If nothing else panned out, perhaps Sam and I could be friends.

"And your sister?"

"Maude is a feminist. Not a very good one though. I like to think she confuses liberation with indiscriminate sex. Otherwise I would have to acknowledge she slept with my husband out of pure familial perversity." I got up from the couch and paced the room.

"If what you say is true, about Maude and Travis, you're a fool to stay."

"I've been a fool for lesser things."

"Me?"

"The first of a long string." I sat down again and looked at him long and hard. "Tell me about *The Witch's Teat*."

"You've read it?" he asked.

"Yes," I answered noncommittally.

"Well, its reviews were good, its sales abysmal."

"And the girl, Corinne. The one who wants desperately to be close to someone or something and yet keeps everyone away with one-liners, that's me?"

"Yeah. What'd you think?" He smiled broadly.

"I hate the name Corinne."

"So do I," he admitted. "I used it to keep objective distance."

"You failed. You were clearly wild for her. The narrator's reasons for leaving her don't wash, by the way."

"Now who's being subjective?" He took my hand and rubbed it softly. "The narrator was plagued with thoughts of her for years."

I smiled coolly. "Just deserts, I'd say."

"I left because I couldn't commit."

"Oh, puhlease . . . you sound like a character in a Doonesbury comic strip." I did not, however, yank my hand away. It felt good. I wanted more.

"You told me I could make you whole. It was too much responsibility."

"Did I really say that?" I asked with embarrassment. I knew I believed it, but didn't think I'd been fool enough to say it.

"It seemed kinder to leave."

"Try not to sound so noble. I cried for months."

"The minute I saw you duck-walking towards the elevator at Woolsy and Balzac, I knew I was still crazy about you." He rubbed my palm purposefully. "I could love you with very little effort."

I took offense. Love should require some effort. "Don't be so casual. Once you love someone, you're stuck. Their ionized molecules buzz around you forever, stinging and taunting. Mother's and Travis's are dive-bombing me as we speak."

"And mine?"

"You're the one that got away," I said, trying to minimize his ions.

"Your mother 'got away.' "

"So will Travis, in time." A triad of despair.

"Why?" he asked, puzzled.

"The way of the world," I answered brusquely.

His posture straightened slightly. "I'm married," he said cautiously.

"Good for you." It made no difference.

"Elise and I have an open marriage."

I laughed. "Still can't commit, huh?"

He had the decency to look embarrassed. "What I meant was, I would very much like to take up where we left off."

"With me wailing in the wings, begging for your genitals? I think not."

"Every year when the new phone books were issued I looked up your name, but there was never a listing."

"I hadn't the credit rating."

"I wrote a book about you. Doesn't that say something."

"Indeed it does." I was here, wasn't I?

"And," he concluded, "there is certainly no reason to be faithful to a man who screwed your sister."

Couldn't that point have been left unvoiced? "If I go to bed with you, it is because I want to—not because Travis hurt me."

"If? Mallory, please."

"Don't beg, it's unseemly." I laughed. "Have you any contraceptives?"

"Aren't you protected?"

"I'm trying to get pregnant. Do you have any rubbers?"

"Yeah, I think I have some old ones kicking around somewhere."

"How old? It isn't your child I want."

"I'll go down to the pharmacy. Why don't you get comfortable?"

While he was gone, I went to the bedroom, turned on the air conditioner, and tested the bed. Nice and firm. I opened my purse on the night stand, combed my hair, and applied Ecusson perfume. There was a small picture of Sam and Elise on the bureau. She looked quite sensible: thick bangs, a sturdy jaw, and dark brown eyes. I tried to work up some guilt but couldn't.

Sam returned with a gross of rubbers.

"My, aren't you being optimistic?" I laughed.

"No sense in stinting."

Sex with Sam was plentiful but not especially rewarding. After he had peeled off the second rubber, wadded it in

Kleenex, and tossed it, I realized I wasn't enjoying myself. Travis had spoiled me for other men.

Sam moved over me again. This afternoon had been a dreadful mistake. I couldn't even be friends with him after this. I wanted out, but I couldn't think how to end the session gracefully. Sam was murmuring that I was beautiful, that he loved me, that he had always loved me. I looked out the window and felt his ionized particles lifting from my sphere.

Three rubbers later, he sighed, "I'm totally spent." I eyed my clothes on the chair.

"Isn't fate amazing?"

"How so?" I said, standing.

"I've been looking for you for years with no success and then your sister calls out of the blue."

I stopped dressing. "Maude called you? I thought your agent submitted the book to her."

"Yeah, but only after Maude called him and expressed interest."

An alarm went off in my head. "Has she read *The Witch's Teat*?"

"She compared it to Irving's *The Water-Method Man*."

I sat down in a heap. "We've been set up."

"What do you mean?"

"Our meeting two days ago was no accident. Damn! I should have known. Maude does nothing without design. The only question is, does Travis know?"

"I'm afraid I've lost you." His mind was still in post-coital glide.

"Maude intended us to go to bed."

"I'll have to thank her," he replied with a yawn.

"Did you tell Maude we were meeting today?"

"No. I think you're paranoid. She wouldn't give me your number, remember."

"She was simply whetting your appetite. Damn!" I stood up and felt a squishy Kleenex underfoot. "I'd advise you to pick up your rubbers before Elise comes home," I added distastefully.

"When can I see you again?" he asked, stretching an arm towards me.

"In court, when you are named as corespondent," I said, buckling my belt.

Sam sat up abruptly. "You don't think Travis would drag me to court!"

"No, probably not," I answered. Sam sagged with relief. "The man's medium is horror. Divorce court would be too pedestrian." Sam restiffened. "Travis is a perfectionist," I said, putting on my shoes. "It may take him a while to come up with a suitable punishment. But then, that is his specialty, dangling the victim over the fiery pit." I looked over at Sam, who couldn't decide if I was serious.

"You're kidding, right?"

"You would be wise to avoid red ant hills bearing stakes, and deep fat." I turned to leave.

"Cholesterol?" he asked, confused.

"Boiling oil, a medieval favorite." I turned to go. "Mallory, wait." He scrambled out of bed. "You forgot your purse." He snapped it shut and handed it to me. Then he took my hand, looked into my eyes, and said, "Darling, no matter what happens, we'll have had today."

I withdrew my hand abruptly. "Right." The afternoon wasn't bad enough, he had to heap platitudes on it. Did he kiss-and-tell, too? "Sam, you are toying with a dark force."

He smiled. "What was it D.H. Lawrence said, 'To fuck is to go to the dark gods'?"

"Not *me*, you fool! Travis."

"Honestly, Mallory, one would think you believed in devils."

"Devils of the heart, yes." I drew in a deep breath for courage. "I can only hope Maude isn't in the lobby." Sam followed me to the door and kissed me with lingering intensity, trying to draw me back to the bedroom. I just wanted to escape.

I cursed sex as I rode down in the elevator. How could I ever have believed Sam would 'make me whole'? If anything, Sam had exacerbated my disjointed sense of self. And the worst of it was, he had only done what I wanted.

The Smoking Gun

The lobby was clear.

I fairly flew home. A crazed adulteress in a wood-paneled station wagon. At the Triborough Bridge, I hurled money from my coin holder to the exact change machine and roared out of the gate, nearly colliding with a trailer truck. I wondered why I was rushing to my execution, but I couldn't slow down.

Leger de Main was quiet. Maude would have been there had she expected to trap me. I had snuck past disaster. I took deep gasping breaths trying to calm myself.

I would never see Sam again. And if he didn't boast about our brief liaison, Maude's plan was foiled.

Wart came into greet me, wagging his stubby tail. "Hello, wump-dogger. Time for dinner." Feeding him, I couldn't get over the joy of performing a daily chore. I was mad to have risked this for the sake of an old hurt.

After he ate, Wart and I went for the mail and then waited by the pool for Travis to finish his work. I heard him before I saw him. His sneezes practically shook the mountain laurel.

I jumped up to kiss him but he put out his hands. "Don't. It must be the plague." I kissed him anyway.

"You're in a good mood. Did you get the part?"

"Huh? Oh no. Not even a call back. You look miserable, come into the kitchen. I'll make you some soup."

"You'll make it?" he said with disbelief.

"Well," I laughed. "I'll open it."

"Umm," he grumbled, but he followed me into the kitchen. He sat at the table and looked through the mail.

"Did you talk to Maude today?" I asked innocently.

"Twice. The Japanese rights were sold for a tidy sum."

"Anything else?"

"Oriana is teething and Esperanza has a boyfriend who Maude thinks is a dope dealer." Travis sneezed. "Have you got a Kleenex?"

"Check my purse." I poured the soup into a saucepan.

I heard Travis open the catch on my purse. An unmistakable odor filled the room. With terror I turned and looked. One of Sam's used rubbers, loosely wadded in Kleenex, had landed in my purse. Travis had almost blown his nose in it.

Travis held it in his hand. The smoking gun. He continued to stare at it but said nothing.

My body shut down in fright.

The room was silent. Travis's jaw muscles rippled and strained. And still he held the damn rubber.

"Travis," I said quietly. "I'm sorry. It was a dreadful mistake."

His body clamped down in the chair as if trying to prevent itself from eruption.

I went over to him and put a hand on his shoulder. His skin was humming with anger. He looked up at me, his dark eyes nearly black. Suddenly his body seemed to cave in and he wailed. It was a sound I hadn't heard since a production of *Playboy of the Western World.* A true Irish keen. I had expected him to be furious but somehow detached. The rubber dropped to the floor. Gingerly, I picked it up and carried it to the garbage disposal. I turned on the tap and flipped the switch. The irrefutable evidence disappeared in a grinding whir.

Travis continued keening for several minutes. I stood there stupidly trying to comfort him.

Finally it subsided. "How could you?"

"I don't know. It was dumb."

"Who was it?"

"Sam Morrow."

Travis looked puzzled. "Maude's 'latest hot pick'?"

"Yes, I knew him years ago. I even told you about him one night when Maude and you and I went to that Armenian restaurant in the East Village."

It took him a moment to connect. "He's the one who gave men such a bad name?" he said incredulously.

I nodded. "He apologized."

"And that's all it took?"

"I can't explain it. It was just something I had to do. It's over now. I'll never see him again."

"I can't believe this. Haven't I been good to you?" I nodded abjectly. "Was it too much to ask that you be faithful? My God. We've been married less than a year. Maybe Trehune was right."

"Look," I answered angrily. "I said I'm sorry, which is more than you've done, buster."

"What have I got to apologize about?"

"Oh, come on. It's a little late to play coy."

"What's that supposed to mean?"

"You're no saint. What I did was wrong, but it doesn't hold a candle to incest."

"Incest?" he bellowed.

"Maybe not technically, but it amounts to the same thing. How do you think it felt knowing you'd slept with my sister—barely two days after our honeymoon?"

"Maude?" he interjected.

"Yes, Maude, damn it all. Or did you sleep with Claire too? It was a busy weekend, I didn't have a scorecard."

Travis looked thunderstruck. "You think I slept with Maude?"

"Everyone *knows* you slept with Maude."

"But I didn't!" he declared.

"Right. Oriana arrived by Federal Express."

"Oriana?"

"Why did you do it, Travis?" I started to cry. "You could have given me a chance."

"Oriana is not my child. My God! What kind of monster do you think I am? Why didn't you ask me?"

"Ask you? Ask you what? If my sister is better in bed than I am?"

"Mallory, I have never been to bed with Maude."

"So you say," I challenged.

"Oriana is not my child," he declared.

"She has your coloring," I accused.

"I am not the only blond male in the world. Besides," he added, "I had a vasectomy two years ago."

I found my way to a chair. A vasectomy. How one little snip could change so much. "If you aren't the father, who is?"

"I always thought it was Gowf."

"Gowf?" I repeated, trying to picture Claire's boyfriend. It made sense. Maude had tapped the family resources again. "I feel sick."

"You're not alone," he said dispiritedly.

"Did Maude know you had a vasectomy?"

"Maude's a good friend, but I don't recall discussing my state of reproductive readiness with her."

"A good friend?" I said snidely. "To whom? Travis, she set me up with Sam."

"Why would she do that?" Travis jumped from his seat and sneezed en route to the paper towels.

"She arranged for me to run into Sam at her office."

He appeared disturbed by this bit of intelligence. "She may have set you up, but you fell on your own."

"Yes," I responded sadly. "But you see, I thought you were sleeping with her."

"Then why not say something! You have a tongue," he accused angrily. "Instead you skulk off and screw the Ghost of Christmas Past. Christ, Mallory! I didn't even get a fair hearing. You just presumed guilt."

"But the circumstantial evidence . . ."

"Life is full of circumstantial evidence, Mallory! You have to learn to trust." He stopped pacing the floor and turned to glare at me. "You don't trust me."

I lowered my head. "No, I don't."

"Why?" he asked with anguish. "What have I ever done but be good to you?"

"Nothing, I guess I've never believed I deserved your kindness. It wasn't as if you loved me . . ."

"What does *that* mean?" he asked angrily.

"It means I know you didn't marry me out of love but expedience."

"Expedience?" he demanded.

"To get custody," I explained with exasperation.

"I can't believe this," he said, determined to ignore the obvious.

"Well, it hardly matters now."

"You're sick," he accused, glowering at me.

"There is that theory," I said lightly.

He grabbed me by the shoulders and shook me. "Damn it, Mallory, just because your mother died is no reason . . ."

"Leave my mother out of this!"

"You and your goddamned orphan complex. You've never felt safe loving anything but a stray."

"And you're no stray."

"No," he said, releasing me. "I most definitely am not."

I had the awful feeling I was about to be.

He sat down and buried his head in his hands. He muttered something and then looked up at me and said, "You were so different from them, I thought it would work."

"Them?" I echoed.

"Mother. Sarah. They were incapable of giving love. You, it seems, are incapable of taking love. In the end, it all works out the same."

"An irreconcilable difference?" I guessed.

"For sure. Will you contest the divorce?"

"No," I said, crying. It seemed I had been living under the unspoken threat of divorce for ages. After all this time I should have been prepared, but I wasn't. Part of me would have preferred being boiled in oil. Then at least there would have been none of the messiness of survival.

"I want to be civilized about this, Mallory, but I'm finding it exceedingly difficult. When someone you love betrays you there is a visceral reaction," he said, I thought, rather clinically.

"Can't we work on this," I pleaded. "I didn't know you loved me."

"How could you have not known?" he asked angrily. "Are you telling me my love was so ineffectual you didn't recognize it?"

"It was a mistake, Travis, I'll never do it again."

He ignored my vow. "This marriage cannot thrive if you don't trust me," he stated.

Wasn't that backwards? "Travis . . ." I implored.

"I don't want you in this house a minute longer than necessary."

"But . . . where will I go?" My brain was scrambling. I had no money or family worth the name.

"It's a big world . . . use it."

And with that he whistled for Wart and pushed me out the door.

Life in the Fire Lane

Wart and I moved into Nell's playhouse and did some keening of our own. I ached from crying. Wart's mournful sighs punctuated the gloom. Wart had never been fond of Travis, but he missed his bone room with its plush bed. Stretched out on the hard floor of the playhouse, he glared at me reproachfully.

The furniture in the playhouse was dwarved. It was impossible to sleep for any length of time on a four-foot play bed or to sit comfortably on kindergarten chairs. Mostly I cried and paced around Wart's sulking presence. The first two nights, I was able to sneak into the Leger de Main kitchen and steal some food. On the third morning, a locksmith came and thwarted my entry.

Despite this, I still believed Travis had a generous nature. With time he would relent and take us back. I would outwait the hurt. And if that didn't work, I planned to hurl myself at his feet and beg. But I never saw him. Either he was taking a circuitous route to his office or he was not working.

On the afternoon of the third day, Father Holmes delivered four bright pink suitcases to the playhouse. The luggage still had price tags.

"These aren't mine."

"Consider them my farewell present. Teddy said you can take the car. Lord knows you haven't the decency to leave it." Wart growled. Father Holmes backed up.

"I want to talk to Travis."

"Can't," he smiled. "Teddy's long gone."

"Gone? Where?" I asked with panic.

"Where you can't get to him, Squatter Hattie. Now clear out before I call the sheriff." He saluted and left.

If Travis was truly gone, there was no point in staying. I pulled the suitcases into the playhouse. Three were surprisingly light. They were empty. Someone had stuffed all my old clothes into the fourth.

I was leaving this marriage practically as I had entered. Interest accrued on eleven months matrimony was four ugly pink suitcases and a wood-paneled station wagon.

The day I left Leger de Main I had $27.56, including the change in the car. I kept the change but threw out the coin holder, which I held responsible for the breakdown of my marriage. If I'd have had to open my purse for change at the toll, surely I would have noticed the used rubber.

Twenty-seven dollars would carry me through about an hour in Fairfield County. It was time to consolidate my assets. I took the pink luggage back to the discount store for a refund.

The cashier balked, citing my lack of receipt. The presence of their price tags on the suitcases carried no weight. The store had been lucky enough to unload the eyesores once, they were not about to take them back without a struggle.

I, on the other hand, had a hound to feed. Irrationality was the only answer. I waved my arms in large looping circles.

"The henny bit the crow. Can we all go home? Put a penny in the old man's craw. I want my money." I pounded the counter. The cashier fled and returned with the manager. I judged the manager to be one tough cookie. She had at least three pens stuck in various parts of her shellacked bouffant hairdo. Black bands of eyeliner circled her eyes. She planted her hands on her skinny hips and said, "We do not accept merchandise without a receipt."

"I want my mother!" I shouted. The manager looked around to see if anyone would own up to being my relative.

"Where is your mother?" she asked calmly.

"Dead, dead, dead!" I shouted. People from other lines were staring now. "All the little worms and fishies are feasting now," I said conspiratorially. "She died of the blue fever. Swept through her like a razor flash, it did."

I realized with a start that not all of my madness was an act. I was pushing the fine line to hysteria with careless disregard.

I straightened up. "I want my money."

"No receipt, no money," she reiterated.

I slammed my fist on the counter. "Now! I'm late for my medication!"

The cashier whispered something. I caught the words

"Benedict Glen," the name of the local looney bin. Obligingly, I sat down on the floor and sang, "You, with the bars in your eyes . . ."

"Oh, very well," the manager said with disgust.

Wart and I lived in the station wagon for two months. The only jobs I could get paid minimum wage. And Fairfield County had no housing for people thus endowed. We parked in fire lanes and on lonely country roads every night. The police ran us off twice. Occasionally, we were joined by teenage lovers. I prayed no one would look in and see me snuggling with a Weimaraner.

Personal hygiene became a spotty process. I showered at the outdoor facilities at the public beach and squatted in the bushes.

The first week we ate out of supermarket Dempsey Dumpsters. I had come full circle. But now instead of sharing the pickings with Ben Meeks, I was fighting Wart for my fair share.

Eventually, I found part-time work in two different fast-food chains in Norwalk and Danbury. Wart spent most of his time chained to the door handle of the car. For entertainment, we sat in the lighted parking areas of shopping malls every Saturday night and watched couples stroll. I couldn't help but wonder what Travis was doing.

After a month I called him, only to be told the number had been disconnected. The new number was unlisted. Maude would have it, but I would sooner cut off my tongue than ask her. My system was in enough pain. I couldn't think of Travis without my stomach knotting. Worse, I couldn't stop thinking of him. The night manager of one restaurant began making inquiries as to my health. I straightened my "pretzel posture," but that made every step a torture. The manager of the other restaurant was less solicitous; he fired me.

I had to see Travis. Maybe he had changed his mind and didn't know where to contact me. Travis was methodical. Chances were good he still shopped on Thursday.

Wart and I had been in the parking lot only ten minutes when the old blue Mercedes pulled up. Maude stepped out and stretched. She was wearing a pale pink running outfit. She reached into the car and put something lumpy and purple around her neck. Then she opened the back door and lifted Oriana out of the baby seat. Clumsily, she maneuvered the baby into the purple canvas papoose around her neck. Oriana squalled. Maude had trapped one of her arms inside the papoose.

I turned on the ignition and drove out of the parking lot.

There was a cold snap in early September that made me realize a Ford LTD was no place to spend the winter. That afternoon Wart and I moved to the Mecca of people without prospects, New York City.

I sold the car, all of ten months old, for a fourth of its value. The car dealer explained depreciation to me. Not a new concept, given my life of late, I muttered.

Wart hated the city. We found a room that allowed animals, but it was directly above the IND subway line. The building rumbled and shook more often than not, sending Wart into repeated panic attacks. His nails would skitter across the linoleum floor as he ran from the window to the door looking for a way out. When I returned from job interviews, he threw himself at me as if I were the last solid thing on earth.

If Wart was skittish inside the apartment, he was terrified out on the street. The noises and smells unnerved him. He didn't walk so much as whirl around me in circles, grabbing at his leash. I knew he was frightened, but the rest of New York seemed to think him a whirring wall of canine protection. The street people gave us wide berth.

He was so aggravated most of the time I feared I would have to move back to the country. The decision was postponed by a stroke of garbage. I had tied him to a tree while I went into the deli for a newspaper. As usual, he whipped around the tree until there was no leash left. But there, right before him was a caramel candy. I came out in time to see him sniff the caramel suspiciously. He looked up at me and then gingerly took it in his mouth and chewed. After that he was miserable only inside the rumbling apartment.

A poster for the "New York is Book Country" fair announced Travis was to be a guest speaker at a symposium held at the New York Public Library. I could have gone alone but felt the need of a friend. Wart and I walked the fifty-six blocks to the library. We arrived very late because Wart had insisted on smelling every particle of litter along the way. He had found nothing of gastronomic interest, but he had found a willing basset hound. In the ensuing struggle to keep him celibate, I had injured my wrist and loosened my right shoe heel. By the time I tied him to the bus stop sign at Forty-second Street, we were both anxious and discouraged. I bought him a hot pretzel and then climbed up the long steps of the public library.

People were leaving the seminar when I arrived. I spotted Maude and ducked behind a marble pillar. When Travis came out I followed him. He had a knot of people around him and he was laughing.

"Travis," I called.

He stopped and turned. "Mallory," he said with surprise. By then Maude had spotted me and strode over.

"The press is here," she said angrily. "Don't do it."

"Do what? I simply want to talk to my husband."

"Hello, Mallory," Travis said stiffly. "You look very . . . ruddy. You are well?"

"Travis, the people from the *Times* are waiting," Maude interjected.

"Travis, please, we have to talk," I entreated.

"Maude, steer the press people out front, I'll be there in a minute."

"Are you sure you want to do this alone?" Maude asked, in a tone which declared her the self-appointed Defender of the Faith.

"He's a big boy, Maude." I glowered at her. But she didn't leave until Travis signaled her.

"Where have you been, Mallory? I've been looking for you."

My heart gladdened. "Oh, Travis, if you only knew. God, I've missed you."

"What's your address?"

"I'm not exactly set up to receive company."

His jaw tightened. "Trehune needs your address so he can serve the papers."

"The papers?" I said stupidly.

"The divorce papers. You said you wouldn't contest it, but then you disappeared. I had expected you to be more cooperative."

"I don't want a divorce," I said, rendered almost breathless by broken shards of hope embedded in my lungs.

"Damn it, Mallory, you promised."

"So? You promised to cherish me till death did us part."

"Aren't you dead?" he said coolly.

"Sorry, I can't oblige," I retorted.

"We're not going to get anywhere sniping in public. If you don't want to do this nicely, get a lawyer. I'll tell Trehune to expect his call." He turned and strode out of the library. We couldn't leave it this way. I went after him.

"Travis," I called, but he didn't turn. He was out on the front steps by the time I caught up with him. Two photographers were aiming their lenses at him.

It was as if we were trapped in a slow-motion dream sequence. I reached out for Travis, calling his name. My shoe heel, cracked from tussling with Wart, broke, hurtling me towards Travis. He inadvertently blocked my fall, but the thrust of my weight toppled him forward. Travis seemed to fall forever, but in fact Maude caught him only four steps away. The photographers' flashes punctuated the scene.

Maude screamed. Travis struggled upright in her arms. A man called for the police. I started down the stairs to apologize, but Maude yelled, "Stop her, she's a crazy." Someone's arms buckled around me in a tight grip. I heard Wart barking furiously.

"I'm not a crazy," I said indignantly. "I am Travis's wife."

"Ex-wife," Maude shouted. A security man from the library was leading Travis back inside.

"Travis, tell them!" I begged. The cameras were still clicking and whirring. People with notepads were asking my name. Wart continued his frantic barking. I ground my good heel into my restrainer's foot. He yowled and let go.

Escape was hindered by uneven shoes. Someone was running after me. I pulled off my shoes and hurled them over my shoulder.

Wart had wrapped his leash around the sign pole. There was no time to unwind it. I unsnapped the leash from the halter collar and ran barefoot across Forty-second Street with Wart by my side.

People Who Read People

Employment remained elusive. Nearly everyone had seen the *People* article. The cover story, "Horror Master Plunges to Own Horror," made it sound as if I had cannonballed Travis down three flights of stairs. And while the article did not come right out and say I was psychotic, it insinuated that I'd howled at the moon with Mozart on more than one occasion.

So I continued filling out job applications, always wondering why under "marital status" there wasn't a box for "limbo." If something didn't show up soon, I would have to apply for welfare, which I was loath to do. It was not merely a matter of pride. Trehune would be sure to scan the welfare rolls looking for my name and address. It was essential I keep a low profile. This meant I could not sue *People,* work Equity, or contact Mort Steiner.

Travis had cut off my father's supply line as well, necessitating the sale of the Wilmet Avenue house. The latest nursing home administrator called to report that Father had been quoting the ruder bits of the *Canterbury Tales* to the Ladies' Canasta Club. It was a familiar pattern. Soon he would expose himself to said ladies and be asked to leave.

Trehune finally tracked me down through the A.S.P.C.A. Wart had gotten hold of some rat poison and went into convulsions. In my panic, I gave the vet my real name and address. Wart survived but our cover did not.

Weeks later, when we were coming home from a walk, there was a well-dressed man loitering at the mailboxes. He wasn't flashy enough to be a pimp, so he had to be a process server. I was thankful for the wool hat that covered my red hair.

"Are you Mallory Delaney Holmes?"

"Nah," I snarled. "But this here's her dog. Ya wan him? Bitch took off to Chicago and left him clawin' at the door. Jeesus, sum people . . ."

"Do you know where in Chicago?"

"If I knew, do ya think I'd still have this here damned dog? Ya know what this thing eats?" Wart began nosing the process server's leg. "Raw meat's his favrit, but he takes what he can scrounge. Are ya a relative or somthin'? I sure would like to unload this dog." Wart sniffed the man's groin area.

The process server backed away. "Thanks for your help."

The next morning, we were gone. En route to the West Side Drive, we stopped at a hardware store to buy a white cylindrical curtain rod. At the Ninety-Sixth Street entrance, I put on dark glasses, hung a sign reading "Boston" from my neck, and prominently displayed my curtain rod/blind cane. Wart lay meekly at my feet.

We didn't have to wait long. A Volvo station wagon

stopped beside us. A woman got out and came back to ask if I'd like a ride to Westport. She boomed the invitation, apparently assuming the blind were deaf as well. I let her help us into the car.

On the way to Westport, I spun a sad saga. It was rather overwrought but seemed to be just what she wanted to hear. She insisted on buying me a hearty lunch.

It certainly would have been easier to get to Boston without a dog in tow. But traveling with Wart had its advantages. The trucker who took us to Hartford expected a little slap and tickle for his kindness. Each time his hand neared my thigh, Wart growled ominously.

We had trouble outside of Hartford. The only people who stopped looked like they would slit our veins for the pure joy of it. It was early evening and a light snow was falling. My hands were raw. I was cursing my lack of foresight. Boston was a stupid destination in winter. I was about to seek shelter for the night when our luck returned. A gray limousine glided to a stop. The chauffeur came back to ask if I required transportation.

He held the door for us and Wart bounded in ahead of me. A small cry of alarm was quickly stifled.

The passenger was a white-haired lady wearing an army coat, wide-wale corduroy pants, and sneakers. I judged her to be in her early seventies. She did not meet my expectations of a dowager, but since I was supposedly sightless I kept mum.

"You are not blind," she announced as I took a seat.

"I beg your pardon?"

"You do not move like a blind person. This," she said, prodding Wart with her cane, "is not a proper seeing-eye dog, and I am quite certain you looked at me as you entered." The limousine had not started up yet. "Have you no shame?" she demanded, poking me with her cane.

"No, I can't afford it," I answered. "We all have handicaps of one sort or another. Mine, at the moment, are homelessness and poverty. But as these do not elicit charity, I have borrowed blindness."

"Well, at least you are clever." She surveyed me. "Remove your glasses." I did. "Poverty is common enough these days. Why are you homeless as well?"

"It's a long story."

She rapped on the driver's window and said, "Home, James."

I laughed with delight. "I've always wanted to say that."

She appeared slightly embarrassed. "His given name is Alfred, but I call all my chauffeurs James."

I smiled. "May I ask your name?"

"Audrey Dillingworth Hampton Gresham Gresham Bains," she announced.

"Are you a law firm?"

"No, I am much married. Why are you traveling to Boston?"

"It seemed like a good idea at the time," I replied.

"Have you legal trouble?"

"No."

"You must be in jeopardy to be out on a night such as this."

"I need a job is all."

"How dreary." She waved her arm in a dismissive gesture. "The answer is to marry well."

"I tried that. It was no answer."

She tittered. "It is true that many financially capable men are emotional eunuchs. My second husband had anhedonia."

"I beg your pardon."

"An inability to experience joy. It was during the Depression. How was I to know he was incapable of laughter? Frankly, I married him for his placidity—and, of course, for his money. All around us men were jumping off buildings, but not my Harry.

"Later I realized he was more than a little dull. The doctors considered it a chemical imbalance. But I knew better." She leaned over and said in a whisper, "His mother breastfed him until he was six!" Then her body snapped upright and her face displayed a most satisfied smile.

"Do you have any children?" I asked politely.

"Certainly. Haven't you?"

"No."

She peered at me suspiciously. "Why not?"

There were several good reasons, but none I felt like sharing with her. "It's a long story."

"Do not consider that an excuse." Her eyes bored in on me. "I like you, young lady. Though heaven knows you've given me little enough reason."

"Thank you, I guess . . ."

"I will employ you," she announced.

"As what?" I said, startled.

"A dogsbody."

"You are too kind," I said dryly.

"It means one who is generally exploited."

"I know."

"You could refer to yourself as a companion if you'd rather."

A companion? The term rang a bell. Hadn't I been a companion before? No, that was in a play. I laughed aloud. My life had become that of the heroine of *Rebecca,* but played out in reverse. Ousted from the bed of the dashing Max de Winter, I was to serve as companion to Mrs. Van Hopper. Wouldn't Travis be amused.

"I find my own company distasteful. I hardly think you would find it any better."

"Merely the result of malnutrition," she said airily.

"What exactly would the job entail?"

"Oh, a little of this and a lot of that . . ."

As job descriptions go, I had applied for worse. "Is it a live-in position?"

"Certainly. I have many whims." She paused for a moment, then said, without a trace of apology, "And they nearly all collide at odd hours."

"Oh," I said, shifting uneasily in my seat. "Is there any other staff?"

"There's James—and Olga, his wife. She cooks, though not well. The rest of the staff comes and goes . . . frequently. I am hard to please," she said with pride.

"My dog . . . he needs a home, too."

"From the looks of him, I should think he could commandeer his own," Mrs. Bains replied archly.

"He's actually quite shy. We go together," I insisted.

"Like an old vaudeville team, I suppose. Does he like cats?"

"Not especially."

"That should be jolly. I have sixteen."

"Sixteen cats?"

"Yes, I believe they breed readily. So. Will you be my companion?"

"Why not," I conceded.

"Very good. What is your name?"

"My name?" I mused. "It's Mallory de Winter."

The Dogsbody Shuffle

Audrey Bains lived in a white-columned brick mansion in Winchester, Massachusetts. All the houses on Everett Street were of equal grandeur. It was like stumbling upon a passel of palaces. With luck, I would be very comfortable.

Mrs. Bains exited spryly from the limousine, declining my offer of help with an animated gesture of her cane. I did not take offense. If she was mobile, that would lessen my load.

The house was beautifully appointed. I wandered the bedrooms upstairs wondering which would be mine. I had stopped a floor too soon. Mrs. Bains rapped her cane on the attic door and said, "You'll be quite cozy up there."

"In the attic?" I replied indignantly.

"There is always the basement," she replied.

"And my dog?"

"There is little better than body heat to keep one warm. The buzzer will sound twice if I require you."

Wart and I climbed the narrow stairs. The attic, full of trunks, boxes, old furniture, and garment bags, was the size of a bowling alley with a partitioned area in the far corner—the bedroom. A bare lightbulb dangled from a beam over a narrow cot. Thankfully, I spied a radiator. But there was no reassuring gush of steam in the pipes when I turned the knob. I climbed into bed with my coat. Wart sat by the cot staring at me. When I didn't acquiesce to his mournful sighs, he pushed his large, cold, wet nose against my cheek.

"Oh, very well," I said, lifting the blanket. He leapt up and stretched out, nearly forcing me off the cot. All the same, I was grateful for his presence. "We've known worse, Wartie," I reflected, wrapping the blanket around him. He buried his nose under his paws. "And if it's truly awful, we'll find something else." Suddenly Wart's ears perked.

Night creatures, momentarily silenced by our arrival, now reclaimed their territory. Legions of them skittered noisily over the floorboards and inside the walls. Wart moaned.

When summoned several hours later, I was still awake, as was Wart. The vermin had been marching all night. Try as I might, I could not forget the scene in one of Travis's novels where a girl is gnawed to death by small rodents.

What Mrs. Bains had described as a "buzzer" sounded more like the spray from a machine gunner's nest. Its effect, coming as it did on already frayed spirits, was unnerving. I screamed. Wart bailed out and burrowed under the cot. And still the alarm blasted. It continued to ring as I left the attic. Wart bounded after me.

Mrs. Bains was sitting up in bed, smiling regally, with her index finger poised on the buzzer.

"Yes?" I said angrily.

"Let's talk." She released the buzzer button.

Wart growled ominously. Something on the bed whined. "Oh hush, Hortense," commanded Mrs. Bains. The whining continued. With an impatient gesture, Mrs. Bains swiped at a hairy object and pushed it to the floor. There, shaking, stood a tiny excuse for a dog. Wart began to bark. Hortense sneezed wetly. Surprised, Wart wagged his tail.

I glared at Mrs. Bains. "Couldn't you have summoned me with something less traumatic. Say a sonic boom?"

"Some people are deep sleepers." She patted her white hair lightly, almost as if she were primping for a suitor.

"I was too busy listening to the Rodent Cantata to consider sleeping," I said pointedly.

"Are you a student of music?"

"No." She was evading the point. "Your summons was grossly overstated."

"Russell required a gong at two paces."

"Russell was doubtless deaf."

"Russell was my third husband. He was impossible to rouse—on any occasion."

"Mrs. Bains, this arrangement will not do. Either you give us better lodgings or we leave at first light."

"Cheeky little thing, aren't you." She reached over to the night table and retrieved a pair of half glasses. Peering over the top of them, she asked, "Tell me, what do you young people do for fun nowadays?"

"I assure you, I wouldn't know. Come, Wart." But Wart was otherwise engaged. He and Hortense were sniffing one another's privates.

"They will be at that a while, if I am any judge of canine lust. Come sit." She patted the edge of the bed. It was better than returning to the attic.

"You need less sleep as you get older," she announced.

"I can hardly wait," I said, from the foot of the bed.

"As to your earlier accusation, we have neither rats nor mice."

"That will come as a surprise to the troop strength upstairs."

"Those are squirrels."

"Squirrels are still rodents. They carry disease and, worse, big teeth. And when they tire of electrical wiring and insulation, their tastes run to human flesh. That's a fact."

"Nonsense. My squirrels are very happy."

"*Your* squirrels?"

"Of course, they are mine. You don't think I'd allow William Devrod's squirrels in my attic!"

"I don't know William Devrod's squirrels," I said cautiously.

"The man has no taste, no taste at all."

"These squirrels of yours, do you feed them?"

"Someone must." Her response was maddeningly ambiguous. Did she mean it was a moral imperative or that she assumed her staff fed the squirrels?

"You don't clothe them or have little squirrel beds, do you?" I asked.

"Just because I am old does not mean I am deranged. The presumption of youth is quite intolerable."

"I am sorry," I apologized. Wart and Hortense had left the room. I jumped up from the bed and called him.

"Oh, let them indulge," Mrs. Bains counseled.

"If Wart indulges in Hortense, she will need reconstructive surgery."

She waved her hand in a gesture of unconcern.

"Won't he bother the cats?" I asked.

"Cats?" She looked puzzled.

"Yes, your sixteen sexually active cats."

"I haven't any cats. Horrid little creatures. Always spitting up hairs balls. So like Thaddeus."

"A cat?"

"A husband," she said airily. "He who left me the electrical utility."

"You told me you had sixteen cats," I argued.

"Well, I don't."

"I think we will be leaving now," I said, edging toward the door.

"I thought you would be more fun," she said wistfully.

"I can be fun, but not when you expect me to live with squirrels and lie to me . . ."

"I took you in from the cold," she interjected.

"That was very decent of you, but . . ."

"Consider my position. Defying common sense, I assist a woman hitchhiker. First, she presumes blindness, then she prevaricates about something as basic as her name. Mallory de Winter, indeed. Did you think me illiterate? And I should bed you in satin sheets? Bah. I give as good as I get!"

"You don't want a companion, you want a sparring partner."

She smiled coyly. "I believe you'll do quite nicely."

We came to more equitable terms. In exchange for my maiden surname, I was allowed out of the attic and put on a first name basis. For the fabricated story of my life, I was quoted a generous salary. I had spun a variation of the orphan of the windy plains saga. My husband, Max, lived in Utah with his two children and faithful collie. Our marriage had dissolved when he caught me messing with one of the ranch hands during shearing season. Audrey took this in without even raising an eyebrow.

My dogsbody duties were simple: twenty-four hours a day I was to attend to Audrey's whims. This might entail anything from reading aloud at three in the morning to brushing suede shoes or chasing William Devrod's squirrels off Audrey's property. Wart assisted with the squirrel patrol, although Audrey thought he lacked discrimination. (Unlike the rest of us, Audrey could tell one squirrel from another.) Much of the work was menial and even demeaning, but I was drawn to Audrey, this moving mass of contradictions. Her life story, spun out to me in snippets, held me in thrall.

When Audrey moved it was in high gear, whether she was fussing at the servants, railing at Mr. Devrod (who had the "good gall" to adore her), or spinning plans for travel and action. Yet on other days, she suffered from "funks" and would remain motionless for hours. I found her once sitting in the dark after a prolonged "funk." As I started to slip away, she called to me plaintively and asked if I could do something about the light.

"What's wrong with the light?"

"It refuses to illuminate."

I went to the dimmer switch and punched it on. No light, it was obviously at the dark end of the scale. I turned it to bright.

"Ah," she sighed happily. "I was right to employ you. You are so clever."

I was about to say something sarcastic when I realized she was serious. The woman who claimed to have controlling interest in a utility company could not work a rheostat.

There were other inconsistencies. In a house easily worth a half-million dollars, Audrey insisted on recycling paper towels. The kitchen held a special rack to dry the towels between uses. Occasionally Audrey could be found rooting through the garbage for prematurely discarded towels. If she thought she had found one, Olga was swatted with a broom.

Whether from age or swatting, the broom was a sorry item. It was missing a good third of its straw and the handle was bound in tape. Yet Audrey refused to authorize expenditure for a new one. She rode herd over the household accounts, scrutinizing every receipt, accusing Olga daily of food theft and "gross mismanagement" of funds. But it was Audrey not Olga who heated an outdoor pool she never used.

Audrey had closets full of gowns and dresses, but most of the time she looked like her body was at war with itself. I was puzzled by the source of the incongruity. It wasn't that she wore plaids with stripes, it was something far subtler. A matter of texture and time. Audrey often looked as if she had been pulled back and forth through a time warp. One day, I found her wearing a pale green velvet Balenciaga skirt with a Jordache scrubbed denim jacket.

My days off were determined without rhyme or reason. Two weeks after I had arrived, I came to Audrey's door punctually at 8:15 with her tea and croissant. On the door was a bronze plaque reading "Go away!" From the permanence of the material, I had to assume the sign had been posted before.

Downstairs, I asked Olga what Madame was doing in her room. Olga rolled her eyes, jiggled her breasts, and sighed. From this I inferred Madame was with a man. Audrey had no shortage of suitors, but none she held dear. Who was she in bed with? It was not William Devrod, for he had just called to see if she would dine with him. Perhaps it was the married patrician from Beacon Hill whose spats Audrey seemed to covet.

Two days later I was summoned in the early morning hours. Audrey was sitting up in bed and looking quite pale. I searched for tell-tale signs of the patrician.

"Cocoa with marshmallows. And not those itty-bitty ones," she directed.

I returned with a pot of cocoa. "Olga only had the itty-bitty ones."

"If you had any initiative, you would have thought of a way to reform them. What am I paying you for?"

"So far you have not paid me," I said pointedly.

She waved her hands, dismissing this petty technicality. "What day is it?" she asked abruptly.

"Thursday." As she still looked vague, I added, "November 22."

"Reagan still in office?"

"Yes," I said with alarm. "Are you all right?"

"Who could be all right with that twit in office? I knew him once. In my salad days. He is one of the reasons I forswore newspapers. Reading of his hijinks was intolerable."

"Is that why you have no television?"

"Partially. Bad news addles the brain."

"I thought the wealthy liked him."

"Your biggest fault, Mallory, is that you cogitate categorically. The old are deranged, the squirrels are rabid, the wealthy are pro-Reagan. Bah. You young are all alike."

"If you say so."

"Timing is everything," she said wistfully.

Gears shifted rapidly when conversing with Audrey. "Are we talking comedy, birth control, or boiled eggs?" I asked.

"Gypsies."

"Oh," I responded hesitantly.

"When I was young, I saw a gypsy fortune teller. She was wonderfully exotic for Boise, Idaho."

"I thought you grew up in Baltimore."

"I did. Now hush, I am trying to impart the wisdom of my years. My mother died young of tuberculosis. For a long time, I had a bad cough. Perhaps it was psychosomatic, but the gypsy told me I too would die young."

"You don't believe that hokum!"

"Disbelief is aided by the distance of fifty-five years. But at the time, I did believe her. I surely did." Audrey looked off dreamily and then suddenly snapped back. "I was going to have a full life, brief but explosive."

I got up from the foot of the bed and went to straighten a picture on the wall.

"You are not paying heed."

"Yes, I am."

"Have you any idea how dreadful it is to outlive yourself?" She sighed and slumped back on the pillow.

"Clinically speaking, I'm not sure such a thing is possible."

"Timing, my dear. The prediction threw off my timing. I paced my life poorly, and now I must pay for it with these spells. It is so exasperating."

"My mother lived a 'brief but explosive' life. All in all, I would say, you fared better. At least you're still around to complain."

"I never complain. Do you still miss her?"

"Probably more the idea of her. Someone to turn to when the world falls in."

"Won't I do?" Audrey asked querulously.

"Compassion isn't your forte," I answered lightly.

"Nonsense. I am the right age," she said, as if that were all that mattered. "Think of me as your mother."

"I think I would rather be paid."

As the holidays approached, the "go away" plaque hung for days. With little else to do (I still had not been paid), I dragged out the cartons of decorations I had found in the attic. Some of the ornaments made of wartime glass reminded me of Christmases at the Delirium.

When Audrey finally emerged from her funk, she was energized. After a morning on the phone, she announced that we were going to Mexico for Christmas.

"We?" I asked uncertainly.

"Yes, we."

"I've never been out of the country," I stammered.

"I rarely stay in it. Come, get my trunks packed."

"Trunks? How long are we staying?"

"One never knows in Mexico."

"Mexico," I sighed excitedly. Beaches, sun, fiestas, margaritas . . .

"Pack for winter."

"Winter?" I asked, startled.

"We'll be with Hector in the mountains."

"The Mexican mountains in winter," I said, not warming to the image.

"Perhaps we'll find a Mexican for you."

"Excuse me," I asked, appalled.

She looked down at her feet. "I'll need a new pair of walking boots. Hector has requested that we bring him a carton of Glad Bags. He can't get them in the mountains. You'll adore San Miguel de Allende. It's an artists' colony.

Oh, and see about getting an oxygen tank. The air is dreadfully thin up there."

I did not want to go, but Audrey was insistent. She claimed I needed some fun in my life. I wasn't fooled. Audrey, I knew, would have me clambering up the mountains like a human pack horse.

I could quit, of course—she still had not paid me a farthing. But my physical needs were met, and since I couldn't be with Travis there seemed little else worth wanting.

Milady Malingerer

Standing in the Mexico City airport a week before Christmas, I saw tourists toting tennis racquets and golf bags. Enviously, I hoisted our luggage of garbage bags, heavy sweaters, Pepto-Bismol, and hiking shoes onto a cart and pushed out into the crowd.

Audrey tugged at my sleeve. "There's Pepe."

Pepe rushed at Audrey exclaiming, "Señora Bens, Señora Bens." He embraced her awkwardly and then backed off. She smiled and patted him on the head. Pepe took the luggage cart and used it as a wedge to cut through the throng of Mexicans hustling taxis and exchange rates to an aged Chevrolet. Could this junker make the three-hour climb up into the mountains?

We inched our way out of the city through near-gridlock traffic. Pepe and Audrey chattered in Spanish. I felt ill, either from the sudden intense heat or the noxious fumes of so many cars. The era of the catalytic converter had yet to reach Mexico City.

Audrey was laughing, ignoring the fumes and the view. I concentrated on the sights. Slums and more slums. I hadn't known I was so rich.

We went past a wealthy district, a park, many factories, more slums, and finally reached the interstate. Pepe paid the toll and chugged out of the gate.

"I'm going to be sick."

"*Ahora no,*" Audrey muttered.

"What?" I squeaked.

"*Mas tarde.*"

"I need a bathroom."

She turned to look at me. "You should have spoken earlier. The only powder rooms are at the tolls."

"Tell Pepe, I'm about to vomit."

"I will not discuss bodily extrusions with Hector's servant."

"Pepe," I said authoritatively, "stop at the next toll."

"*¿Qué?*"

"In Spanish, if you must," Audrey quarreled.

"I don't speak Spanish."

"Certainly you do."

"No, I don't."

"Everyone speaks Spanish," she argued.

"Fine. Have it your way. Pepe, stoppay la chevay."

"Why are you being difficult?" Audrey asked.

"I am going to be ill."

"Then you should know the next toll booth is an hour away. Chew this." Audrey handed me a stick of peppermint gum. I chewed quickly, fighting the surges of nausea. She was peering angrily at me over her half glasses. "You might have informed me of your linguistic inadequacies earlier."

"I thought I had," I said weakly.

"Perhaps you did," she conceded. "I speak nine languages and seven dialects. If one is going to travel in a foreign country, one owes them the courtesy of learning their language."

"On two days' notice?" I objected.

She looked thoughtful for a moment and then asked, "Did I tell you to get a typhoid inoculation?"

"Typhoid!"

"I gather I did not," she sighed. "I forget these things."

"What if you get sick?" I asked with alarm.

"Oh, but I shan't. Before journeying to Kenya this fall, I had a whole host of injections. There'll be no yellow fever, infectious hepatitis, malaria, typhoid, plague, or dengue fever for me. But Mallory, dear, you really should have had your shots," she scolded.

Five miles up the road, I spied a covey of big black birds pecking at a large brown lump lying on the shoulder. As the car approached, the birds lifted off and circled.

"What is that?" The stench was unbearable.

"Hmm?" said Audrey, turning to look. "Oh just a dead burro, pay it no mind."

I never made it to the toilet.

Dead burros were not an uncommon sight. There were two more before we reached our destination. The stretches between the burros offered little of interest. The countryside was brown. To my New England eyes, the land looked too barren to support life, but small shacks of piled stone and adobe dotted the hillsides. Most of the tiny shacks were surrounded by many children, reminding me of clowns pouring out of a circus Volkswagen.

I kept expecting the terrain to change to something more conducive to life. But, burro after burro, it was more of the same.

I looked nervously at Audrey. She appeared exhilarated by the arid climate. Why then did I feel my bodily fluids receding?

"Almost there, Mallory." The car came down around a steep curve and there was San Miguel de Allende, a rough jewel of church spires and houses, set into the mountain.

Soon we were in the middle of the town, driving down bumpy stone streets through colored canyons of fortress-like adobe structures. Much of the adobe was crumbled, exposing layers of age.

Pepe stopped in front of an unpromising faded pink building.

"This is Hector's *casa*. That's Spanish for house," announced Audrey. From what I knew of Audrey, I was amazed she would travel this distance to see a man of no wealth.

No sooner had we gotten out of the car than we were besieged by Mexicans. Pepe barked something at them and they dispersed.

Audrey went to the massive wooden door and rang.

A Mexican woman opened the door and, seeing Audrey, smiled broadly. "Señora Bens!"

Audrey clearly had better relations with servants here than in the States. This woman hugged her and began speaking rapidly in Spanish.

I took my bag from the trunk, leaving Pepe to struggle with Audrey's luggage, and followed my employer inside. There, I received my first pleasant surprise of the trip. The outside of Hector's *casa* belied the beauty within. I dropped my bag and stared.

Audrey and a silver-haired Mexican, presumably Hector, stood in an open courtyard of geometric tiles, adobe arches, and water fountains. After the miles of barren landscape, the profusion of plants and flowers in the courtyard was almost a physical blow to the senses.

Audrey brought Hector over and said, "*Hector, querido, le presento a mi hija, Mallory.*"

"*Mucho gusto.*" Hector pumped my hand.

"*Mucho gusto,*" I repeated, feeling as if I were in a beer commercial.

"*Ella no habla español,*" Audrey said with evident dismay.

"*¿Sí?*" Hector said with disbelief. He stared at me as if I had just turned into a hunk of meat on the auction block.

I was given a large dark room on the first floor. The view was minimal. Instead of a window, there were wooden shutters. When I opened them I found myself eyeball to eyeball with passing Mexicans. We all gawked and then I closed the shutters.

Audrey's suite faced the courtyard. When I went to unpack her clothing, I found Audrey lying on the bed with cucumber slices on her eyes.

"Are you all right?"

"I feel a funk brewing."

"Oh no you don't."

"Hector is not Hector."

"Who is he?" I asked cautiously, bracing myself for tales of changelings and clones.

"An old man."

"He seems like a very pleasant old man."

"But he's my age."

"I am not following this." I sat on the other bed.

"I must be old."

"We all must be eventually," I responded. She looked so comical lying there with her cucumber eye patches.

"Wait until it hammers you."

"Frankly, I imagine it will be a great relief." If only time would hurry and blunt my senses. How lovely it would be not to ache for Travis.

"Romanticize all you wish, but Age does not tread gently," she admonished.

Audrey's funk was not to be deferred. She sent me with an apology to Hector. I knocked on the living-room door and handed him the note, intending to fade back into the dark of my own quarters. But he seized hold of my arm and pulled me inside. I tried to back out of the room.

My retreat was met with a flurry of '*no*'s.' Hector took my hand and directed me to a sofa.

He handed me a clear drink.

We sat in silence and stared at one another. Then Hector began speaking in Spanish. From the intonation, I gathered he was questioning me. I caught Audrey's name and a word that sounded like "eeha." I shrugged my shoulders and smiled. This set him off on a new round of inquiries.

The maid came in, saying something that caused Hector to stand.

"*Adios, amigo,*" I said with little hope.

Hector chose to ignore my television Spanish and escorted me to dinner.

* * *

The next morning Audrey's shades were drawn.

"Go away," she muttered, when I entered her suite.

"Audrey, I won't face Hector alone again."

"Nonsense, it's good training for you. I expect you to be bilingual at the very least by the time I am recovered."

"And at the most?" I asked bitterly.

"In love. Mexicans make marvelously attentive lovers. Ask Hector to introduce you to some nice young men."

"I have no need of nice young men," I said coolly.

"Poppycock."

"I will not be a party to your machinations." Angrily, I released a window shade. With a sudden snap, it flooded the room with light.

Audrey's reaction was that of a heliophobic creature. She scuttled under the covers where she curled into a tight ball. "I need quiet—quiet and dark."

"Then you've made a monumental error in your choice of country."

"This is a lovely country," she countered.

"For insominacs. When do people sleep? Trucks lumbered past my bedroom wall all night, dogs howled, bugs, both terrestrial and airborne, bit. And then just when I was too exhausted to cry, a cannonade of fireworks went off. Tell me, Audrey, why do they set off fireworks at four-thirty in the morning?"

"It's Christmas time."

"For a moment I thought it was one of your more abrupt summonses."

"Wait until you hear the fireworks at Easter."

"Easter!" I snapped, aghast at the idea of staying so long.

"Perhaps not this trip." She moved around under the covers. "Do you imagine you are the only one who suffered inconveniences during the night?"

"You were spared the trucks."

"But little else. Why are you so hard on me?" she asked plaintively from beneath the blanket.

"Because you rearrange other people's lives for your convenience and then refuse to deal with the consequences."

Her head, with her hand shading her eyes, emerged from the covers. "That is simply not true."

"Right. You leave me to dine with your paramour while you brood in bed about life's lost opportunities."

"You have no idea of the pain I am feeling."

As a concession, I pulled down the shade.

"Thank you, Mallory. Consider today a holiday."

A day off, in a foreign land where I knew no one, couldn't speak the language, and had no money. "You're a real pip, Audrey."

"See the *jardín*."

"What's a hardeen?"

"The public square. They have an interesting mating ritual there."

"I will not mate with an itinerant Mexican," I snapped.

"That was merely an interesting side note. You must learn to relax, Mallory. Hand me my bag."

This was it. I was finally going to be paid. She extracted a slim volume from her purse and handed it to me.

"A Spanish-English dictionary?"

"See what you can learn. Remember that 'j' is pronounced as an 'h' and double 'l's as 'y.' The letter . . ."

"Dammit Audrey, I want my money! You owe me six weeks' wages."

"Airfare is costly."

"I did not ask to come here."

"But here you are," she smiled. "It would be unwise for you to carry money. The natives could take advantage of you."

"They'd have to form a line behind you," I grumbled.

"Oh, very well, here are a hundred pesos."

Lost in Translation

In the best of times one hundred pesos were not a fortune. Currently, it was worth about $1.98. Still, it was more buying power than I had enjoyed in a while.

I left Hector's *casa* and began exploring San Miguel de Allende. Eventually I found my way to the town square. No one appeared to be mating at the moment. I sat on a bench absorbing the winter sun and observing the local color. It was lunchtime but I had lost my appetite. Earlier I had seen stores that specialized in deep-fried pork fat. Sides of pork fat hung in the open windows, attracting flies.

Mexicans began to approach me as I sat on the bench. My red hair shone as a beacon in the beggar's world. At first I resisted. I got up and moved away. Then I thought, what was I going to do with a hundred pesos? Send a postcard to Wart? But a hundred pesos might make a difference to a

Mexican beggar. I handed it to a small elderly woman wrapped in dusty black. A cry of gratitude went up and soon I was besieged. I turned my pockets inside out to show I was now of their class and walked on.

The old lady who had received my riches followed me. We wandered through the marketplace. When I stopped to admire the melons and pineapples, she stopped. The sight of all that lush fruit sent a lance of longing through me. I thought of Travis filling his shopping cart in the Ridgefield supermarket.

I was beginning to get hungry. I went out of the marketplace and tried to find my way home.

It didn't take long to get lost and then panicky. Was the old beggar dogging my steps lost as well? A blond couple approached me smiling. I asked them directions, but they responded in a Germanic tongue.

It seemed I was going in circles or rather squares. Hadn't I seen that woman with the bright yellow shirt and red skirt before? Why did everything look alike to my foreigner's eyes?

All my life I had feared being lost. Now, my situation mirrored my sense of powerlessness. I would never find my way home again. And if I did not, who would care but Wart. How had my life become so empty?

I climbed up a steep street. From there I was able to see the spires of what I hoped was the cathedral facing the *jardín*. I tried to retrace my morning route, but all the streets looked the same. My stomach was knotted from hunger and panic. Finally I spotted the police station. A man in a rumpled blue uniform with red trim, black shoes, and no socks sat on a chair in the doorway.

I smiled obsequiously and thumbed through my dictionary for 'lost.' "¡*Perdido*!" I exclaimed. He looked at me drowsily. "*Perdido*," I repeated with urgency.

He answered me in rapid Spanish.

"*Perdido*," I repeated. "Please . . . uh, *por favor*." How did one pronounce Hector's address? "*Pila Seca uno*."

Again, the policeman said something incomprehensible. Absurdly, I had hoped he would break into perfect English.

A voice spoke from behind me. I whirled around to find my beggar. I thought I had lost her long ago. She tugged on my sleeve and motioned me to follow her.

Within a matter of minutes, she had me in front of Hector's *casa*. "*Muchos gracias*," I said, grateful for her show of human kindness. She stuck out her hand. I shook it. She pulled the hand away and turned it up. I pointed at my empty pockets, still dangling outside my pants, and banged on the door. The beggar began chattering angrily and pulling at my shirt. The door opened. I ran past the maid to my room.

Lying on the bed, I began shaking uncontrollably. I took deep gasping breaths trying to abort the anxiety attack. I am an independent woman, I said to myself. I come from independent stock. I can make it through this. But my body wasn't buying my bravura. Images of Mother packing her bags flitted through my head. The desolation of being left again hit me in violent waves. Stop this, I willed my body. You are not alone. Audrey is across the courtyard. Good old silly Audrey. I concentrated on the image of her telling William Devrod to have his squirrels spayed.

When my body had finally calmed itself, I went to the kitchen for something to eat. The cook was not there, sparing me yet another one-sided conversation. There was a large glass bottle of treated water suspended on a pivoting device. I poured myself a glass, stole a pear and some strawberries that were still inside a market string bag, and hightailed it back to my room.

I felt stronger after I ate. Surely I would feel stronger still if I had some command of the language. I opened the dictionary. Where to begin? What was it Hector kept saying last night, "eeha"? From the keys in front of the book I deduced it would be spelled "*hija*."

But an *hija* was a daughter! Did he think I was Audrey's daughter? My mind raced at the possible implications. What was Audrey up to now?

At dinnertime I went to Audrey's suite and entered without knocking. She was wearing her cucumber slices.

"Is that you, Mallory?"

"If you weren't wearing vegetables, you wouldn't have to ask."

"How was your day off? Did you spend all your money?"

"Every peso."

"Oh? What did you purchase?"

"An amethyst ring for myself and a gold collar for Wart."

"Yes, the prices here are quite reasonable," she replied.

"Right," I snapped. Audrey groaned softly.

"Don't die on me, Audrey, I've had a hell of a day."

"One doesn't die from cluster migraines, though it would be preferable. Would you massage my shoulders?" She sat up slowly, in evident pain. The cucumber slices slid to the tiled floor. She applied fresh ones from a dish, but they too fell. She sighed.

I rubbed her back with moderate pressure.

"Harder," she ordered.

"I thought you hurt."

"I do. It helps."

Rubbing harder, I said, "I got lost today, Audrey. It scared the hell out of me."

"I imagine I'd have found you sooner or later. Towering redheads aren't all that common here."

"Would you have looked?" I asked.

"Certainly," she answered brusquely.

"Right. Cheap help is hard to find."

"You are hardly cheap," she objected. Who was she kidding? Not even a wetback would work six weeks for a hundred pesos.

"Audrey, if there were a union for dogsbodies, I'd have you up on charges."

"George Meany had solid gold faucets in his bathroom."

"So?"

"Why pay union dues so a man you never met can sit on a gold toilet?"

"You said faucets," I corrected.

"Mallory, you are too literal."

My hands were tired, but I kept rubbing. "Audrey, why did you tell Hector I was your daughter?"

Her body stiffened. "Who told you that?"

"It's true, then?"

"Of course not, how could I be your mother?" she evaded.

"I know that. But why lie to Hector?"

"Hector wants me to be happy. I can hardly let him think I have to pay someone for their company."

"As it happens, you don't pay me."

"Yes, so you see, it is quite perfect."

* * *

At dinner that night, Hector talked excitedly. Something big was brewing for *mañana.* I smiled numbly and concentrated on the plate of roast pork before me. Hector continued to address me as though I had suddenly sprouted bilingual antennae. I stopped smiling and took to shrugging my shoulders and looking dismayed.

The next thing I knew, I was being whisked out of the *casa* by Hector and into Pepe's Chevy. The beggar lady was still camped on the door step. Hector barked something at her. She cursed in return but moved a few steps away from the door.

Pepe drove through town, past the *jardín* where the mating ritual had begun. Men walked in one direction around the square and the women walked the other, checking each other out. It reminded me of a similar ritual in high school.

Hector took me to a nightclub where we danced for the next four hours. On the few occasions I was allowed to sit down, I greedily eavesdropped on a table of Americans. Their conversation centered on the "appalling poverty" of the country and the various dread diseases available here. One of them had broken out in rosy spots and was sure he was dying of typhoid. By the time they got to diarrhea, I was beginning to understand the term, "the ugly American."

I pantomimed thirst to my companion and soon I was awash in margaritas.

That night I slept through the rumbling trucks, howling dogs, bug bites, and even the fireworks. I awoke early the next morning to the sound of repeated knocking on my door.

"Come in," I muttered. The knocking continued. "Ah, hell." I struggled to my feet and discovered I had a wicked hangover. At the door, the maid spoke quickly and gestured toward Audrey's side of the courtyard.

"Oh, no!" I gasped and ran to Audrey's suite. Audrey, dressed in a long black gown and sneakers, was lying in state. The cucumber slices were in place, reminding me of the ancient Greeks who put coins in the eyes of their dead to pay their passage across the river Styx. Her arms were tight by her sides. "Audrey," I cried.

"Good morning."

"Oh, Christ. I thought you were dead."

"Why would you think that? I told you, I have no intention of dying."

"Then why are you dressed like that?" I quarreled.

"I had hoped to join you at the club last night, but was laid low."

"What do you want now?" I asked suspiciously.

"The day is fast upon us. I thought you would want the schedule."

"Sleeping off a hangover does not require a schedule."

"You leave in twenty minutes."

"Leave?" I asked, bewildered.

"Yes, to find the Sanchez brothers."

"Audrey, let's be reasonable. To me, everyone is a Sanchez."

"Hector will handle the negotiations."

"What negotiations?" I asked yawning.

"For our three-day mule trip down the Santa María River," she said impatiently.

Pulling back the covers of the second bed, I climbed in and pulled the blanket over my head.

The Legacy

Twenty minutes later, I was sitting in Pepe's Chevy. The beggar lady was still by the door. I admired her tenacity.

Drowsily, I leaned against the rear window for the trip across town.

Pepe drove out of San Miguel and began climbing into the mountains. I sat up and looked around in alarm. "Hector, where are we going?"

"*¿Qué?*"

Scanning my shorted brain circuits, I tried to remember the lyrics to an old Top 40 Christmas tune. "*¿Dondes estes Santa Claus?*" I murmured.

"*¿Qué?*"

"Uh, *¿dondes estes Sanchez?*"

"Ah," he nodded with an expansive grin. "Xichú."

That was a great help.

The road to Xichú went up and up for three hours and

then dropped two thousand feet to a dirt road. At the end of this road was a dusty village, presumably "Xichú." Looking around, I saw a church, a square, several houses, and a small building claiming to be a *hotel.* The men got out of the car and stretched. I followed. Last night's drinking had left me with a severe case of cottonmouth. I pantomimed drinking to Pepe, and he led me into the hotel.

Where a lobby should have been, the space was filled with stacked wooden coffins. I staggered at the sight. Pepe didn't seem to notice anything untoward. Perhaps all Mexican hostels doubled as funeral parlors, or perhaps the coffins served as bedding during unexpected surges in tourism.

The innkeeper sold Pepe three warm Cokes. We went back out to Hector, who was talking with some local men and gesturing at the dry riverbed. I drank two Cokes waiting for Hector to finish his business with the Sanchez brothers.

But all was not well. Hector gestured for us to follow as he set off down the narrow dirt road that ran beside the riverbed. I pointed to the locals and said "Sanchez?"

"*No!*" replied Hector. Cursing Audrey, I trudged after him.

Twenty minutes into our trek, Hector stopped, as did Pepe. No doubt they were lost. If this was to be a long conference, I wanted to rest. I went to sit on the rocks and thought about removing my sweater. It had been cold this morning, but now I was hot and cranky. The men were gesturing toward a hillside cabin. I looked about the countryside and then down at the rocks. Two feet from me was an attentive lizard about eighteen inches long with orange and black rings. I stared at it for a moment. The name Gila monster popped into my brain, probably from photos Mother had once shown me. Were Gila monsters dangerous, and if so, should I make no sudden moves or should I run like hell? Suddenly, Hector issued a cry; Pepe grabbed my arm and dragged me back from the rock and into the rocky riverbed. Hector berated me while Pepe hugged me as if I were his sainted mother.

An hour later we reached the Sanchez "ranch," two shacks and three mules. While Hector entered negotiations with the brothers, Pepe and I sat under a tree with a goat, some children, and several chickens. Pepe delighted the children with magic tricks. I talked to the goat. Señora Sanchez brought us some lemonade. Pepe and the children drank it with gusto, and even I was too thirsty to worry about what bacteria might be swimming within.

Nothing happens fast in Mexico. Hector was still negotiating with the men an hour after we had arrived.

I looked at the mules. As there were only three of them, and four of us, it appeared one of us would be walking the three-day trip down the Santa María River.

I could only hope chivalry was not dead in Mexico.

We reached San Miguel de Allende at sunset. I went directly to my room and crawled into bed, but not for long.

I was summoned soon thereafter.

Audrey was sitting up. She looked agitated.

"Hector has just been in to see me. Why did you not report first?"

"What's there to report? I sat in a car for six hours, walked in a riverbed for three, and sat with some Mexicans. An altogether thrilling way to spend a hangover."

"You were meant to have fun."

"Sorry. You should have warned me," I replied.

"Tomorrow you tour Dolores Hidalgo and Guanajuato. See that you enjoy yourself."

"Hasn't this funk of yours gone on long enough?"

"I expect to be well by Christmas. The expedition begins the day after that."

"What exactly are we expediting?"

"Once again, Mallory, you betray a careless disregard for English usage."

"I see we're well enough for petty arguments," I countered.

Ignoring me, she said, "Hector tells me there is a black marble-like canyon where water gushes miraculously from the earth."

"Hot damn," I replied with little enthusiasm.

On Christmas day, the fireworks started earlier and went on longer. I was too ill to care. When they finally stopped, I knew with sudden clarity that I was going to die. I had been vomiting all night. Now I had chills, a severe headache, sore throat, backache, and red spots on my stomach and chest. If it wasn't the plague, it was surely typhoid.

I hadn't been ill a day since my first year in New York City. Now I was going to die in a foreign country far from Travis. I wept tears of self-pity and rage.

I must have passed out because when I awoke, Audrey was wiping me with a cool cloth.

"Hold on, Mallory, we have sent for a doctor."

"No," I protested. Mexican country doctors probably still used leeches. "Tell Travis I loved him," I begged.

"Don't be silly. You will tell him yourself."

"Promise me you'll take care of Wart."

"Hush," she soothed as she stroked my forehead. "You'll be fine. You are merely suffering a momentary lapse of manners."

I passed in and out for days, but Audrey was always there. In my delirium, I saw her astride a huge Gila monster. In saner moments, I realized it was she who cleaned my face when I vomited, rubbed my back with alcohol, and coaxed me to drink my broth and medicine.

After four days, I was strong enough to sit up. I realized with a start that I had been moved to the spare bed in Audrey's suite.

"You will live," she said. "It was not typhoid as we feared, but paratyphoid." Audrey looked like Florence Nightingale after a bad year in the Crimea.

"Oh."

"Satisfy my curiosity. Who is Travis?"

"My husband."

"I thought your husband's name was Max."

"That was just a game we played."

"Well, I did wonder. You kept calling for him." She wrung a cloth in her hands. "I am dreadfully sorry, Mallory."

"It wasn't your fault."

She sighed. "In a way it was. You were brought here for a purpose."

"What purpose?"

Audrey stared out at the fountain for a moment and then said, "To twist the course of your life."

"Oh?" I replied warily.

"Ah, Mallory," she said, looking at me with a small smile. "You remind me so much of myself. My mother also died when I was young. One never fully recovers from that. Long after you think you've gotten on with your life, it continues to infect you in subtle ways. My husbands wanted children, but I refused. To bear children, I thought, was to give others the power to hurt you—to leave you. I didn't want to be left by anyone else."

"Wait a minute," I interjected. "You told me you had children."

"Did I? Well, I don't. Now listen, I vowed I would be independent, so I insulated myself from life—just as you have done. Mallory and Wart . . . you two remind me of an old western about a man and his horse."

"We are not alone by choice," I replied.

"We have no choice. Our mothers left us the same legacy."

"Hardly. You were an only child, or did you lie about that, too?"

"No."

"Well," I mused, "my legacy was more of a load, four brothers and sisters. I had to be their mother as well as my own."

"That, I daresay, was the easy part. The real 'load' as you call it is far more insidious, a sense of worthlessness."

"I'm not entirely worthless," I objected. Though at the moment I did feel so.

"Why did your husband leave you?"

"I had an affair."

"Bosh and fiddlesticks, be truthful."

"He said I was incapable of taking love."

"And whose fault was that?" Audrey asked.

"Mine, obviously." This was dredging up too much pain. I slumped back down on the bed.

"Your mother did not die because you were a loathsome child."

"I know that," I snapped.

"Do you?"

Her question felt like a bludgeon to my head. "I resisted her every step of the way," I said softly.

"What are daughters for?" Audrey asked rhetorically.

"For leaving?" I guessed.

"Do you think she wanted to die?"

"No. But she was always leaving us."

"Perhaps mothering scared her," offered Audrey.

"Mother wasn't scared of anything." Of that I was sure. I started to cry.

"She probably loved you very much."

"I suspect even Travis loved me. But it seemed so unlikely at the time. I thought he wanted something from me." I sighed. "Actually, I'm still not sure he didn't want something."

"A classic pattern. You do for others in order to be accepted and then refuse payment in kind."

"I gather psychobabble is one of your nine languages," I said, warding off hard truths.

"I know whereof I speak," she answered simply.

"When have you ever had trouble 'taking'?" I asked abruptly.

"Perhaps if I'd had siblings to care for I would have been selfless or, as in your case, self-effacing. But I chose a different tack. I married boring men who wouldn't notice I was all shell with a hollow core. Eventually the core was crammed with lovely possessions."

"You never loved your husbands?"

"One of them," she sighed.

"Gresham, the one you married twice?" I guessed.

"No, the Greshams were brothers. It was the first, Jasper

Dillingworth. Dear Lord, I loved him." She sighed wistfully. "I know you think I am a frivolous old woman, Mallory. But I do care for you."

"And I for you, Audrey."

"Well," she smiled weakly. "There you are. Perhaps my meddling was justified."

"I liked you back in the States."

"But you wouldn't take from me."

"Was I to wrest my wages from you by force?"

"I meant my regard." She arched her neck as if to loosen a kink. "You insisted on payment."

"I'm a little confused. Didn't you hire me?"

She waved her hand, indicating irritation. "I took you on as a little project. You were too cheeky to resist. My scheme was to crack your formidable self-reliance. Where better to accomplish this than in a culture where you could not speak the language, knew no one, and had no money. We would have gone to China but Doa Peng was unavailable."

"Then what?" I asked, amazed that anyone would go to such lengths.

"I hoped you might give yourself over to the fear of vulnerability." Her lined face was expectant.

"I have always been vulnerable," I quarreled.

"It is easy to be vulnerable. The hard part is giving that gift to another person."

"It doesn't sound like much of a gift."

"From one such as you, it is the rarest."

I absorbed this for a moment. Perhaps it was true. "Audrey, thank you, I think. But was it really necessary to make me so bloody ill?"

" 'The best laid plans . . .' I had not anticipated paratyphoid. Or Gila monsters. When Hector told me of your near brush with death, I was furious."

"Hector has a vivid imagination. What about your prolonged funk?"

"Did I tell you I was once an actress?" asked Audrey.

"No."

"Well, I should have been. Let's go home."

To Tell the Truth

Despite Audrey's declaration of affection, I was still her dogsbody. Upon our return to Boston, she invited me to clear the basement. The basement contained the detritus of five marriages and a surprising amount of junk. When questioned as to the presence of lamps made from chianti bottles, several rusty basketball hoops, and six broken televisions, Audrey confessed to being a secret tag-sale junkie. I began to understand her unusual wardrobe. The image of Audrey gliding up to a tag sale in her gray limousine amused me as I cleaned.

With the basement in order, I was told to learn French, Spanish, Italian, German, and Russian—before spring. It seemed we were to tour the continent.

One morning in mid-February when Audrey was out shopping, I had the house to myself. I sat with Wart in the formal living room listening to Berlitz records. But my mind was not on the task at hand. Wart had his head on my leg, obliging me to scratch his ears. I thought about Travis and Maude. Was there any point in trying to win him back? Audrey wouldn't live forever. I needed a plan.

Audrey came home early and shut the door with a resounding smack.

"Are you all right?" I called into the foyer.

"A most dissatisfying luncheon. I shouldn't be at all surprised to find I have indigestion. Mallory, never dine with a gossip," she directed.

"As it happens, I never dine with anyone. What's the scoop?"

"One would think Elsbeth had learned her lesson, but quite the contrary . . ." Audrey dropped her sable and purse on the sofa. "Now I suppose I will have to call my daughter."

"Your daughter!" I said with amazement.

Audrey blushed. "Yes," she sighed. "I suppose it was inevitable you find out. Though it was a small enough fib. Just as you once borrowed blindness, I borrowed childlessness. It was all in a good cause."

"I don't know why I ever believe you."

"I have three children."

"A good lie requires details," I said brusquely.

"Richard is in Kuwait, Todd lives in Germany, and Adrienne in California. The boys are stodgy," she sighed, "though a picture of compassion next to their sister, Adrienne. But she'll want to know."

"Know what?"

"That her friend Sarah was murdered. Elsbeth couldn't contain her glee. Claimed she always knew Sarah would come to a bad end. As I recall, Elsbeth's daughter was snubbed at Sarah Bentley's debutante ball."

"Sarah Bentley?" It couldn't be.

"They were at school together."

"Did you know this Sarah Bentley?"

"All too well."

"An icy blonde with green eyes?" I hazarded.

"Why, yes. Do you know her?" asked Audrey.

"I met her once. Who murdered her?"

"They say her husband—or rather her ex-husband."

I felt perilously close to fainting. Wart was looking at me with enlarged amber eyes. I rubbed his head hard, trying to stay conscious.

"I attended Sarah's wedding. He was strikingly handsome, a writer I believe. Taylor Something."

"Travis," I said. "Travis Holmes."

"Yes, that's it." Audrey looked at me with alarm. "You don't mean to say . . ."

"Yes."

"Dear Lord! That does put a new wrinkle in the pudding."

We sat silently for some time. My mind raced erratically. Was Travis already in jail? Did Massachusetts have a death penalty? I felt dizzy with fear.

"I do wish you had told me the truth," Audrey admonished.

"Mistruth is the coin of the realm here," I commented. "What else did Elsbeth say?"

"The police arrested him on suspicion of murder. They say he had the motive and the opportunity."

"And the inclination."

"You believe he did it?" Audrey asked with dismay.

"I don't know," I cried, terrified by my lack of faith in the man I loved.

"Yes, now I remember. He wrote murder mysteries. He could have poisoned her with treated figs or somesuch!"

"Travis wrote horror stories."

"Same thing," Audrey maintained.

"Not at all. We have to find out how she died."

Audrey rang a buzzer.

"James" appeared and was dispatched to the newsstand for copies of all the local papers and *The National Enquirer*.

Sarah had been murdered with a snub-nose pistol in her own living room.

"Travis didn't do it," I said with great relief.

"Where does it say that?" Audrey asked, peering over my shoulder.

"It's not his style."

"Let me get this straight. You believe your husband capable of murder but not this particular felony?"

"I know Travis. If he had murdered Sarah, which I gather he had reason to do, it would have been by far more imaginative means."

"Who then?" she asked.

"Maybe the French mafioso."

"The French mafioso!" Audrey exclaimed.

"During the trial, Travis's attorney accused Sarah of a heavy cocaine habit and claimed she dallied sexually with an array of international thugs."

"Little Sarah Bentley!"

"The judge didn't believe it either."

"But they have a witness, Mrs. Carstairs, who heard him

threaten her. And he was at the house earlier that evening."

"I've met Nanny Carstairs and I'm telling you, he didn't do it."

"Good. Call the district attorney."

"And tell him what? That Travis is too ghoulish to commit murder by snub-nose pistol?"

"A point well taken." She thought for a moment, her brow crinkling. "You still love this suspect?"

"Yes," I said simply.

"Then you must take matters into your own hands."

"I'm not James Bond. I can't liberate Travis with a ray gun."

"Have they set bail, yet?"

"Yeah," I answered glumly. "According to this, one million dollars."

"Why haven't his parents put up the money, I wonder?"

"There was no love lost between Travis and his mother. His father was quite fond of Sarah. I have always suspected that he fed her information for the second custody trial."

"Second custody trial? Oh never mind, the truth will wait. Do you suppose the judicial system has changed much since the days of Perry Mason?"

"Why?"

"As I recall, if one retains a bail bondsman, one need only supply ten percent of the bail."

"That's still a hundred thousand dollars!" I exclaimed.

"Peanuts," she said blithely.

"Audrey, we're talking dollars not magical pesos!"

"This suspect you love," she asked calmly, "is he likely to leave the country?"

I didn't have to deliberate. "No. For all his faults, Travis is honorable."

"Then I have nothing to lose," she replied with a wry smile.

I was waiting for Travis when they released him that afternoon. He walked into the lobby of the police station with his head down, counting the money in his wallet. His clothes were rumpled, his hair had sprung cowlicks.

He had not seen me. In another moment, he would be gone. I was losing my nerve. Perhaps it would be better to let him go.

He pushed on the door.

"Travis!" my voice wavered.

He turned to look at me, his face displaying a mixture of exhaustion, shock and anger. He said nothing.

"Travis," I repeated. He came over and sat beside me on the bench.

"Hello Mallory. What brings you here?" He sounded so very tired.

"I know you didn't do it."

He laughed scornfully. "Well, that makes two of us." He ran his hand through his hair. The gesture, which I remembered so well, made me want to cry.

"Is it too much to hope that you're waiting for someone else?" he asked wearily.

"How many jailbirds do you think I know?"

He shrugged his shoulders. "I thought you were in Mexico."

"How did you know that?" I asked with surprise.

"Trehune keeps tabs on Mexican immigration. I wish you were still there."

"Thanks," I snapped.

"I mean, this can't be pleasant for you."

"Neither was Mexico. Come on, I know where we can get a stiff drink." I helped him to his feet. We walked out of the station to where "James" was standing by the open door of the limousine. I steered Travis towards the opening, he tried to swerve, I pushed him in and followed. "James" shut the door.

"What the hell is this?"

"Relax, my pimp lent it to me."

"Mallory!" he exclaimed with alarm.

"I'm kidding."

"*You* paid my bail?"

"I would like to say yes, thereby cancelling my father's debt. But as usual, I am not in a position to pay. You are beholden to Benny the Bondsman and Audrey Bains. I'm just a conduit."

"I thought it was Maude. She and Trehune were supposed to arrange things with my banker."

"I can send you back, if you prefer to be rescued by a fairer maiden," I said, unable to keep the edge out of my voice.

"Don't be crazy. Who's Audrey Bains?"

"Do you remember an Adrienne Bains, a friend of Sarah's?"

"No."

"How about Adrienne Dillingworth, Hampton, or Gresham?"

"Gresham, yes. I didn't like her."

"Well keep that to yourself. Her mother put up the money."

He shook his head in puzzlement. "Adrienne loathed me. Why would her mother spring me?"

"She enjoys unexpected twists of fate."

"Am I supposed to understand that?" he asked.

"No."

"Good. I thought I was losing my grip." He put his head back on the upholstery and closed his eyes. I suppressed the urge to kiss him only by biting my tongue. This, I reminded myself, was a reprieve, not a reconciliation.

The brief nap in the car seemed to revive Travis's charm. As we pulled into the gravel drive, he smoothed his hair and said, "Whatever your part in this, I thank you. You are a good friend."

Did one divorce friends, I wondered?

Wart, scenting the enemy, bounded out of the house barking. Travis stooped down to pet him affectionately. Wart was nearly as surprised as I.

Audrey glided into the entryway wearing a brown velvet hostess gown over a yellow cotton turtleneck.

"Mr. Holmes, how good of you to come."

Travis smiled at her irony. "The pleasure is all mine."

"Won't you join us for tea? Olga poured it when she heard the car arrive."

We followed Audrey into the library. I started to sit in the leather wing chair but Audrey said, "Come sit by me, dear. Mr. Holmes may require that chair's sturdy comfort after his ordeal."

"Please call me Travis," he invited.

"Very well. I suppose that is in order. After all, I danced at the deceased's wedding." She hid her mouth with the tea cup, but I could see the smirk.

Travis's eyebrows rose, a sure sign he was going to retort, but he must have thought better of it, for he took a sip of tea. Then his whole face reacted with startlement.

"You are new to Red Zinger tea?" she surmised.

"Yes. I see where it comes by its name. One could hide arsenic beneath its citric wallop."

"A most curious thought, sir."

I could not speak during this interchange. I was mesmerized by the sight of two people I loved mentally circling one another.

"How is Adrienne?" he inquired politely.

"Much the same, I fear."

Travis fought to stifle a laugh.

"I should not laugh if I were you," Audrey cautioned. "I may have birthed Adrienne, but you married Sarah."

Again, his eyebrows rose. Then he smiled. "I married Mallory, as well."

"That would be a point in your favor had you not thrown her out," she said mildly.

I felt like a tennis ball being lobbed back and forth. "I have to feed the dog."

When I returned ten minutes later, Travis was asleep in the wing chair. He had looked so vital a few minutes ago. Audrey was hanging up the phone.

"We must hurry," she urged.

"Why?" I asked with surprise.

"The car should be here any moment."

"What car? Is Travis all right?" I had never seen him asleep before, but something about the jaw looked peculiar.

"He will be fine," she smiled broadly, "in a few hours. I slipped him a 'mickey.' "

"You did what?"

"You must hurry to catch the last boat." She was flushed with excitement.

"Audrey, what on earth are you talking about?"

"Did you know that males fantasize about being kidnapped? I gather it has something to do with their subliminal desire to be raped by a woman. I read that once. It has always intrigued me. I expect you to tell me all about it when you get back."

"What are you babbling about?"

She opened a drawer and shuffled through some papers until she found a key ring. "It is obvious to me that Travis is going to go to prison, innocent or not. His career will weigh heavily against him. Soon the press will get wind of his departure from jail. I want you to take him to my house on the Vineyard and enjoy him while you can. Travis still loves you." She paused. "I think. Anyway, you still love him . . ."

"You are mad. Absolutely mad."

Ignoring me, she continued, "Your bag is ready, Olga has packed some provisions. Here are the directions and the keys. The house is a Victorian beauty set out on the tip of Chappaquiddick. At this time of year, there won't be anyone around for miles."

"I am not going." Travis would be furious when he awoke. A "mickey," indeed! I was not about to compound his anger with abduction.

"Mallory," she said sternly. "Maude is on her way to Boston. Go now, while you have the chance."

Ménage à Trois

"James" and I carried Travis out to the car Audrey had rented. I looked at the VW bug and laughed. On its dented bumper was a sticker, "Rent-a-Wreck." Only Audrey would spend a hundred thousand dollars on bail and then rent a budget getaway car.

Wart jumped into the car via Travis's lap. I thought for sure his weight would rouse the sleeping beauty but it didn't. I took it as a sign from above.

"Come on Wart, get out." Wart thumped his abbreviated tail on the back seat. "Come on. Not this trip." But Wart wouldn't budge, and given past experience, I gave up trying.

Audrey came out and stood shivering in the driveway. "I haven't had this much fun since Prohibition. Did I tell you my daddy was a rum runner?"

"No, a town clerk," I smiled. "And a country doctor and

a railroad engineer." Audrey was a fiction chameleon. Her life took on the protective coloration of whatever novel she was reading at the moment.

"Your memory is too keen," she replied grumpily.

I stored the last of the food and clothes and turned to look at her.

"Audrey, I am scared. What if he's furious with me?"

"Oh, there's no doubt he will be furious." Panic must have flooded my face. She patted my arm. "If nothing else comes of it, Wart will enjoy the long runs along the beach."

"Oh, well," I replied sarcastically, "as long as one of us profits from the experience."

"Would you prefer James haul your young man back into the library? When Travis awakes, he'll be none the wiser."

If I said no, I would become a party to this madness. If I said yes, I would lose him forever. I could almost feel Maude closing in on us. I looked at Audrey's lined face. She would get a chill standing out in the cold. I couldn't think.

"Be audacious. If all goes awry, you can always come home to me."

"I love you, Audrey."

"Doesn't everyone?" she replied airily. "You will need money," she said, handing me a tightly rolled green cylinder, which I shoved into the pocket of my jeans. "Remember, dear, I want to know all the sordid details!"

Somewhere along Route 3 South, we lost a gear. The engine made an awful grinding protest each time I tried to shift into fourth. And then the steering wheel would shimmy frantically. It seemed safer and simpler to trot along in third.

At the ferry office, I pulled out Audrey's money to pay for

the car and passenger tickets. I handed the rolled bill to the ticket agent and picked up a ferry schedule.

"Lady, this is winter."

"Hmm? Yes, so it is." Odd, the conversation these Cape Codders made.

"I can't cash this in winter." He pushed the bill back at me.

I looked and gasped, "That's a thousand-dollar bill!"

"I know that lady. Why didn't you?" he said suspiciously. Any minute, the gendarmes would arrest me for counterfeiting.

Grabbing the bill, I said, "I'll be right back." I went to the car and picked Travis's pockets for cash.

The seas were rough. Wart threw up on deck. I took him below and checked on Travis. Shouldn't he have been churned awake in the hold? What if Audrey had given him too much "mickey"?

Leaving Wart in the car, I went topside again. I walked the deck, delighting in the sea air. The cold cut through my jacket and numbed me.

Once on the Vineyard, we followed the shore road through the fog to Edgartown. Here Audrey's directions were a bit hazy. We went the wrong way down a one-way street but eventually found the ferry to Chappaquiddick.

No one was on duty. Winter hours were in effect: the last boat had left, according to the sign, at nine. There was another small sign with an emergency phone number. Was this an emergency? I was stranded in a rented VW with an estranged, drugged husband and a fretful Weimaraner. I hadn't seen any open hotels. And even if there had been one, dragging a comatose male in through the lobby would be sure to arouse suspicion.

I pleaded emergency.

The ferryman was quite pleasant about being rousted at this cold hour.

I drove onto the ferry, an open three-car barge. Would Wart's stomach endure another sea voyage? I was about to get him out for a walk when the front end of the ferry hit a dock bay.

"Two-fifty," the ferryman said, collecting my fare.

"This is it?" I asked, horrified at having dragged him from his home for a two-minute crossing.

"Yup. Take care. Thar's a nor'easter brewin'."

"Can you tell me how to get to the Bains house?"

"Folla the macadam till it turns to dirt. Folla the dirt to the end."

We followed the dirt to the end. There in the moonlight sat a Victorian hulk of a house. Travis was still not awake. I started ferrying food and clothes through the back door. I flipped the light switch in the kitchen and was not surprised when it didn't work. Electricity, to Audrey's mind, was a minor detail.

The house was icy cold. There were no storm windows or insulation. Like the Delirium, it had been built for summer use. The furnace was probably of the same makeshift ilk. In any event, it did not turn on when I moved the thermostat. I could only hope Travis, when he awoke, would be in the mood to provide body heat.

I wandered through the house looking for the linen closet. The rooms were large and, in the summer, would have been delightfully airy. The furniture was draped with sheets. Wart sniffed warily. The only sign of life was an abundance of mouse droppings.

I started a fire in one of the seven fireplaces. The wood was wet and smoke filled the room. I crumpled up old issues of *Town and Country*. When the fire finally took hold, I dragged a mattress from the downstairs bedroom in front of the fireplace.

Taking some blankets out to the car, I got in before I realized Travis was awake. He was sitting stock still staring out at the windswept headland.

"Hi," I said cautiously. The car was no colder than the house. We might as well hash it out here. I spread the blankets over us.

He grabbed my arm and pinched it so fiercely I could feel it under my coat. "Ow!" I hadn't expected physical violence.

"You're here," he exclaimed. He released a deep breath.

"What's the matter?"

"Nothing much. I thought I had entered the Twilight Zone. Weren't we drinking tea a moment ago?"

"Several hours ago. We're on Chappaquiddick."

"The Vineyard? Why?"

"You've been kidnapped."

"Who would want to kidnap us?"

"No. I kidnapped you."

"Ah!" He rubbed his hands together.

"Aren't you mad?" I ventured cautiously.

"Should I be?" he asked pleasantly.

"Yes," I quarreled. Where was his anger? "You've been abducted—and drugged."

"My, you have been busy. My only quarrel is with the locale. Couldn't you have spirited me to the Bahamas?"

"Dammit, Travis!"

"You shouldn't have bothered."

"Bothered!" I hollered.

"I know what this is all about, Mallory." He blew on his hands.

"You do?" I was beginning to realize I didn't.

"A man bound to prison makes a wonderful stray. You couldn't resist. I can count on you to visit me faithfully on Death Row."

"Being a stray has nothing to do with it!"

"No?" he asked lightly.

"No." I lowered my head. "This wasn't my idea."

"Whose then?"

"Audrey's. She thinks you want to be raped."

He laughed. "Surely I'll get enough of that in prison."

"By a woman," I mumbled into my lap. I looked up and stared out to sea. "She thought kidnapping might do the trick. Deserted beaches, cozy fires, enforced sex . . ."

"Enforced sex? Did you bring a machete with you?"

"Audrey did the packing. It wouldn't surprise me to find a howitzer."

"I don't suppose it occurred to either of you that I might have come willingly?"

Startled, I turned to look at him. "You would?"

"No."

My face remained still, belying my anguish.

"But not for the reason you suppose," he added. "This little stunt could cost me dearly in court. It might be construed as jumping bail."

"Oh, my god! I never thought! Is it true what they say in all those old movies, 'don't leave town'?"

"I'm afraid so. We have to go back."

"We can't. There's no ferry until morning."

"You could call Trehune with a ransom demand," he suggested with amusement.

"The phone's been disconnected."

"Ah," he said somberly. "Well, then, come have your way with me."

Sex had been briefly attempted. I could only marvel that there were second-generation Eskimos. Fully dressed, we had clung to one another with only our zippers undone. Finally when we had removed our pants out of sheer awkwardness, Wart started humping Travis from behind.

"Wart!" I screamed.

Travis rolled off me and sighed. "Perhaps he's trying to give me a taste of prison life."

"Dammit, Wart," I cursed.

"He'll have to go to sleep sometime, we'll outwait him."

"You're talking about a dog who when asleep can hear a jar of Planter's peanuts being opened three rooms away. Maybe if I come on top . . . Ned said he thought Wart had homosexual tendencies."

"It's worth a shot."

I clambered up on Travis and turned to Wart. Gruffly, I said, "Try it and you're out on the mean streets." Wart made a piteous moaning sound.

"Think of it as violins," Travis urged.

But Wart persisted. "I'm sorry, I can't." I rolled off Travis.

Travis got up, dragging one of the blankets with him. "Here, Wart."

"What are you going to do?"

"I'm going to p-u-t him in a-n-o-t-h-e-r r-o-o-m."

Wart followed his sex object to the adjoining room. Travis

darted back around the door and slammed it. Then he put a straight back chair against the door. Wart, realizing he had been duped, barked angrily. I could hear him clawing at the door.

Travis and I were in mid-lay when Wart hurled himself against the door, toppled the chair, and came crashing into the room. He bounded over barking furiously at Travis. Baring his teeth, he bit at the air near Travis's shoulder.

"What the hell is his problem," Travis groused.

"Perhaps this is his primal scene."

"Well I bloody give up," Travis said with disgust.

"Thanks a heap, Wart." Wart came and licked my face wetly. Dispirited, I pulled on my pants and snuggled with Travis under the blankets. Wart, content that our lust had been foiled, settled down in a coil between our feet.

"I had my heart set on being raped," Travis complained.

"Join the club," I fretted.

"If they think I jumped bail, I'll be incarcerated the minute I hit Boston."

"Audrey will fix it," I said firmly. I could hear her now, explaining her amorous plot to the judge.

"What a lot of faith we've placed in Audrey." He was studying me. "She struck me as missing a few cogs."

"Audrey's not crazy, she just has her own style. She told me a story once, it was probably apocryphal, but it will tell you as much about Audrey as the truth. Her college roommate took all the towels and clothes from the communal bathroom while Audrey was bathing. All Audrey had was a washcloth. The security guard was between the bathroom and her bedroom. Now, had this happened to me I would have used the washcloth and my arms to cover strategic areas and made a dash for it. But not Audrey. She put the washcloth over her face and marched boldly down the hallway."

Travis roared with laughter.

"Audrey said it was better to bare all anonymously than to give ownership to a single part."

"How ever did she produce a prig like Adrienne?"

"Husbands have genes, too."

Wart stood, circled his small area between our legs and sat down again, this time with his head on Travis. We both watched him and then drifted off into companionable silence. The wind was howling outside and hail was pelting the picture window.

"Does this remind you of anything?" he asked. I frowned. "The birthday party."

"I didn't lose that custody case for you purposefully, you know."

"I know."

"Poor Schuyler. What are you going to tell him when he asks 'where's Mommy?' "

"I just hope no one has to explain where his Daddy is."

"Do you think you'll be convicted?"

"Well, I didn't do it, if that means anything. I had Trehune wire all that information he had from the second custody trial to the district attorney's office. Sarah had many dark layers. But who knows? God I'm tired . . . Tired of lawyers and entanglements and legal hassles that never end."

"I'm sorry I messed up the divorce. I just couldn't let go."

He rolled over on his back, put his hands under his head and stared at the ceiling. For a long time, he was silent. Then, he said, "There is no divorce. I stopped the proceedings when I got over my anger."

"Oh? When was that?" I asked, trying to keep my voice level.

"Right after you pushed me down the steps."

"Most people would have taken umbrage." My heart felt like it was doing wheelies in my rib cage. "What exactly does this mean?"

"It means we are still married and likely to remain so. I hired a detective to find you but you were in deep cover, as they say in the spook trade."

The man in New York wasn't a process server but a detective, I realized with a jolt. I had been running all these months when I could have been with Travis.

"Do you love me?" I demanded.

"Of course," he said matter-of-factly.

"What about the children?"

"Perhaps they will grow to love you. If not it's their loss. But I don't intend it to be my loss any longer." He shook his head with amusement. "It's ironic really, like a banner headline in the *New York Post*, 'Motherless Mallory Mothers Motherless Moppets.' "

"That's ironic all right," I said uneasily. It would be just like Travis to secure childcare in the event of prison. If that were his motive, I wanted nothing to do with him. "How do I know you didn't change your mind about the divorce in jail?"

"Ask Trehune," he offered.

"Trehune would lie for you."

"Ask Maude."

"Right! She's a beacon of impartiality where we're concerned."

"Then ask yourself."

"That's a low blow," I accused.

"You're the only one with the answer. Use your head. Mallory," he said reasonably.

There was little point in using my head. Loving Travis would always be a Leap of Faith.

Off I went, with battered wings, praying for an easy fall.

Cindy Packard is most often found in Bethel, Connecticut, where she lives with her husband, Harvey Richmond, and their children, Amanda and Ned.

Ms. Packard prefers writing to housework, although she admits they pay about the same. She has been a New York book editor, a researcher, a Head Start volunteer, and a realtor. She once spent a summer digging up dead Indians.

Whereas the major honors and awards have thus far eluded her, Ms. Packard wryly notes that her first novel, *Hell's Bells,* was named one of the year's ten best—by the Ocala, Florida, *Star-Banner.*